Gulf of Deception

KELLY HOPKINS

CHAMPAGNE BOOK GROUP

Gulf of Deception

Published by Champagne Book Group
2373 NE Evergreen Avenue, Albany OR 97321 U.S.A.

~~~

First Edition 2021

pISBN: 978-1-77155-347-6

Cover Art by Juan Padron
https://www.juanpadron.com

www.champagnebooks.com

Version_1

To David and Kelsey: Never give
Up on your dreams.
To Dave: You're the best time I've
ever had.

Chapter One

Coconut Champagne roared through my brain as Maynard Ferguson's ridiculous, upper register trumpet work raced chills down my back. I kept my hands steady until the baritone sax solo cued. At the first note, my fingers flew over the imagined keys, trying to imitate Dennis DeBlasio's brilliance as I read the runs printed on the sheet music in my mind.

Thump. Thump.

I yanked the headphones off my ears. They dropped and settled around my neck. In the office doorway, with his knuckles against the jamb, my father raised his eyebrows. His smirk told me he'd been there for a while before he knocked.

Great. He'd seen me playing the air sax.

"Practicing for your summer audition? It's this week, right?"

"Ugh, yeah." I wiggled my fingers to distract him from my blush. I wasn't *entirely* lying. The audition had nothing to do with the local university's wind band and everything to do with our beachy jazz ensemble scoring the prime summer slot at Sun Runner's on Fort Myer's Beach. Our band was in high demand for the upcoming graduation party season thanks to some well-placed flyers and a couple of successful free gigs around town. News about our chops traveled faster than a marlin with a boat of tourists on its tail. We'd been granted a tryout performance at Sun Runner's—a huge deal for a bunch of teenagers. My heart tripped somewhere between discord and staccato, and my tongue stuck to the roof of my mouth every time I thought about auditioning in front of the entertainment director.

He wagged a finger at me. "College is coming up. Freshman year is going to be tougher than you think. You won't have much time for the sax next year, but I do love when you play."

Uh-oh. *Fantastic.* Here comes another getting-into-law-school-is-no-joke lecture. I longed to tell him the truth about my audition and future plans, but how could I let him down? Music was more than a hobby, and he should accept that. Dad had attended every one of my concerts since elementary school, yet he couldn't envision me playing beyond the end of my high school career—or that staying true to my music meant a lot more to me than following in the family footsteps to Boston College and law school.

"I'll find the time," I told him with an innocent smile.

He folded his arms and half-frowned. To my relief, rather than continue our argument, Dad dropped the subject. His gaze roved over the desk and the white marker board behind me where I listed names, dates, times of cases, and upcoming court appearances. "This place looks fantastic. You've cleaned up the backlog and then some."

He gestured toward the near-empty paper basket on his absent secretary's desk, but ignored the monstrous, towering piles covering half the floor—my effort to convert his legal office chaos into some semblance of sanity. Each stack, a tiny island of instability, listed to port on the coral carpeting.

"If you keep it up, I'll have to tell Monica she's out of a job."

I grimaced at the threat. My entire summer would go up in smoke if he fired her. No way. Especially if we got this job. Brass Tactics—the name we'd given the band—was poised to take the summer tiki bar scene by storm. Not my fault his secretary had been absent for six weeks thanks to popping out twins. The last thing I wanted was to spend my final summer before college buried under a mountain of legal paperwork. Besides, I needed to figure a way out of the pre-law trap waiting for me in Boston. The clock was ticking.

Activating my best innocent smile, I said, "Are you kidding me? She's gonna have a freaking heart attack when she sees her desk. I haven't even touched the mail yet." Stacks of unopened envelopes mocked me from the top of the filing cabinet, and a vortex of papers flapped in a sudden gush of air conditioning. "There's at least two weeks' worth of unfiled briefs, continuances, and other assorted legalese to scan, sort, and file. You need to hire a temp," I told him for the hundredth time as I shoved loose strands of hair back toward the messy knot at my nape.

The corner of his mouth lifted, crinkling his eyes. He tucked the back of his polo shirt into the waist band of his jeans before stepping inside to give the top of my head a brief kiss and my shoulder an affectionate squeeze. "Nah. I have my favorite attorney-in-training to make sure this place doesn't fall apart. You're doing great, future-attorney Lily Harmony." He sighed, a dreamy expression on his face. "Doesn't that sound nice?" He fished in his back jeans pocket, withdrew the brown leather wallet I gave him last Christmas, then handed me a fifty-dollar bill for my three hours of work.

"Dad! I'm not even in college yet." I clenched the bill in my fist and stuck out my tongue, refusing to bite the hook he dangled. True, I grew up in the office and could find my way around a case file—hence the reason he assumed my future lay in the law. "You do know it's Saturday? It's an official day of rest." *And* sunbathing at the beach, but I didn't tell my father *that* part.

"Well, the day's not over yet." He rubbed his stubble-darkened cheek, his beard rasping beneath his fingertips. On Saturdays, Dad refused to shave. When I was little, he used to chase me around the dining room table trying to rub his scratchy cheek on mine until my mother got tired of the shrieks. My lips twitched in amusement.

"What's so funny?" he asked, one eyebrow arched in a perfect, mocking curve.

Schooling my features to innocence, I lied smoothly. "Nothing. Just admiring your ankles."

Saturday also marked the one day he didn't have to wear the official lawyer uniform, and he went all in—jeans and no socks. "Huh? I work hard on these babies. Check out the even tan lines." He tugged up on his pants leg.

"Oh my goodness," I murmured. "That's messed up."

"Really? Mom likes them."

I covered my burning cheeks with my hands. "I need you to leave, now, before I'm scarred for life."

"Uh-uh. It's catch-up day, and I appreciate you helping me catch up." He gave me a one-armed squeeze, careful to avoid my sorted piles. "You're doing fine, Lil. I mean it. I appreciate this. And I'm sorry about the beach."

Ugh. I hoped he didn't hear me swear under my breath. My father didn't miss a trick. His perception skills made him a fabulous lawyer. He could spot a lie in the pitch dark with his eyes closed. Somehow, I'd been able to keep my true feelings about college from him.

Or had I? A flutter of unease set up a rumba in my stomach.

"You didn't find anything on a Dorminy Holdings, did you?" He thumbed through the files.

"I don't remember the name, but it could be in the Leaning Tower of Mail over there, or on the filing cabinet. What are you looking for?"

With a frown, he shifted his weight onto his left foot. "Anything that comes in. It's a complicated case. If you see something, let me know. I'm waiting for some stuff." A shadow drifted over his face, swift as a wind-swept Florida thundershower, before his normal reserved appearance reverted. Maybe he'd tell me about the case when I discovered the papers. Although I didn't share his passion for the profession, I loved learning the intricacies of the law from him and hearing the dirt.

There was *always* client dirt. "I'll keep an eye out for it," I told him.

With a knowing smile playing across his tanned face and dancing in his blue eyes, he jerked a thumb in the direction of my mother's office. "Mom's itching to leave too."

As if on cue, my mother appeared in the doorway. "Someone forget to invite me to the family meeting?" She peered at us over the glasses perched on her nose.

"I was just telling Lily what a great job she's doing in here."

Mom's hazel gaze scanned the room and my improvised organization system. Her blonde-streaked curls bobbed as she nodded. "I can see there's a definite plan." Her dry wit came through. "You know, I did some research. We should remodel this space while Monica's out. The sand-colored paint is dated. So is this carpet." She scrubbed her toe on the worn coral shag with a yuck-face. "I bet she'd like a make-over."

"What are you thinking?" Dad asked her. "New furniture? I've always wanted to break through the wall and get a window in here."

"I don't know about demolition," she said with a shrug. "Will we have time for construction before she comes back? Maybe we should talk to a decorator. Or ask Liz for suggestions."

"I love what she did to her office. Attorney Monroe has great taste," I piped up. Liz Monroe was their junior partner. I loved her bright, airy office.

"That's a good idea," Mom said. "I'm not good with this side of the business. Give me bankruptcies any day. I'm willing to entertain redecorating proposals."

I cleared my throat. They chuckled as if remembering I was there. "All this will get filed quicker if you two vacate my office."

Dad backed into the hall, holding up his hands in surrender. "Watch out. She's getting territorial."

Mom stopped him from leaving with a fingertip on his arm. "I came to ask if you wanted to take the boat out tonight. They're calling for storms over the Gulf but to our south. Should make for a spectacular sunset." She glanced in my direction.

I was supposed to spend the evening with Jazz, our band's wicked trumpet player, on Estero Drive. We had burger and ice cream plans followed by three hours of intense rehearsal time.

But a ride on the boat? That didn't happen often. I sighed.

Decisions, decisions…

Through Monica's door, I could see Fort Myers Beach beckoning just beyond the hallway windows, the ocean sparkling in the distance as if infused with a sprinkle of diamonds. There was nothing like spending the waning hours of sunset on the boat, drifting with the tide.

Dad must have seen my hesitation because he cleared his throat awkwardly. "Why don't you ask your friend to come along? It's time we met him, don't you think?"

"He's right," Mom agreed. "Bring him. He'll come, right?"

I hated it when they put me on the spot. Like sharks sensing blood in the surf, they waited with sharp gazes for my response. "Uh, yeah."

"Does he have a real name?" my father asked.

"It's Jason," I said, treading carefully. Jason Sumner was his full name. I kept the rest of the details to myself. *If I give them too much information, they'll run a background check before dinner.*

Mom leaned into the room. "And he's a student?"

"Yes, computers."

"And you met him at music practice?" She raised an eyebrow. "At the university?"

Swallowing, I pried my tongue free and said, "Yes. Wind ensemble. He's a sophomore, and he plays trumpet."

"An older man and a musician. Sounds like trouble to me," Dad said with a sigh. "Your sister dated an older man once." He leveled a semi-serious glare in my direction.

Mom rolled her eyes. "Annabelle was six. Tommy was seven. It wasn't a date."

My sister's movie date story was a family legend. No wonder Belle decided to go to college in Georgia. At least she had a prayer of privacy. Some days, I'd kill for twenty minutes out from under their scrutiny.

I folded my arms across my chest. "Will you two please leave?"

"We'll do steaks and have dinner on the boat." Dad winked and exited the office.

The Saturday night grill event in the Harmony household was a standing tradition, one I rarely missed—especially if we took dinner on the water. Dad's steaks were amazing, and Mom's homemade biscuits? Yum.

When he'd gone, Mom said, "Finish what you can. We're out of here by noon. I don't care what he says." She waved and left.

They wanted to meet Jazz. That was good and bad because they only knew half of the story. Yes, I liked Jason, aka Jazz. He *was* a trumpet player *and* a software engineering major at Florida Gulf Coast University. But he was also one of the top video game streamers in the area on the cusp of having enough views to go legit, all while building an eSports company. Best plan was to keep the conversation to music—much safer territory.

Getting my parents and Jazz together was inevitable, I supposed, since we'd been spending more and more time together. They'd have to meet him sooner or later. Offshore, on the boat, watching the sunset and the distant storms might be a good way to break the ice, if we kept his video gaming off the discussion table.

I dreamt of warm sand and Gulf breezes, but the last stack of files beckoned. I dug in and plowed on.

~ * ~

"Damn it!" Blood welled from another cut, and I jammed my latest paper-sliced digit in my mouth. Four hours. I'd been stuck at the law office for four freaking hours, filing briefs, motions, and injunctions in this windowless bunker of a file closet, excited for time spent at the shredder because hey, at least that room had a window. Paper cuts had transformed my fingers into a patchwork of bloody slices. I ran my aching finger over the top of yet another manila file then slammed the drawer with a shot from my hip.

That's it. I'm d…o…n…e. Done. On cue, my phone buzzed with a *where are you?* text. Except instead of a regular text, I gazed at a recent picture of the beach. He sure knew how to torture a girl. Instead of sharing in Jazz's beach bliss, I ground my teeth and glared at the framed photograph of Monica's last crowded ultrasound.

I shouldn't blame a couple of babies, but really, who else was there to blame?

The only thing saving my sanity in this airless room was the double mocha latte I procured before dragging my butt to the office at the crack of eight. I sniffed the unappealing congealed coffee in the bottom of my take-out cup before tossing it in the trash.

Ten minutes until noon. Time to get out onto the beach. Another text rattled into my phone, and I smiled at the screen. Jazz. We'd flirted on the edge of more than friends, even fell into a serious make-out session once after too much beach party. Somehow our friendship had survived our near miss at a relationship. Maybe because neither of us talked about it.

Ever…as if the night never happened.

But I remembered the hour we'd spent together in the sand, far enough away from the party bonfire to do more than talk. Every last moment. My skin tingled with memories too vivid to file away in some dark, subconscious corner.

You home?

My fingers flew over the screen. *No at work. Leaving at noon. Streaming at two. Watch?*

You bet.

Legal indentured servitude would be over by then, and I'd have to choose between a fleeting hour on the beach, practicing our new material, or watching Jazz's stream by our pool before Dad wanted to shove off. *If* I left on time. If not, I could always view Jazz's stream on my phone. He was so close to nailing down those streaming sponsors. He needed every view he could get with the Fort Myers Storm eSports team growing like a depression in the Gulf. Still, between his gaming and his music, he barely made enough to squeak out rent and tuition.

If the team took off, he'd be set.

I smirked at his next emoji-laced text. The boy had a way with smileys. I decided to tell him about the boat after his stream. No reason to make him nervous. I had that end covered enough for two.

Filing done, I cranked up Post Malone in my headphones. With a gleaming letter opener from the secretary's drawer, I attacked the first envelope. Inside lurked another wretched continuance. Great. The change meant moving Dad's schedule around and calling clients to switch appointments. I glared at the color-coded schedule on the white board.

Maybe I could pretend I hadn't seen the notice. But who else opened the mail these days? I unfolded the document with careful fingers, stamped it with a received date stamper, entered Friday's date, and then neatly stapled the sheaf of paper. Just like Monica always did.

Dorminy Holdings. Yep. The same company Dad had been after earlier. I set it aside to slit the rest of the envelopes, sorting and stapling as I went.

Fifteen minutes later, I finished. *Finally.* I uncapped a tepid bottle of water and took an unsatisfying draw before switching musical gears to Van Morrison. With the documents sorted into piles for each of the firm's members, I sighed in relief. No more schedule busters lurked in the mail.

Smiling, I sang along to the chorus of *Brown Eyed Girl* as I danced down the hallway carrying the partners' mail. I let myself into their offices and deposited the correspondence in their in-boxes, lingering in Liz's office. She'd gone for a lighter, more Floridian vibe than the cherry-wood paneled offices of my parents or the more masculine hunter green and black of Patrick Malvern's man cave.

A collage of beautiful Gulf photographs covered the wall behind her desk. Brilliant sunsets, dark forbidding storms, and lush, overhead jungle shots of thick mangroves—plus a picture of her smiling from the deck of a fishing boat holding a massive tarpon. I adjusted the vase of flowers on her desk and checked the water, pausing over the stunning Bird of Paradise blooms.

Mom *had* to ask for the name of her decorator.

Sunlight streamed through the windows, and pang thudded deep in my chest. Hard to believe I was leaving this stunning scene in a few short months for college. A thousand miles north in Boston, away from the sun, the sand, and the balmy breeze. At least the ocean was nearby—except it would be the lumbering, lead-colored, frigid Atlantic, and I'd be wearing an unflattering parka with boots up to my knees. Maybe when the snow melted in June, I could trick myself into believing I was standing on the Gulf.

All so I could one day add my name to the Harmony Law letterhead. Except that was the last thing I wanted.

My feet stopped short as a shock reverberated through the walls, like something heavy crashed down in another part of the building. But there were no other offices on the top floor. I pulled my headphones from my ears and turned off the music.

At the office door, I peered into the hall. A gust of humid air rushed down the narrow passage and ruffled my hair. Now where had the breeze come from?

Delicate music came from the speaker system—some unnamed melody that sounded familiar and should have vocals. Another blast of breeze hit me as if someone had forgotten to shut a window.

"Mom?" I called. The law office answered me with soft strains of piano wafting down the hall.

"Dad?" My father's door stood ajar at the far end of the building. Next to it, my mother's office door was shut. Maybe they were both in Dad's office. His was the only one with a balcony. They could have gone outside and left the door open.

Another violent crash came from the direction of his office. A gunshot rang out. Then another. Followed by a blood-curdling scream.

Mom!

Dad!

Terrified, I crept down the hallway, my back pressed against the wall, my cellphone pulled from my pocket and clutched in my shaking hand. My heart pounded, making me feel faint. I blinked away the sensation. Sharp blasts of unintelligible conversation drew me toward the office as wind whipped down the corridor.

I hesitated at the door and gasped.

Mom knelt beside Dad, a gun in her hand. Blood colored the front of his polo shirt—a crimson stain spreading from his chest and down his left side on a backdrop of stormy blue fabric. Strangled sobs ripped from my lips. I rushed in, dropped to the floor beside my father, and took his limp hand.

Glass shards bit into my knees as a terrible gurgle erupted from his throat. Bloody froth colored his chin and lips. The room spun around me.

"Dad? Please, Dad. Can you hear me?" Spots popped in my brain, and another wave of vertigo hit as my abdomen heaved. I forgot how to inhale.

His bewildered eyes were wide, his mouth moving soundlessly, his fingers splayed against the floor. I couldn't tear my gaze from his face as I laced his fingers in mine and squeezed. "Dad! What should I do?"

"William?" Mom whispered. She pressed a wad of orange fabric—the scarf she'd worn this morning—over the wound on his chest. Fresh terror gripped me as blood dripped down her cheek, and I couldn't tell if it belonged to him or her.

Dad struggled to lift his other arm, but it fell back to the floor.

"He's gone, William," she said. "You're going to be fine."

Somehow, I unlocked my words. "Who's gone?"

She ignored my question, or maybe she didn't hear me. Tears and blood trickled off her chin, making pink spots on her white shirt. "Call for an ambulance. Oh God." The gun slipped from her hand and landed on the carpet with a thud. "William." Her voice broke on his name.

My heart tore from its moorings on a crash of agony. "Dad? Dad." For a split second, his gaze fixed on mine, then he was gone as if a candle extinguished in a sudden, sharp wind.

"William!" Mom gripped his arm.

His head lolled to the side.

Chapter Two

I sat crumpled on the floor of the hall outside my father's office door, my body numb. Police officers took pictures and whispered together, their gazes flitting toward me every once in a while. Tears dropped off my chin, darkening the faded denim of my shorts in an ever-widening stain. I forced myself to breathe, to hold on to the screams swirling inside my brain as my fingernails dug into my thighs.

Dad. My Dad.

A clean sheet covered him, but the pure white cloth would never be able to erase the bloody horror lying beneath. My father, cold, dead. His breath gone, his life drained, his death indelibly etched inside the darkest corners of my brain.

My guts flipped like a funhouse ride, gone to acid as tears choked off my air. I rocked on the floor, my body a boneless heap.

Dad. How had this happened?

I buried my head in my arms. His death played over and over and over in my mind like a horror movie on infinite rewind. The crash. The glass sparkling from the floor. My mother in the center of it with a gun clenched in her fist.

Dad kept a pistol in his drawer.

Did she shoot him?

It *had* to be an accident.

Dazed, I hiccupped as I wiped away the tears with the bottom of my shirt. Thoughts crashed like sadistic swells in a frenzy of impossible questions in my unfocused brain. The person who could answer them sat in Dad's office surrounded by severe and sober cops. From where I sat, I could see Mom slumped in a chair, her head in her bloody hands. We'd not spoken in the minutes before the police arrived; the grief we shared was too fresh.

Crimson stained my fingers. She wasn't the only one with my father's blood on her hands. I shuddered and hugged my knees.

"Lily Harmony?"

I jumped when a police officer tapped me on the shoulder. He didn't wear the sharp pressed uniform some of them wore. Dressed in a black Fort Meyers Police Department collared shirt and jeans, he sported a gleaming gold badge attached to his belt. His stern demeanor retained a shadow of sympathy beneath a day's growth of beard, but my guard leapt up. I'd lived my entire life with a pack of cautious lawyers.

"I'm Detective Jed Stephens, Fort Myers Special Investigative Unit. Can I talk to you for a few minutes?"

My gaze lingered on the activity in the office while I remained silent and hoped for a glimpse of my mother. Never agree to talk to anyone without counsel present. Don't self-incriminate. The rules were the rules, but the terrible, clotted blood and the glittering glass swayed my resolve by fractions.

"Lily?" he asked.

I have the right to remain silent...

Jaws welded together, I said nothing but shoved my spine into the wall to stop the trembling in my bones. A woman with a similar dark polo shirt and a blonde ponytail collected glass samples from the floor with silver forceps, dropping the shards into small plastic bags. Two men lifted my father's body into a dark bag and then strapped him to the gurney. The gun lay where my mother had dropped it.

"Come on. You don't need to watch this." He raised me by the elbow as the attendants packed up the medical supplies they hadn't needed to use. They removed their crimson-stained gloves with sharp snaps.

Too wrung out and shocked to know if my legs were strong enough to support me, I didn't resist.

"I'm sorry for your loss. Look, um...they're going to take him now. We should move away from the door."

I hesitated for a moment when he released my arm. My knees went soft beneath me, but I stayed upright with a hand on the wall. "I want to see my mother." My chin came up in defiance. She could explain this nightmare to me, like she'd done when I was young and suffered from night terrors.

The muscles in his jaw clenched and released. "In a bit. We're taking her statement." He paused but took a firm hold on my arm as I stepped toward my father's door.

I needed Mom to talk to me. To tell me we would be okay. To explain why Dad was dead. To make sure I didn't say the wrong thing.

His sympathy for my loss didn't extend to patience. "Lily?" The detective lingered, waiting for me to move with him. "I need you to come with me now."

"Okay." He was right. I didn't want to stand there and watch them wheel my father away. Thankfully, the EMTs used the rear office entrance and didn't come past me. I followed the detective toward the reception area. The gurney clanged over the threshold. The distant ding of the elevator sounded as the doors slid shut on the madness.

Daylight shone through the skylights, filling the reception area with midday Florida sun. Rosewood trim glowed like burnished gold. Even inside, the rays warmed my chilly arms, and I rubbed the skin wishing the heat would settle into the cold center of my core as my body collapsed onto the nearest chair.

The detective took a seat opposite me on a tan leather couch, his hands clasped in his lap as he leaned forward, perhaps waiting for me to catch my breath. He had close-cropped hair and a square chin. His chestnut brown eyes were kind, and his face trustworthy even though I knew I shouldn't trust him. I had the impression he was a man with a lot of things to do, and I was holding him up.

A shaking breath burned into my lungs. Why couldn't someone, somewhere, fix this? I was too old to believe in fairy tales. No magic spell would bring my father back. He was gone, and the grotesque, hunched witches of my nightmares danced with glee. I cupped my elbows to mask the trembling in my hands.

"Are you okay? Can I get you something? Water?"

If I unclenched my teeth, I'd never stop screaming. I shook my head.

A marble-topped coffee table separated us, gleaming like obsidian glass. He shifted the overbearing floral arrangement out of our line of sight. "Again, I'm sorry about your father. You were here when it happened?" He removed a notebook from his laptop bag and set it on his knee. The pen hovered over a fresh page.

Throat tight with tears trying to claw their way to the surface, I nodded. I'd been down the hall the entire time, music blasting into my brain, worried about stupid things like rehearsals and college. And I'd done nothing to save him.

How could I tell this man what finding my father was like, when the impossible truth clung to my vocal cords? My mother had a gun in her hand. I hadn't been there when someone—I couldn't say *she*—shot him.

If I'd been in Dad's office, would I have jumped between the gun and the bullet? Offered my life for his? Or stood mute as now, unable to process the scene?

The detective dipped the notebook between his knees. His body shifted over his lap as if goading me into talking. In his line of work, he must be used to dealing with emotional wrecks and people who'd lost the will to speak.

"Do you think you can tell me what happened? What you remember?"

My lids squeezed shut for a moment, but the image of my father dying crashed into my mind like a wrecking ball taking out a house of playing cards. I blinked, breathed in through my teeth, and summoned strength from the abyss of my soul. "I was filing in the secretary's office. Then I went to deliver mail to the partners. I heard—I mean I felt a big crash."

"A crash?" His left brow arched. "Like something fell?"

"Yeah. The floor vibrated like something heavy fell or…exploded."

"Exploded like a bomb?" He studied me for a moment. I chewed on the inside of my cheek and tried not to squirm under his scrutiny. "Where is the office where you were standing?"

Blood leaked into my mouth as I bit through the delicate skin. I waved toward the office door wishing I could go back inside the file room and never come out. "Over there. That's Attorney Monroe's office. I was inside."

The detective made a note of this. "How many lawyers are in the firm besides your parents?"

"Just two. Liz Monroe and Patrick Malvern." I wished I could spit out the copper taste.

"They weren't here when it happened?" he asked.

"They don't usually work on Saturdays."

"But you do?" His tone turned clipped, direct.

My eyes narrowed before I could bland my expression. He questioned—accused me when my father was dead. "I've been helping in the office. My parents' secretary is on maternity leave."

"Are you in law school?"

"No. I'm a high school senior at Dunbar High. I graduate in two weeks." Reality hit me like a blow to the chest. Dad wouldn't be there to see me receive my diploma. A fresh surge of tears strangled me. I struggled to compose myself before the next question.

The detective tapped his foot as he wrote. "You didn't hear anything before it happened? The crash or…explosion?" His face betrayed nothing as he glanced up from his notebook.

Swallowing, I said, "No," remembering to guard the inflection in my voice. There might not be an attorney present, but that didn't mean I shouldn't watch the words coming out of my mouth. The gun had been in her hand. I was her best and worst witness.

"No yelling? No conversation or arguments?"

Tears dripped off my chin. "I had headphones on." I wiped the moisture on my shoulder sleeve. "My mother screamed. After the shot, I think."

"How did you hear your mother if you had headphones on?"

"I don't know. I took them off." The timeline scrambled in my mind, and I couldn't recall if the scream came before the shot or after I took them off. Where were the headphones anyway? Why couldn't I think?

"You're bleeding," he said, gesturing toward my legs.

Glass sparkled from my bloody knees. The shards had embedded in my flesh when I knelt beside my father. I didn't feel them—then or now. "I'm okay."

He removed a clear plastic bag from his laptop case. My bright yellow headphones were sealed inside. "Are these yours?" He handed me the bag.

"Yes. Where did you find them?" I stared at the headphones like strangers.

"In the hallway. Outside your father's door. There was no cord with them."

"They're Bluetooth." I didn't remember dropping them on the floor. Those first moments after the shot remained hazy, slightly out of focus, like rain cascading on a car's foggy window at twilight.

"I guess I lost them when I saw…" I couldn't continue. I averted my gaze, intent on the potted palm in the corner as fresh tears took my ability to speak.

"That had to be tough." The sympathy in his tone, laced with a note of sincerity, begged me to tell him more.

"Awful," I agreed, refusing to meet his gaze. What would happen now? Did Mom know who did this? My upbringing kept the questions glued to my tongue.

Several seconds passed before he asked, "You were delivering mail when you heard something?"

"Yes." My spine stiffened a notch. We'd been over this already.

He leaned back. His brows drew down as if a curtain of suspicion descended between us. "Okay. So, you felt a crash? You didn't hear one."

"Yes. And no." A hint of annoyance filtered into my words. Again, he'd already asked me this more than once, in differing ways. Anger brought my weepy emotions under control for the moment, and I glared at him.

"Was it a thud? Like something fell? Or more like a boom?" He glanced at his notes. "You mentioned an explosion."

My breath hissed out in frustration. "I don't know. Does it matter?"

Stubble crunched under his scratching fingers as he studied me. "We didn't find anything tipped over," he said, his comments measured. "Nothing that would create the impact you're describing. No blast or explosion. Nothing burned or scorched."

"I'm not making this up," I said. "The floor vibrated under my feet." Once, when we had traveled to California, I'd experienced an earthquake. Although a small one, maybe a four on the Richter scale, the experience had stuck with me. I knew what I meant.

"Okay. I'm not blaming you. It's a mystery. The crash happened. What did you do when you felt it?"

The moment rushed back, and I saw the events with pinpoint clarity. My finger on the pause button on the front of my phone. The shock before my feet moved in the direction of the sound. "I shut off my music and went into the hall. Maybe that's when I lost these." The sequence unraveled in my mind. "The wind blew down the hallway toward me. It shouldn't have been windy. He never opens those doors."

"The balcony doors?"

"Yes."

"The glass door in your father's office appears to have been smashed by one of the shots," the detective said. "That's why you noticed the wind. From the balcony."

The logic didn't flow. He sounded reasonable enough, but something in his version of the truth wasn't connecting. "No. That's not right. First came the explosion, then the wind. But the office was quiet until—"

He raised his eyebrows.

My heart thundered behind my ribs. "Two gunshots. Quick, one after the other. And a scream. My mother screamed."

The detective tilted his head. "Two shots?"

"Yes. Two. One after the other. Why?"

"Well…" He paused as if trying to choose his thoughts. "Your father was shot once. As far as we can tell, the gun on the floor had been fired once. Only one bullet missing."

"Where'd the other shot come from?" Had I gotten it wrong? Maybe I was in shock. Maybe I couldn't trust my memories. But I was so sure I'd heard a second shot.

His brows drew down, but he didn't answer my question. "Did you hear any voices? Before or after the shots? Anyone saying anything when you got to the office?"

The twisted threads of my memories slipped through my fingers. "No. Just a scream. I kind of... I called for my parents. That's it."

"A female or male scream."

"Female."

He took some time to write my details into his notes. I wished I could read what he wrote, to make sure he got it right. "Okay, after the shots, what did you do?"

The hallway outside my father's office loomed in a dark tunnel of doubt. "I went to my Dad's office. He was on the floor next to my mother." I clutched the bag. "I must have taken these off," I said again, unsure of how the headphones mattered.

After a contemplative moment, he asked, "Did you say anything after you called for your parents?"

"No."

"How about your mother? Did she say anything to you?"

"She said his name. William." I choked on the word. I'd never hear her call him William again.

He turned back a page in his notes, checked something then paged back. "Okay. Let's go back to the moment you first looked into the office. Where was your mother?"

When I was a kid, my grandmother used to embroider intricate designs on everything. Scarves, towels, even my third-grade purse. The H on my bag had been wrapped in vines and blooming daisies. Though the bag had fallen apart years ago, I could close my eyes and conjure the image perfectly. The picture of my parents together on the floor knitted into the fabric of my mind, much like my grandmother's precise stitches.

In my memory, my mother knelt on the floor, the wind whipping her curls, the blood splattered on her face, the wildness as she saw me, then stared through me. "She was kneeling next to Dad with the gun in her hand. I don't know if it's my dad's. He had a gun in his desk drawer."

How many times had he warned me about the dangers of a weapon? *Never open the drawer. Never pick it up.*

"We didn't find a gun in his desk." The detective tapped his pen against his notebook. "We're checking the registration, but we're pretty sure the gun is his."

"Did she tell you what happened?" I whispered. "Did Mom see what happened?"

"We're getting her statement now." He paused, studying me. He had no intention of telling me what my mother said. If he did, I could corroborate her story. "Did your mother say anything to you after you entered the room? Did she appear frightened? Angry?"

I tried to picture her in the moment, leaning over Dad, trying to keep his life from spilling onto the carpet. She'd been crying, screaming his name, pressing her hand to his wound. "Just to call for help."

"How did she seem?" He sat forward, waiting for my response.

I wished I could answer his question. "Upset. Frantic. She was trying to stop the bleeding."

More notes on his page. "You have a sister?"

I blinked, stunned at the abrupt change of inquiry. "Yes. She's at law school."

"Does she know what's happened?" The leather creaked when he shifted his weight, reclining back. Giving me space.

"Not yet." Tangled knots of despair twisted my thoughts. I'd have to call her. Sometime soon. She needed to know. She needed to come home and help me with the disaster of our lives. "She's in Georgia."

"Do you have her contact information?" he asked. "We'll have to speak with her."

How could I tell her? Where would I find the words?

"Lily? Do you have her number?"

"Yes, in my phone," I whispered.

Stephens closed his notebook and then set it on the table. He clasped his hands and leaned his elbows on his knees. His chestnut eyes darkened to ebony when a cloud occluded the sun. "I have to ask you some questions, Lily. They're hard questions, but we need answers, and you might have them."

My fingers gripped the armrests. I shivered in the sudden shade.

"Did your parents fight?"

I dragged my lip through my teeth. My parents used to have knock-down, drag-out brawls when we lived across town in a neighborhood full of identical ranch houses with bad landscaping and tiny backyards. Once, when I was ten, the argument had gotten so bad the neighbors called the cops. The worst of their battles ended a long time ago. The detective would be able to find that out. Of course, he would. There had to be a report of the police coming to the house.

"Sometimes," I told him. "When I was little. They had arguments."

"What were those fights about?"

Good question. I learned at an early age to make myself scarce when the screaming started. I couldn't count the times I'd fallen asleep in the back corner of my closet where their quarrel couldn't cut me. My sister used to lock herself in the garage and sit in the car. Maybe she wished she could drive away but wasn't old enough to leave.

"The firm, maybe, when they first started the business. They didn't fight in front of me." *Because you hid.*

"Not recently?" he asked.

Over the last few months, there'd been several arguments in my parents' home office. Instead of listening or hiding in my closet, I bailed out when the fireworks began and drove to the solitude of the beach with my saxophone in tow.

When they noticed my convenient absences, they'd become more discrete.

"Have they fought lately?"

What was he thinking? He wouldn't give up until I answered.

I chewed on my ragged cheek before working up the courage to answer. "Yes," I said and braced myself for what would come next.

"Okay. Do you know your mother and father were having marital problems? That they'd been in counseling?"

Shock, then irritation tore through me at his revelation. "No. When?" How could I live in the house and not know?

"Last summer." He consulted notes on another page. "Your mother told me they entered an intensive thirty-day program to save their marriage."

My chest constricted, making it difficult to breathe. "I was in Europe last summer." They'd hid it from me while I toured Italy, France, and Germany. Waited until I left the country to deal with their problems in private while I lingered in the Louvre.

"That sucks," he said. Empathy laced his tone. "I'm sorry you have to find out about their marital problems this way."

His bombshell surprise brought my defenses up and cleared some of the fog from my brain. I straightened my posture to stare him down. "So? Lots of parents fight. What's the big deal?"

"Because if your parents weren't getting along, there would be motive for what happened here this morning."

"You think my mother did this?" My stiff spine crumbled, and pain ripped through my lungs. "No way. It's not possible."

"Did your father and mother fight this morning?"

I imagined them arguing in his office, other times, other days. Over what, I had no idea. "I don't know. No. We went to breakfast. They were happy and laughing. We had dinner plans." An hour ago, my father laughed from the doorway, talking about sunsets and the boat.

My throat closed.

"You're sure?" the detective pressed. "Think. Think hard."

Enough. Don't be stupid. Shut your mouth. The last thing I needed to do was talk anymore to the police. I was a lawyer's daughter, and some traits were imbued in my DNA. Somehow, my brain kicked into legal mode, and my tone sharpened as I said, "I didn't hear anything. Like I said, they were happy today."

The detective's mouth twitched. "You said your mother was the only one with your father when you entered the office."

"Yes," I said through clenched teeth.

"You didn't see anyone else?"

The punchline was coming, and I didn't like where it led. "No, why?"

"Because your mother claims someone else was there. Someone who went out onto the balcony and disappeared. Now we haven't located anyone who could scale a six-story building, so we have to ask if you saw or heard another person in the office this morning. Someone who could have wanted to hurt your father."

No amount of legal genetics could help me answer a yes-no question like that. "No. I didn't see anyone else in the office." The corridor was the single way in or out of the offices. I would have seen someone take the back exit. Was my mother lying? In her grief and shock, maybe Mom imagined seeing someone.

A weighty pause stretched out between us. "Your mother also has bruises and scratches as if involved in a struggle."

I saw the office. The glass. The disarray. He was pursuing the wrong path with this. I had to believe that. He had to believe me.

"My mother did not kill my father." Impossible. They might argue, but not murder. I needed to convince us both.

He sat back as if satisfied I concluded the same thing he had. "I think your father and mother argued. I think it got physical. Something happened between them. The gun was pulled."

Defensiveness stiffened my back. "You're wrong. My mom didn't do this. I *heard* two shots."

She didn't. She couldn't.

But then, who fired the shots?

"I need to talk to my mother."

"I'm sorry, Lily. I can't allow you to speak with her right now. Your mother hasn't been able to explain what occurred. She was allegedly in possession of the murder weapon. You were here but arrived after the fact." He rose from the chair. "We're going to take her in for more questions. She's a suspect in your father's murder. Is there someone you can call? Does she have an attorney?"

Murder. The letters spun and whirled in my brain, drenched in waves of blood.

Murder. Blood spilling across the carpet, pooling on his blue shirt...

"Lily? Did you hear me?"

Liz. My parents' partner. That's who I would call.

I choked the answer out. "Yes. I can call someone."

"Are you able to get home?"

Home. The hollow word rang in my mind. "I have my car here." Pins and needles pricked my fingers. An hour ago, I wanted nothing more than to be alone. Now the drive home to an empty house with nothing but the memories of my father's last moments loomed.

"Did your mother drive separately?"

Nodding, I said, "Yes."

He removed a card from his wallet. "If you think of anything else or remember something that can help us help your mom, please call me."

My fingers gripped the edges of the card, the crisp, white paper biting into my skin.

"What about your sister? Do you want me to call her?"

She was in Georgia, finishing her last two semesters of law school. I hadn't considered her in the moment when I knelt beside my dad—of what this would do to her. They'd always been so close. Mom and I were tighter. "I'll call her." But I didn't want to. No matter what happened, my sister would find a way to blame me. She always did.

"Go home, Miss Harmony. We'll be in touch." He rose from the chair.

"No, you're wrong." Panic threaded through my brain. "She didn't do this!"

"She's going with us." He stepped into the hall, dismissing me as he tucked the notebook into his back pocket.

"Wait! She's being arrested?" *Not possible. Not.*

"Go home," he said again, the moment of sympathy over, his supportive air lapsed into unreadable and cold.

He assumed my mother could have fired the shot—with no regard for my pleas.

"Call your attorney."

What was I supposed to do now? My parents were the lawyers—the ones with the answers. I could call Liz from home. Or my car. Not from here.

I retrieved my backpack from Monica's office and stuffed the headphones inside. A uniformed officer kept his eye on me. Without a glance at my mother's door, I ran from the office to the parking garage. Air ripped through my lungs. I pounded down three flights of stairs until I reached the door to my level and burst from the building into the Gulf

Coast heat. Tears blinded me as I staggered toward my black Audi A3.

Across the parking garage, two cops moved around my mother's car, taking pictures.

My view twisted, and I clung to the trunk. A wave of nausea hit, and I vomited my latte behind my car. Spots popped in front of my vision, dancing around images of my father. Smiling. On the beach. On the floor…

Somehow, I opened the door, fell into the driver's seat, then pressed the button to start the car. My clammy skin chilled in the blast of air conditioning. I chewed a handful of mints to erase the sick taste lingering on my tongue. Clutching the wheel, I sobbed. There was no one to help me.

Maybe I should text Jazz. He'd be there for me. I tapped on his contact information. His picture smiled back from the screen, but the phone slipped into my lap.

Not yet. I couldn't form the words.

Chapter Three

It took several minutes to collect myself enough to walk from the car to the house with a mass of soggy tissues pressed to my grief-swollen face. I let myself in through the garage and grabbed a tissue box from the kitchen counter before I slumped into the family room and collapsed onto the couch, chest heaving, nose running.

Every fiber of my body hurt. The ache below my sternum clenched and released in torturous waves.

My father grinned from the mantle, and his mischievous smile stabbed straight through my heart. Mom had taken the picture the day he bought a plane. He'd been so excited. Beside his photo sat a small watercolor I'd painted of a sunset, his birthday present in February.

Our family's history marched across the wood beam, each picture a separate knife to my soul. Last year's Christmas photo with all of us in front of the tree. Belle's college graduation before she left for law school. A family vacation on Oahu when I was twelve.

Shredded, raw, I lay on the couch, staring at the French doors and the pool enclosure beyond, unable to summon an ounce of energy to lift my hand off my clammy forehead or wipe my running nose.

There would be no more grilling by the pool. No heart-to-heart talks on the patio as the sun set behind our house. I'd never again hear his swift footfalls in the hallway outside my room as he brought some interesting case to me to share. I'd never get to tell him the truth: *Dad, I don't want to be a lawyer.*

I needed to tell my sister he was gone. My inner debate raged over calling her tonight or waiting until tomorrow when I learned more. What should I say? She'd think me weak and hate me more than she already did if my voice cracked. As the baby sister, I always wanted her attention. She was the cool older sister who wished she'd been an only child, as if wishing could erase my existence.

My sister always said Mom and Dad didn't fight until I was born.

She blamed me for their unhappiness.

With shaking fingers, I sent her a text. *Call me pls*

Ten minutes crawled by, beyond our family's agreed on window for responses. Fifteen. Twenty. Silence. Then again, Belle never accepted the roll of conformist.

Finally, my phone buzzed. *What do you want?*

My fingers hovered over my phone. *You to not be such a bitch.* Except I couldn't say it. Not today. I needed her. *Just do it. Important.*

I wiped my sweating hands on my shorts as I stared at the phone, waiting for the ring, pacing from family room to kitchen and back a dozen times. Finally, I let myself out the patio doors into the screened enclosure and sat on the edge of the pool, my feet in the water. The tinkling of drops over a small waterfall soothed me a nerve ending at a time, leaving me grateful for the privacy fence separating our yard from the others around us. No one would see me weeping into the water.

The sky bled orange into deep purple in the east, and planes' trails streaked in a crisscrossing pattern of vibrant vapor. I breathed in the fragrance of an early summer evening laced with gardenia and oleander and missed my dad with every ounce of blood in my heart.

A half hour later, she called.

"This *better* be important. I'm in the middle of exams."

No hello. No sorry I didn't send you a birthday card this year. Or last year.

My paper-dry throat closed, and I gripped the blue tiled edge of the pool. Over the last hour, I prepared myself for this moment, but the truth turned to lumps in my throat.

I could do it. I could. "I have to tell you something."

My sister didn't disguise her snort. "Well? Clock's ticking."

I should slam the phone on the ground. Shut her off from the terrible thing I endured while she sat in class hundreds of miles away. Take away her chance to grieve because she was too busy to give a crap about anyone but herself.

Sweat dampened my shirt, and a flash of heat crowded against my skin as the awful truth burst from my brain, fresh and sharp as if it occurred a moment ago. "Dad is dead."

Silence. No gasp. No cry.

"Did you hear me?"

"What did you say?"

My thoughts swam with bloody images, staining my memories with unbearable pain. "Daddy...he got shot. He's dead."

"What? How? Who shot him?" A strangled sound between a sob and a curse choked off her words, the most passion I heard from my sister in years.

I blocked out her grief and the ever-present picture of my father dying on the floor to answer. "They think Mom shot him."

Silence. We Harmonys were so good at silence.

"Belle? Did you hear me?"

Rage flew through the phone, vaporizing her sudden tears like a nuclear blast. This was the sister I feared. "That's bullshit. Why would they believe such a thing?"

Here was the part of the conversation I dreaded. I had to tell her I'd been there and couldn't back Mom's story of a mysterious shooter. "Mom had the gun in her hand. The cops say they were fighting over it when it went off." The charge sounded vulgar on my tongue. Like I accused our mother of a terrible crime.

The detective's claim echoed in my brain. *She has cuts, scrapes, like they fought...*

"You're wrong. It's a lie."

Belle couldn't see me, but I shook my head anyway. Did she know Mom and Dad went to marriage counseling? I lived in the same house blissfully ignorant. "What if it's not? What if they were fighting again?" The words tumbled out, unbidden. They tasted like poison.

"No." She sniffled into the phone, proving my sister had a heart somewhere under her impenetrable granite shell. "Mom and Dad are tight."

"It's true. They went to counseling last summer. When I was in Europe."

She said nothing for several seconds. "None of that matters. Marriage counseling doesn't mean she killed Dad. Tell me the rest." When I finished, my sister let loose a streak of crisp obscenities. "You incompetent idiot. Why did you talk to the cops?"

A chill brushed over my damp skin. She'd caught me in a mistake. Suddenly I was six, and my fifteen-year-old sister caught me in her room playing games on her tablet. "I had no choice. I was in the office. What was I supposed to do? Lie to the police?"

Maybe I should have.

"How about shut your mouth until you had a lawyer present. Didn't you learn anything living in this family with a bunch of lawyers?"

"I'm not guilty of anything." My terse reply reminded her. "I had nothing to hide. And I'm not stupid. I didn't tell them anything to hurt her." Still, my conscience asked, *Did I?*

"Maybe, maybe not. But you didn't help Mom with your interview."

She had me there. If I helped her with my comments to the cop, my mother would be home right now. I chewed my trembling bottom lip.

"Where is she?"

"They took her. I don't...to the police station, I guess." I never asked the detective specifically where. I never demanded to know what happened next or when I'd see my mother again. Maybe the shock *had* stripped me of my common sense.

Or maybe I believed she could have aimed a gun at my father's chest and shot him. My stomach heaved up behind my tonsils. I grabbed a wad of tissues from my shorts pocket to cover my gag.

"Are you sick?" she asked.

"It's nothing," I croaked out. The afternoon sun darted behind a cloud. Chilled, I dragged myself up and inside as the grandfather clock rang four.

She swore, but she must have taken the phone away from her mouth because I caught part of her vivid wording, not the full blistering tirade.

I brushed away a stream of tears. Mad or not, I wanted her with me. "Are you coming home?" I finally asked, afraid she'd hear my fear. I didn't want to be alone. No Dad. No Mom. I needed my sister to help get through the next week, day, hours.

Who would I talk to so I wouldn't go insane?

"I'll be on the road in an hour. Be smart. Don't talk to anyone else, okay?" She paused until I thought she'd hung up on me. "Lock the doors. Don't let anyone in. Not even the cops." The call ended abruptly.

I stared out the windows to where the pool sparkled in the afternoon sun. I should be on my way to band practice, planning my summer, dreading my first semester of college, and figuring out what I would wear to my graduation party. Instead, grief immobilized me. This morning, we'd gone to breakfast at our favorite place. We'd eaten too many banana pancakes. I'd been aggravated because Dad wouldn't hire a temp. Mom had been preoccupied with a fundraiser she would chair for the local library and paint colors for the office.

Dinner, the boat, sunset, and Jazz. All so normal. There'd been no hint my life was about to go sideways, or both of my parents would be taken from me by lunch time.

Even exceeding the speed limit, it would take Belle at least nine hours to make the drive from Atlanta to Fort Myers. More if the traffic backed up along the route. I'd be alone tonight. What about Jazz? I'd missed his stream. I fired off a text. *Please don't hate me.*

Minutes ticked by as I stared at the screen. The phone buzzed his reply. *Not a chance. You okay?*

A wave of agony crested on my breath. Not okay. Never okay

again. My body shuddered as I typed an answer. *No. Something terrible happened. My dad got shot.*

Instead of texting, the phone lit up and rang. Tears blocked my throat. Jazz *never* called me. We existed in a universe of disconnected texts and poorly timed emojis.

"Hello?"

"Lily! Is he all right? Are you?" He sounded out of breath as if he'd been running. The wind rushing by the receiver told me exactly what he was doing.

"No. He died." I wiped the tears with my sleeve as I tugged another wad of tissues from the box on the coffee table beside me. The clumps of tissue in my hands did little to absorb the fresh onslaught.

The snapping wind stopped. He heaved his breath into the phone. "Oh my god. I'm sorry. How?"

My lips parted, then shut. The words I needed to say refused to divest themselves from my mind. Maybe if I didn't say it, I could pretend none of this was real. Instead of explaining, I asked, "Can I see you?"

"Yeah. Sure. You want me to pick you up?"

All the times I'd avoided having him come to the house—I didn't want him to have to deal with my parents. I didn't want to answer questions I hadn't asked myself like *did I really like him that way* and *what would the parents say if they found out I liked a gamer.* We'd been close for months. Best friends outside my gated community. I was pretty sure my mother suspected we were more.

Now I wished we were.

"Could you?" Did he hear the sadness in my voice? Even I could hear my need. "I'll send you the address."

"Yeah. I'll be there in a bit. As soon as I shower."

"Thanks." After he hung up, I stared down at my father's blood on my hands, the dark, dried spot of it filling the edges of my index fingernail. He'd been alive when his blood stained my hands. For seconds, he'd still been there.

~ * ~

I ignored my sister's demand to do nothing until she got home. Instead, I left a message for Liz on the answering service. My sister was right about one thing. We needed legal help.

I was in the kitchen with a steaming mug of tea when the doorbell rang. My heart thudded in time to my steps as I crossed the gray-tiled foyer. Taking a deep breath, I opened the door.

"Lily, I don't know what to say." His blond hair was damp and darkened from his recent shower.

I slipped into his arms without hesitation, buried my face in his shoulder, and breathed in his scent from his clean T-shirt. He hugged me hard. I didn't cry. Gratitude swelled in my chest, and some of the loneliness eased. "Thanks for coming." He closed the door, and I grabbed his hand to lead him back to the kitchen.

"You look like hell. That all you've eaten today?" He gestured at my teacup.

A sigh escaped my lips, rough and ragged on the end. "Yeah. Pretty much. I had breakfast." Breakfast felt like two years ago.

"There's gotta be someone who delivers in this area." His gaze drifted over the granite counter tops and the gleaming hardwood floors.

My spine stiffened a notch. He lived in Fort Myers, and not on the pretty beach side. At eighteen and on his own after his parents' divorce, he'd finished high school online. He rented a neglected bungalow consisting of one bedroom, a living room, and a closet-sized kitchen. The entire house could fit inside our three-car garage.

His presence in my huge house made me self-conscious, and I worried he'd think less of me because of what we had, which was completely messed up.

"How about pizza?"

My appetite roared at his suggestion. Food. Pizza. How could I be hungry after what happened today?

He saw my indecision and took charge. "I'm ordering food. You're gonna eat it." He drew out his phone and searched for local restaurants. "This one sounds promising. What do you like on your pizza?"

I smiled in spite of the dark train of my thoughts. "Everything but fish."

"A girl after my heart," he said with a wink and a grin. I collapsed onto a kitchen stool while he ordered on his phone app.

When he finished, he dragged a stool next to mine and took my hands in his. "We have a feast coming."

"Thank you."

His thumb circled on the back of my hand. "So, you want to talk about this? Tell me what happened?"

I didn't want to, but someone had to share this burden with me. I took my time, trying to remember details as I lived through those minutes. While I talked, he stroked my hands and offered me napkins to dry my endless tears. "So that's it. That's what happened."

He shifted in his seat and crossed his arms. "You said your father's balcony door was shattered. There was glass on the floor. Any idea how it got there?"

"Not really. Maybe one of the shots? There were two shots, but my dad was hit once."

"So, where'd the other bullet go?"

I chewed my bottom lip, distancing my thoughts from the horror of my father's death and instead imagining how it could have happened. I refused to glance at my father on the floor of my memories. "If a bullet fired inside the office had hit the door, wouldn't the glass break outside, on the balcony? Glass was all over the carpet and the desk." In my mind, I saw the shards winking across the carpet in the sunshine.

He played with my hand, brushing his fingers over my bright, melon-painted nails. "You'd think so. Anything else weird you can think of?"

I didn't want to go back there, but like the glass, maybe something important would come from my memories. Something I could contribute to help clear my mom. I closed my eyes and pictured the office, keeping my focus away from the blood. "My dad's chair was pushed to the far left and facing the balcony."

"Like he was looking in that direction?"

Nodding, I blinked back tears. He gripped my fingers, sending tingles up my arm.

"And you didn't see anyone else in there, but your mom said she saw someone. How could they get out of the office if they didn't use the door?" he asked.

"Or into the office. No one walked by me," I said.

We stared at each other. The answers to our questions remained elusive while the clock ticked in the hall. He ran a hand through his damp hair, his expression curious. "Do you have any pictures of your father's office? Where the furniture is and the layout?"

I glanced at him, wondering if he thought I'd imagined what I saw and heard—because I doubted myself. "Yeah. I have a couple on my phone. I used to sneak up on him and take candids when he worked." My voice caught. Dad had chased me away from his office, even as he smiled for my photos. For one Christmas, I'd made him a collage book of pictures of him deep in thought as he worked on a case or busy on the phone. He'd loved it.

Jazz squeezed my hand again and gave a gentle tug. I missed his warmth when he let me go. "Do you have any paper around here? And a pencil? It might help if we draw the office on paper, to figure out the sequence of events."

"You're right," I said, my heart full of thanks. Belle might be miles away, but the person I needed was here. I had help.

By the time the pizza arrived, we'd cleared the dining room table and taped together six sheets of computer paper. Jazz served up steaming slices while I sketched the basic layout of my father's office. It felt good to be doing something, anything, to help my mother. Dad would want me to help.

Then there was my sister. Maybe if I had something useful to offer when she got here, she wouldn't hate me so much.

For the thousandth time, I checked my phone. No call back from Liz Monroe. Our band mates had texted their condolences and graciously rescheduled practice.

"Can I see your phone pics again?"

"Sure." I handed it to Jazz.

He studied the pictures on the screen, compared them to the sketched layout, and nodded his approval. "Nice job on the drawing. You're good at this."

"Thanks," I said with a smile. "Painting's my thing." I gestured to the watercolor on the distant mantle.

He walked over, lifted the painting from the ledge, and brought it back to the table. "You did this? It's really good."

"Thanks." With the smell of garlic and cheese in the air, hunger took over, and I became human again—as human as possible with a dead dad and a mother in jail.

"You'll have to show me sometime." His gaze clung to mine for several seconds until I pretended to be interested in the remnants of my pizza crust. "Okay. Now for the bad parts. Where were the glass and the chair?"

This was the hard stuff. I indicated the area. "Here. On the floor. Some scattered on the desk, too."

He hesitated, and his brows drew down into a studious point. "Did you go out on the balcony? Did you see anyone outside?"

"No," I said, shaking my head. "I stayed with my dad."

"I'm sorry." His fingers brushed against my arm before he took his hand away. "I'm a total idiot. This must be awful to talk about."

I bumped his shoulder with mine, wishing his fingers had lingered. "Talking helps. I feel like I'm doing something, not sitting in the corner crying—which I can totally do." I held his gaze for longer than I should have. The pain in my heart or the compassion he gave made me lean closer.

"Can you draw the rest?" He offered a pencil severing the tenuous string tugging us together.

"Yeah. I can do it." Clenching my teeth against the hurt, I sketched my mother first, kneeling on the floor. The gun had been in her left hand. My pencil hovered over the paper. "Wait a minute. This is wrong."

"We can erase it." He searched the pile of colored pencils. "I think there was an eraser in here."

I stopped his searching hand with mine. "No, that's not what I mean. The gun was in her left hand. My mother is right-handed." A surge of hope warmed my chest. I had to call the detective. Immediately.

Jazz scowled at the paper. "I know you're not going to want to hear this, but could she have switched hands? What was she doing with her right hand?"

"She had something—her scarf—pressed on my father's wound. *Wait a minute.* She said, 'he's gone,' to my dad."

"Who was she taking about?"

"I don't know. I never had a chance to talk to her. They wouldn't let me see her."

"But your mom and dad were in the office alone?"

"Yeah. I keep thinking about it…running through those seconds in my mind." I pressed my fists to my eyes and gritted my teeth. "Why can't I remember?"

"You will," he soothed. "Take your time."

My hands dropped to my sides. "No. You're right. She could have switched hands to make tending to Dad easier." The excitement of a possible solution deflated. So much for my big find. "Why would she try to stop the bleeding if she'd shot him?"

"I have no idea," Jazz confessed. "What about your dad. He was here? In front of the desk?"

"Yes," I said, my throat tight.

Tugging on the neck of his T-shirt, he said, "Don't you think the positioning is odd?"

"Why?"

"Well, if someone aimed a gun at you, would you go toward them? And see how his face is leaning this way? Doesn't it make you wonder why he was looking toward the balcony door?"

Right again. I didn't understand why the scene had ended that way. My brain had the consistency of cold, day-old oatmeal. I ran my finger over the pencil lines, smearing them.

"You mentioned the glass. Do you know if your dad had any on him? Like the glass hit him?"

Digging through the resistance in my mind, I concentrated on the awful moment. "He had small cuts on his skin. I was in a car accident once, and the passenger window blew in on me." I ran my fingers over the faded scars on my forearm. "The cuts reminded me of the accident."

"Is that what happened to your knees?"

"I forgot about my legs." I glanced down at the array of cuts and dried bloody smears on my knees. "After the car accident, my arms were covered in slices. Like my knees."

"You should clean those—"

"Wait," I said. Why didn't I realize it before? "My mom had cuts on her face too."

"Well, that means the glass came into the office. Your dad was hit with it. I wonder if the first shot was the glass breaking—maybe from the outside."

"A gust of wind blew through the hallway, fluttering magazine covers. The door must have blown out before the shots. That's where the wind came from in the hallway." The tremor in the floor could have been caused by the window. "The door is hurricane glass. It's supposed to withstand a hundred and forty miles an hour."

He gazed at our patio doors as if wondering whether they were also as strong. "I've read about it. The glass is supposed to stop projectiles. A single shot wouldn't have gone through." He went to the sink, soaked some paper towels then wrung them out. "You need to clean those cuts."

"I'm fine."

"Shhhhh. Prop your foot up here." He slid the flip flop off my foot and lifted my ankle with careful fingers. "They're not too deep, but you might have glass in some of these cuts. You probably should have gone to the hospital."

I clenched my teeth as he cleansed my wounds with cool water before drying the fresh blood with clean paper towels.

"I think there's something in this one," he said with a grimace. "Do you have a first aid kit? Tweezers?"

"In the hall closet. Outside the bathroom." I wiped my tears on a clean towel.

He returned with antiseptic and gauze. "I'll try not to hurt you," he promised.

Once he removed the glass and bound my knees in clean white gauze, I swallowed some ibuprofen and picked up our storm door conversation.

"No, I don't believe a shot would go through. They had those doors installed after one of the Gulf hurricanes made a mess of the offices."

"Then what came through the door?" Jazz twirled the pencil between his long fingers. "Maybe something explosive?"

"Some sort of blast might explain the crash. I wonder if the police came up with anything." A new set of worries erupted in my chest. Horrible enough that we were searching for a murderer, but whomever had done this had an arsenal.

"Did you smell smoke?"

"No." If there had been smoke, the gusting breeze took care of any traces.

"That means we might be trying to find someone experienced with explosives."

"Maybe the person who did this came in from the balcony? Dad's office is on the top floor." I tried to imagine a person coming in from outside.

Jazz nodded grimly, his remark mirroring my worries. "Any idea how someone could get out on a top floor balcony?"

The sixth-floor corner office had a view of the ocean. So many times, I'd stood outside on the balcony with my dad, gazing up at the edge of the roof and imagining how cool it would be to climb up there. "Wow. From the roof. All they'd have to do is drop over the side and onto the balcony."

"This was very well planned, Lil," Jazz said, his tone grave.

My heart thumped; my brain too terrified to consider what we were suggesting. Someone had planned my father's murder. Meticulously. Someone had blown their way into the office, through hurricane windows, and killed him.

"You know what I know?" he asked, his gaze on the office's floorplan.

"No. What?"

"I know your mom didn't do this. And I know we're right about how they got in and out of the office."

Hope flooded my mind, lifting a thousand pounds of burden from my shoulders. How did Stephens not see what we did? They'd have to let my mother go once I shared what we uncovered. "Um. I should call the cops."

"Yeah. Might be a good idea."

Jazz sat beside me as I fished out the detective's number and dialed. The call went to voicemail. Some of my exuberance deflated.

"Detective Stephens. This is Lily Harmony. I need to talk to you about my mother. Can you call me back?" I left my number and ended the call. "Hopefully, he'll call me." Sighing, exhaustion weighed me down as I remembered Belle's vibrant anger. "I don't even know where they took her." I shuddered. My sister's reaction to another conference with the police was likely to be as unhelpful as the first one.

His fingers brushed over my hand again. "You know more than you did an hour ago. Talk to the cop. Explain what you know." He tucked a comforting arm over my shoulders. I leaned against him, relieved we'd come up with a plausible explanation. "Then you can spring your mom," he said.

That would be a reunion like no other—I'd pick up my mother from jail, both of us knowing what I hadn't remembered put her there. Both of us pretending finding her with a gun in her hand didn't make me wonder for a minute.

"Lily? Did you hear me?" he asked with a gentle nudge.

I started at his question. "What?"

"Your phone's ringing."

I snatched it off the counter and hit the button. "Hello?"

"Lily? This is Detective Stephens. Sorry I missed your call. I was in a meeting." Conversation behind him told me he was at work.

"Thanks, uh, for calling me back." My throat went dry. Talking to this man made me feel like a five-year-old caught drawing on the dining room wall with a Sharpie. Not as if I'd ever done anything like that.

"You mentioned you wanted to talk? Do you want to talk on the phone? Do you want me to come to the house?"

I glanced at the diagrams spread over the table. How much damage could we do to Mom's case if we showed him our visual aids? He could charge me with something—evidence tampering or sticking my nose where it didn't belong. The hesitation in my gut answered my question. "Um...can we meet at the City Coffee House in Times Square? I can be there in fifteen minutes."

The coffee house had always been one of my favorite places, just steps from the beach. At this time of night, we'd be able to get a table on the deck, overlooking the Gulf. It would be dark, but the ocean sounds never failed to soothe me. And I was in desperate need of soothing.

"That's fine. It's on my way home. I'll see you there."

"Well?" Jazz asked as I stared at my phone, unsure I made the correct choice.

Inhaling, I said, "He's going to meet me."

"You want me to go with you? We're kind of in this thing together."

I pecked him on the cheek, lingering beside him for a moment and breathing in the smell of his shower and minty soap. "I better do this on my own."

His blue eyes filled with worry. "Okay. But you call me when you're done."

"All this calling. What happened to texting?"

He wrapped his arms around me and squeezed. "Don't argue."

I was so grateful he'd come over tonight. "I won't."

Chapter Four

The City Coffee House sat just off Fort Myers Beach's majestic pier, giving the bistro a heart-rending view of the Gulf of Mexico and the wide, white sand beach. The area was known as Times Square, although the collection of restaurants and shops bore little resemblance to the neon-signed version up north. After I parked next to the Sandal Factory, I made sure to lock my car and hurried past the open-air restaurants and ice cream stands to the coffee shop, my puffy eyes hidden behind dark sunglasses. Every step took conscious effort, like my limbs had been infused with concrete. Inside, my soul lay tattered and torn. On the drive over, I'd promised myself I would not cry. I'd hold it together to meet with the detective.

He was seated beneath an umbrellaed table, his gaze fixed on the last vestiges of sunset bleeding into the horizon. Boats bobbed offshore, their cabin lights twinkling like earth-bound stars. The detective shredded the label from his sweating water bottle leaving the frayed paper in a soggy pile. "Miss Harmony," he said when he saw me.

His sunglasses sat on top of his head, and with a clear mind I saw him for the first time. I guessed him to be around thirty, closer to my sister's age than mine, and a little young to be handling my father's murder case.

"Sorry it took so long." I fanned my sweaty face. "The drawbridge was up. I had to wait."

I'd taken the time to change into knee-length shorts and a sleeveless white polo, but I couldn't do anything about my blotchy complexion, or bandaged knees. Only time would fix those. I removed my sunglasses hoping he'd empathize with my appearance and listen to me.

"It's fine. I was enjoying the view." He waved to the waitress in super-short shorts. I wondered which view he meant as my opinion of him descended a few, frosty degrees. "You want something? Coffee?

Water?" He lifted his bottle to me.

"Iced tea would be great." I fidgeted under the table, nervous that he might think I wasted his time and not hear me out.

"How are you holding up?" he asked.

On cue, tears filled my eyes. I swallowed the wave of grief and took a moment to collect myself. So much for the self-pep talk. "I'm okay. I needed to get away from the house."

"Is your sister home?"

The waitress approached, order slips in hand. "Not yet. She's on her way."

After I ordered, he removed the notebook he'd used earlier from his bag beneath the table. "You said you remembered something?"

This was the moment. I inhaled a deep breath. "Yeah. Something I can't figure out."

He tensed. I suspected this was not the conversation he'd been expecting. I was not here to relay cold, hard facts, but to offer my suspicions. "Okay…"

"How did the balcony door get broken?" I blurted out.

Stephens stared at me for a full minute before he answered. "Why does it matter?"

I rolled my eyes. Great. The answer a question with a question routine. But I needed information, and he needed to listen to what I had to say. My mother's freedom depended on this meeting. "It's hurricane proof glass. I read an article where the guy tried to get through a window but couldn't even with a dozen shots. The glass was inside the office, scattered over the floor—on my dad. My mom was cut too. How did the window shatter? Something on the outside had to break it in."

"Miss Harmony, do you know what the wind speed was today?"

I lifted a shoulder. "No."

"Eight knots. At the elevation of your father's office, my guess would be ten to twelve knots, blowing off the ocean, right at your father's balcony door. If the door shattered because the pane had been shot and weakened, where do you think the glass would go?"

I swallowed. "Inside?"

"Yes. Most of it would blow back into the office."

"Was there any glass outside?"

Curiosity blossomed on his face. At least I piqued his interest. "No. Not much." Then he shifted in his seat, and I sensed I was losing him as the waitress deposited my tea onto the table.

"That's not fast enough to break those windows. And the broken glass was mostly inside. Hurricane winds weren't blowing today, and the door is supposed to be strong enough to withstand a gunshot." Strings of white lights winked on overhead, bobbing in the humid sea breeze. Goosebumps rose on my arms.

The detective tapped his notebook. Was he at least considering what I suggested? "What are you getting at?"

I had to make him doubt what he thought he knew. "I believe my mother is telling the truth. Someone came in from the balcony and shot my dad."

His lips drew down, a definite you're-wasting-my-time frown. "How would they get there? Are you implicating Spiderman?"

"This isn't funny." I let my anger flare into my tone.

"Neither is trying to work a case when you're not a cop. When you don't see the entire picture."

I gripped the edge of the table with my fingernails. "What is the entire picture?"

"Go home, Miss Harmony." He glanced at his cellphone. "Is there anything else?"

"Did you even go up on the roof?" I asked him.

He paused the conversation until a man loaded down with fishing gear lumbered by on his way to the pier. "There was no need."

So much for the unbiased opinion I hoped he'd have. I decided to toss out my other piece of ammunition. "My mother's right-handed."

The strings of lights dipped and bounced in the breeze. He crushed his empty water bottle in his hand. "So?"

"When I saw her in the office, the gun was in her left hand, not her right."

The cords in his neck stood out, and I sensed I was close to pissing him off. I had to give him credit, though. He kept his tone patient even when he asked, "Do you think she could have switched hands?"

I couldn't stop the tears. "Why would she try to stop the bleeding? Why not just let him die?"

With a sigh, the detective got up then pushed in his chair. He dropped a five-dollar bill onto the table. "Miss Harmony. I am truly sorry for your loss. Both of them. I can't imagine what you're dealing with. But the mind has a way of changing what we see to fit the picture we'd rather see." He picked up his laptop bag and slung the strap over his shoulder. "Go home. Get some rest. Talk to your mother's attorney in the morning. I'm sure they'd appreciate knowing what you know."

"But you're going to leave her in there. She's innocent!" A couple stared in our direction.

"Call the attorney," he said again.

"I did," I snapped.

"Then let them handle this. Get some rest." His strides took him to the corner of the complex, away from the beach. He never glanced back. I waited until he receded into the darkness before dragging myself out of my chair. The police had no intention of entertaining the possibility my mother didn't do this.

I had to believe in her innocence. Otherwise, I'd live the rest of my life without her.

Instead of returning to my car, I opted for the comfort of warm sand beneath my feet and the quiet hum and shush of the waves breaking on the shore. At the pier, I stepped onto the sandy planks that stretched out into the Gulf, past the gift shop perched high above the receding surf. The tide had ebbed away from the shore, and the ocean was calm— totally opposite of my pulse and blood pressure. Lights winked on the water's surface, and music thrummed from the restaurants along the beach. The man who strolled by our table with his gear earlier stood by the rail fishing, his cigarette a bright, burning star against the night.

This morning, I'd been annoyed I couldn't get to the beach. I'd given Dad a rough time. Now he was gone. What would happen to the firm? To me and my sister? She had law school to finish. I was beginning my life. High school graduation loomed, plus my summer internships. Then there was the dream of confessing to my mother I didn't want to move to Boston and go to law school.

None of those dreams seemed possible now. None of it mattered.

I'd been so stupid. Tears dripped down my cheeks, blending salt with pain and the ocean air.

Inhaling, I breathed in the perfume of sea and distant cigarette smoke, algae, and fishy brine. After a time, my breathing leveled, and my brain cleared as I leaned my forearms against the railing. The frantic thoughts of the day brushed against the sea's solace like waves touching sand on the shore, and I heaved out one last cleansing exhale. Sailboats bobbed on the tide west of the pier, their yellow cabin lights soft pinpricks of comfort.

Still, as much as the call of the Gulf fastened me to the pier, I had to go home, alone. Belle would show up eventually. The way she drove, sooner than later. It would be a good idea to try to sleep, to brace myself for the next violent storm hovering just off the horizon of my life.

I moved to leave. Darkness cloaked parts of the pier, but the lights from the shore outlined the fisherman's shape against the dark water.

His cigarette glowed as he sucked in, his tattooed forearm visible against the darkness. He exhaled in two thick streams. "You have a hell of a problem on your hands, Miss Harmony."

My feet froze to the pier.

"You're not going to get anywhere talking to a cop. He's already made up his mind." His voice was low and guttural. I had to strain to hear his whispers rasping against the noise of the tide. "Or maybe he's not who you should be worried about."

"Who are you?"

He chuckled, his face in shadowy profile, his hat pulled low. "Someone who knows what you need more than anything." The man rubbed out his cigarette on the rail, sparks flashing and dying like fireflies.

"What's that?" I asked him, sure he could hear the thundering of my heart.

"A friend. Someone who understands what it's like to be in a position like yours."

My feet shuffled back and to the side, trying to skirt the edge of his reach. Stupid! So stupid. I was out on a pier in the middle of the ocean alone with a strange guy who knew my name. Had he followed me? Stalked me while I sat at the coffee house? How did he know Stephens was a cop?

He could kill me and dump me over the side. No one would ever know what happened to me. The reality of my vulnerability fed anger into my blood.

"What do you want from me?" I demanded, my fists clenched, my feet planted.

"Nothing. I want to help you. Didn't you hear me?"

I moved back another step to put a bit more distance between us. Terror clogged my throat, but I had to answer. Keep him talking. That was what they always said, right before the guy jumped off the side of the building or detonated the bomb. If he was talking, he wasn't trying to kill me.

So I hoped.

What if this guy had killed my father? Hot tears flooded my eyes—tears I didn't need distracting me. I blinked them away. "I don't know what you mean," I stammered.

The man tracked my progress as I tried to get by him. Something in his stance told me he was more than a fisherman, more than some random guy. He stepped into the middle of the pier, closing my path to escape. "You know. Your parents. This was no accident—no murder your mother planned. Don't let the cop tell you otherwise."

"How do you know this?" I gasped.

The man lit a fresh cigarette, and for a second the glow of the match illuminated his beard in a flash of flame. He laughed. The sound fell harsh and unpleasant, the notes laced with menace. "Your father hired me."

My father. Why would Dad employ a creepy guy with a skull and dagger tattoo on his arm? "What do you want?" I squeaked. The raucous music on the shore guaranteed no one would hear me scream. Soaked in chilly sweat, my sleeveless polo shirt clung to my back.

"Your father hired me to investigate something for him."

Stunned, I asked, "What?"

"Hmmmm…that's where things get interesting. See, I was supposed to deliver my report today, but I had a dead battery. By the time I got my car going, I was a half hour late for our meeting. And then I heard the call on the police scanner. I put two and two together. Someone at your parents' law firm figured out what I was researching and didn't want me to deliver the report to your father—that's my guess. But your dad paid for my work. Paid a lot for it. I figure you and your mother deserve to have what might have gotten him killed."

I stared at him, aghast. "What? So they can come after me next?" The shadows on the pier took on a darker hue. I glanced behind me. We were alone.

The man puffed on his cigarette. "I'm sorry, but it's a matter of time. You Harmonys are standing in their way."

"Who's way? What do they want?" My body went stock still. "Why? I don't know anything."

He bent to his fishing gear, pulled out a plastic bag, and tossed the bag toward me. I jumped as it landed at my feet. "What you're going to need is on the flash drive. I'd keep that drive safe if I were you." He took a drag and blew out the smoke. "You might want to get out of town too."

"Who are you? Really?" I demanded.

"It's better if you don't know," he said, his words a whisper above the waves.

I gingerly retrieved the plastic bag, my fingers playing over the shape of the drive inside. "You said you wanted to help me."

"I just did."

I glared at him—which was ineffectual in the inky darkness. "Then we have a different opinion of help. You said my father paid you. Does my mother know?"

The man said nothing for a moment. Finally, he stubbed his cigarette under his toe. "No. She doesn't. She shouldn't. When you view those files, you'll know why. That's all I'm going to say."

My fingers clutched the drive. "Does this prove she's innocent?"

"It doesn't prove she's guilty."

"You're not helping," I ground out through clenched teeth.

He angled his body against the railing. The fisherman tugged his Marine's cap farther down, covering most of his face. Who was this guy? A private detective? A spy?

"I am helping you, but now I'm questioning the logic of doing so. Take what I gave you and get the hell out of here," he snarled.

"Wait. How do I talk to you again? I might have…questions."

"You don't. The questions are your problem, not mine." He picked up his gear.

I couldn't let him leave, not if he had information that might help get my mother out of jail. "I'll pay you to work for me, like my father did."

The man stopped. His cap dipped toward the pier as if he considered his choice of shoes. I had his attention.

"How much do you want?" I had my college fund and the money in my savings account.

"What could you need me for?"

Reggae music blared from a dockside bar as a new band tuned up.

"I need you to find who killed my father," I said.

"Honey, that's a subject you might not like to study."

Rage ripped up my throat, vaporizing the tears. "Don't call me honey. You want the job or not?"

"Tell you what. You check out what's on the drive. You decide what you want me to do for you." He faded into the darkness.

"But how do I find you again?"

He murmured over his shoulder, "I like the crab cakes at The Whale. They serve them on Sundays, starting at eight. Chances are, I'll be there drinking a Key West Sunset Ale." Whistling, he strode away.

I pressed the drive into my palm, digging the edges into my skin. What had my father hired this man to investigate? Someone at my parents' law firm?

There was only one way to find out.

I jogged down the pier while I dialed on my phone. "Jazz? It's Lily. I need your help."

Chapter Five

Jazz whipped the bungalow door open before I could knock. He wore black gym shorts and a sky-blue tank top that deepened the color of his eyes. One side of his hair was flattened as if he'd been sleeping. "What's wrong? Is your mom okay? You have an accident or something?" He darted a glance toward the street where my out-of-its-element Audi sat against the curb.

My body trembled as if in the throes of a fever even as goosebumps erupted on my arms. "I wish that was all it was."

He took my arm and led me inside. "Come on in and sit down. What happened?" His Bach trumpet sat on the coffee table made from a milk crate and a green painted board. My voice seized up as I tried to put into words what I experienced since he left my house. I shivered. The air conditioning chilled the air to snow level, and my damp shirt clung and cooled against my back. "Do you have a sweatshirt I could borrow?"

"Yeah, sure." He dug around in his closet. "I...it's pretty clean."

Clasping the thick cotton to my chest, I breathed deeply. It smelled like home and safety. Good enough for me. I tugged the shirt over my hair. "It's perfect." I rolled up the too-long sleeves and followed him into the kitchen. The room consisted of an apartment-sized refrigerator, microwave, and two-burner stove. A set of cabinets flanked a stainless-steel sink, and the countertops used to be blue before most of the finish wore away.

"How'd it go with the police? You look like you saw a ghost." He offered me one of his two mismatched chairs and took a seat on the other side of his tiny kitchen table.

"Not good. He basically told me to mind my own business." My throat closed on my anger. I wanted to cry more than a couple of ineffectual, inconvenient tears. A genuine crying jag—a rant and rave, throwing fragile things, hating the world for what it had done to me—a true fountain of pain.

He took my hands between his. The contact soothed. Between his comfort and the warm sweatshirt, the shaking in my body eased. "He'll come around. Maybe we can find actual proof somehow. Did you ask him about the roof? Did anyone go up there?"

The detective had brushed off my ideas like yesterday's dog hair. "He didn't seem impressed."

"Well he's an asshole," Jazz said.

"Agreed." Stress pounded in my temples on the cusp of a full-blown migraine. "You know, someone could get up to the roof without coming into the law office. There's an access door from the stairwell."

His blue-eyed gaze shifted to seriousness, a gesture out of character for him. "Why do I think your upset is more than the cops giving you the brush off?"

I tugged my hand out of his and dipped my fingers into my shorts pocket, coming up with the drive. "Because you're right." I told him about the man, his job for my father, and what he claimed to have on this drive. "He scared me. I was afraid to open this on my home computer. If someone killed my father to prevent him from seeing this, what will they do when they find out I'm carrying the drive around in my pocket?" The more I thought about what to do on my way over here, the more I became sure the fisherman's investigation was dangerous.

Jazz took the drive from me and bounced it in his palm. "You're right. Who was this guy? A private detective?"

I shrugged. "Something like that. Dad hired him, but the man wouldn't say why. There was more to it, I'm sure. He told me I could meet him tomorrow night at The Whale. I offered to hire him to help me find out who shot my dad."

Jazz gripped the drive. "You're going to meet with this guy again? You think that's wise?"

I grimaced and gestured toward the drive like a hairy spider sat on his hand. "Depends what's on that thing."

"We'll see. I don't like this. You might be going to the cops with this after we're done." He picked up his car keys and lifted me out of the chair with a hand.

"We're going somewhere?"

He nodded. "If you're right about this being dangerous, there's one place to access it, and it's not here."

I ran a hand over my disheveled hair. "Okay. Where?'

"A friend. Someone with a hell of a lot more firewall than I have."

~ * ~

Jazz had a ton of friends in the video game streaming

community, and several of them were involved in his eSports plan. But I didn't know one of the most famous streamers online lived twenty minutes from his apartment—a total gaming badass—someone who might be able to help me.

We didn't say much as we drove across town, listening to our latest set tape. He cradled my hand when he didn't have to shift his Jeep. The sides were open to the tropical night. I closed my eyes, letting the silken, humid air drift over my face. If I went to Boston, I wouldn't have this—the soft strains of *Moondance* and the beat of reggae—plus endless summers. Right now, with my father dead, Mom in trouble, and the future dawning bleaker by the moment, leaving Fort Myers seemed unrealistic. How would I survive? Stuck inside, cold, miserable—without the sunshine and music my soul craved.

Jazz wouldn't be there either, and the agony of missing him cut my battered heart into tiny shreds. It's not like we were romantically involved. Yeah, there'd been that one night we made out on the beach…but we never tried to cross the line again.

Why did we stay on opposite sides of that line? He cared. I was sure as he reached for my hand again. Maybe the hesitation in our relationship was on me. Did I pull back when we got too close for comfort? I searched my memories for times when the air had thickened between us. What had stopped us from taking the next step and letting our lips touch? And would I kiss him back if the opportunity arose again?

I studied his profile as he drove—the irregular cadence of streetlights striping his skin—his hair tousled by the wind. He was my friend, and best of all, he didn't live in my circle or know the hollow halls of my private high school. He didn't judge me because of my family name or what we drove. We'd come to know each other through our music, and we hadn't let go.

He glanced at me before his gaze fell back on the road. "What?"

I snapped out of my reverie. "What? Nothing. Why?'

"You were staring at me," he said.

Smiling, I said, "Can't I stare?"

"Not like vampire over raw meat staring."

I burst out laughing. "Oh my God. You're nuts."

"I wasn't the one staring," he teased.

Busted. I faced out the window, heat creeping up my neck.

"So?" Braking for the light, he gave me the full force of his gaze.

Why, oh why, did the light have to be red? "So what?"

"You were staring."

I held up my hands in mock surrender as I said, "Sorry. I won't do it again."

"Why not?" He shifted in his seat. His dimples twitched.

"You want me to stare?"

His shoulder lifted a fraction as did the corner of his mouth. "Maybe." The light changed, and the air gelled. He accelerated through the gears. "Sorry. I shouldn't be busting your ass today. You've been through hell."

"It's okay," I admitted.

He grinned back. "I gotta tell you. Frankie isn't used to me bringing anyone around. I'll set it up and come back out to get you."

"He's a gamer. Not a super-secret-hacker-dude. Right?"

"Ah, he's not a dude. Technically."

Jealousy roared through my veins. "Frankie's a girl?"

"Used to be."

I stared at him, confused. "So what?"

"Frankie identifies male. Just so you know."

What did it matter? "Okay. No big deal," I said with a shrug.

"I just wanted to make sure you were cool with it."

"Of course, I am. Why wouldn't I be?" Even as I asked, I understood what he tried to say in the most unoffensive way possible. I was a lawyer's kid. A prep school kid. Hanging with a bunch of video game streamers was as far outside my zip code as I could get.

"No reason," he said, like he meant nothing by his comment.

"I can't wait to meet him," I assured him.

Jazz smirked, and I couldn't help but smile in return. "Touché," he said.

We parked in front of a darkened store called Vapes and Videos. A pink flamingo hung in one window, the other advertised an assortment of sun-faded beach balls. Behind the store, apartments stretched across the back of the parking lot as if the building had been connected to an old strip motel. The lone car in the lot was a white Range Rover, but several mountain bikes were chained beside the doors.

"Looks like an interesting place," I said.

"He runs the shop to make enough money to support the streaming habit—among other things. But with his subscribers, he's expecting he can close the store pretty soon. He's my silent partner in the eSports company. Lucky bastard landed some sponsorship deals too."

I detected a wisp of wistful jealousy in his tone. "Wow! That's amazing." The huge step for a streamer of securing a sponsor meant they were legit—on their way to being a player in the big time. Some streamers made millions.

He killed the engine. "Yeah. I'm waiting to see how he makes out with his gigs. I'd like to go for sponsorship next year, and his cred will help us attract more interest in our company." He handed me the keys to the Jeep. "Slide over into the driver's seat. You catch a glimpse of anything you don't like, you lay on the horn. I need to test the waters." I climbed into his seat when he hopped out of the Jeep. "See the window with the *Call of Duty* poster?" He indicated the rear of the building. "That's where I'm going. I'll be out in a minute to get you."

"Too bad there's no doors to lock." Minnows of fear nibbled on my resolve. Sitting in the Jeep alone creeped me out.

"I'll be right back." He kissed my cheek then hurried away.

I brushed my fingers over the spot his lips had occupied. When the door shut behind his back, my senses went on high alert. Every shadow, every set of headlights became a possible threat. Maybe my imagination let the creepy fisherman get the better of me. Maybe I should fear him, not the faceless ghosts he accused of killing my father.

Dad.

This morning I'd been snarky and pissed about working. Now I'd give up the rest of my life at the beach to have him back. And Mom. How was she taking this? The idea of her sitting in a cell alone wracked my insides with biting guilt. My sister was right. I should have kept my mouth shut. I should have called a lawyer instead of filling in the blanks for the police. I'd learned a hard, bitter lesson.

But, if I hadn't met with Stephens, I wouldn't have the fisherman's drive.

I sat up straighter. *Wait a minute.* The fisherman had known about my meeting with the detective and followed me. A shiver rattled my spine. Was the man stalking me? The world had become one giant hazard full of dark shadows and sinister secrets.

A car rounded the corner behind the Jeep. *Crap.* I slouched in the seat, making myself as small as possible. They wouldn't see me until they drove by.

The car crept closer. I held my breath and peeked between the seats. Three car-lengths behind. Two. A horn blared, and a huge orange alley cat ran for cover.

The car drove off into the night.

Gripping the wheel, I dug my fingernails into the leather. This was the fisherman's fault for scaring the hell out of me.

The door on the side of the store opened. My body sagged in relief as Jazz hurried toward the Jeep. "Come on. It's all good."

I handed him the keys and crawled out of the car on rubber legs. Somehow, I managed to follow him toward the strip of light emanating from the doorway.

He closed the door behind us. "You okay?"

I tried to find my ability to speak—last seen lodged under my tonsils. "Yeah. Just a little spooked."

He tugged me next to him. "It's going to be okay. I promise."

"You believe that?" I fought back the terror hovering over my life like a maleficent specter.

"Yes. Come on." He led the way through a musty storeroom piled high with boxes of tourist trap merchandise and papers. Old laminate desks were topped with dusty computer towers and discarded monitors. The uneven floors of the hall had been warped by more than one hurricane surge.

"Nice place," I commented.

"It gets better." He squeezed my hand. The smell of smoldering weed hung in the air. Apparently, his friend went for the real deal, not the CBD vape version advertised in the store's front windows.

Jazz knocked his knuckles on the frame. "Yo, we're back."

"Yeah. I know. I can see you on camera. Get your butts in here."

We entered a gaping space the size of my family room at home. Flat panel televisions wallpapered the perimeter. One wall showed sporting events with the sound off. Another streamed news stations and two different episodes of *Stranger Things*. The last wall displayed proof of his gaming addiction. Multiple streams ran at the same time, but the largest scene had been frozen on a frame from *Call of Duty*. Three black leather gaming chairs faced the array of screens. Slumped into a misshapen couch, the gamer gazed at us from under the brim of a black baseball cap, his eyes glittering.

A video camera blinked from the corner indicating we were being recorded.

"Frankie. This is Lily Harmony." He nudged me forward with his elbow.

I didn't know if I should shake hands or bow to a gaming-god—a sick, skilled assassin in the virtual world. But could he help me with my little drive?

I opted for a simple, "Hey."

"Yeah." He pinched the short end of a joint with fingers that ended in nails painted bright Caribbean blue with black dots. "I hear you have a problem." The gamer took a deep drag, exhaling plumes of fragrant smoke into the air.

I stiffened, lungs flinching in the cloud. Great. Now my clothes would reek like pot. Belle would smell the odor on me and suspect the worst. Didn't matter I didn't smoke. She'd judge me. Accuse me. Just like the detective.

"My father was killed today," I said.

Frankie tipped his head as if he found the news of my father's murder no more interesting than finding the milk out of date in the back of the fridge. He set the joint on an ornate, blue-painted rice bowl doubling as an overflowing ash tray. "It's all over the news. I'm sorry to hear that."

"Me too," I ground out between my teeth.

My new friend's glazed gaze roved over me from hair to toes.

"We have this flash drive I told you about," Jazz joined the conversation. "It might have something to do with why her dad was murdered."

Frankie leaned forward. Maybe the words finally sank into his weedy brain. "Really? Like espionage or something? Your father a spy? You kind of look like the girl on *Alibi*."

I folded my arms. "No. A lawyer."

"Same thing." He waved a hand to dispel his smoke.

Jazz held out the drive. "We don't know what's on it. We needed somewhere safe to look at it."

"Well, my man, you've come to the right place."

I leapt back with a muffled squeal as he bounded out of his seat, his youthful face stretched in a smile. He had deep green eyes and a round chin. His teal shorts beneath a black T-shirt matched his nails, and he wore a wrist full of string bracelets woven in every shade of the rainbow. "Hand it over, and we'll see what's up."

Frankie fingered the drive, his expression thoughtful. "Make yourselves comfortable. I'll bring it up on the big screen. Man, too bad we don't have popcorn." He removed his cap and ran a hand through his thick white-blond hair, standing it up in clumps over shaved sides.

Between the energy drink cans and the joints, I wondered if Frankie ever ate actual food. Maybe popcorn was a main course.

I sat sideways in one of the gaming chairs while Jazz cleared a spot on the paper-covered couch. The gamer slid into the center chair, inserted the drive in a laptop, then tapped out commands on a wireless keyboard balanced on his knees. A diagnostic flashed by on the main screen of the gaming wall.

"What's all that mean?" I asked, as the code flew by. I'd taken some coding classes in school, but this stream of numbers and letters was way out of my league.

"Just making sure my system's not gonna take a nosedive when it reads whatever's on this baby. Running it on a separate partition I set up for just this kind of thing." He waved a hand at the walls of monitors. "Gotta protect my investment."

"You thinking there's malware on it?" Jazz asked.

His friend scratched at his chin. "You never can be too sure—if where you got it is true."

"It's true," I snapped. "Why would I lie?"

"Everyone's got secrets, sweetie, even lawyer's kids." The program finished running. Frankie nodded at the result. "Drive's clean—no bugs. Let's crack this egg and see what's inside." His finger swiped over the screen. The contents of the drive revealed a single folder inside. "Well isn't this a surprise? Doesn't look like much. You sure this is right? Ah…wait a minute. Look at the size of this folder. Almost maxed out the drive. Something big hiding in here."

I squinted at the screen, my heart pounding. "What is it?"

With a few more clicks, the screen filled with filenames. "Uh…got some pictures. PDF files. Nothing executable, so that's good. Won't have anyone dropping in my backdoor. Just documents and stuff. Must be hundreds of them." Another swipe across the screen produced scores of individual pages.

"The names of the files are in code," Jazz said, pointing to the screen. "See here? These have the same initials followed by numbers. Some of the pictures have the same initials. MG. TH. RP. DH."

"Can you access one of the documents and see what it is?" The attention to detail in the organization of this information amazed me. The scraggly fisherman had been very careful when creating these files. Methodical in his naming conventions and organization. He was no amateur.

Frankie clicked on the first one. "I think the numbers are dates—right here. They're sequential and the letters might be initials. At least partially. See? Matches up to the memo. If I sort by date…" A few more keystrokes. "There you go. Now it makes more sense. Pretty straight up filing system."

Sorting the documents by date revealed an obvious pattern. My brain swam. Why did my father pay for this to be compiled, and what was I supposed to do with it now?

"I think these are memos. Emails. Internal documents from a company," I said. "What does it mean?" The company initials didn't ring a bell, even though I'd been working for my parents for several months.

Jazz leaned closer to one screen as the files scrolled and appeared on the other. Some were memos, internal business correspondence. Boring stuff. Not what I expected to find.

I didn't recognize the names as clients of my parents. "I don't know. It's gonna take us a boatload of time to read through this. Do you a have printer?"

Frankie grimaced and slicked back his hair. "You want me to print all this? Man, you're gonna owe me some toner, dude."

"I got something better than toner."

I sucked in a breath when he produced a small bag from his pocket.

The streamer took a deep sniff. "You know where my heart is, man." He stuffed the bag into his pocket. "Load a ream of paper, will you?"

I raised my eyebrows at the payment, but Jazz smirked and gave a half shrug.

A half hour later, we left carrying a paper box full of documents. My new friend waved as we loaded the Jeep. Would we make it around the block before he lit up his payment?

"Frankie's pretty epic," I said.

He laughed. "Oh, he'd like that. He's all about his cred."

"I'll tell him next time."

"You have any idea what all these papers are?"

The box nestled between the front and back seats. There had to be over a thousand sheets of paper. Maybe we were chasing ghosts. Maybe this was a big mistake and had nothing to do with my dad. I laid back against the headrest, not believing my maybes for an instant. "Maybe some. What I looked at were basic files, things a lawyer would have for a client like letters. A lot of business correspondence too."

"Did you see anything you recognized in there? Names? Places?"

"No. I read a couple of pages, but there's a ton to go through. I might find something." I remembered the Dorminy briefs I set aside because I couldn't find the files. Those might be the source of the DH files, but I wouldn't know until I read through them. "But I don't know all of Dad's clients."

We merged into the late-night beach traffic. "Could you get a list from his office?"

I closed my eyes, my brain fuzzy. A sudden, overwhelming exhaustion washed over me. I couldn't bear the thought of driving home to the empty house. Instead of answering his question, I asked, "You think I could crash at your place tonight?"

"Ah…what?"

"On the couch," I said.

"Oh. I thought you were flirting again."

"I wasn't flirting!"

He sighed as he shifted the Jeep. "That's a damn shame."

I stared. "Sometimes I don't know if you're screwing with me or not."

"Which time?"

"Ugh! You're impossible." My stomach picked up a fluttering flop.

The day we'd gotten together, after the party, I blamed the queasiness in my guts on the beer. But neither of us were drinking tonight. I operated stone cold sober, raw and emotionless because of my grief. I couldn't explain the way his teasing tied me up in knots. I'd always liked Jazz. If we willingly opened the door to the chemistry between us, I couldn't be sure I'd be able to close it again.

"Too much?" he asked with a smirk.

"No, no." I sighed as we drove beneath the streetlights and out of town. Weariness pressed my back into the seat. "I'm a mess. I can't get what happened out of my head. I keep seeing my Dad's face this morning, before, after. I want to text him and tell him I'll be home late, but he'll never get it." Tears flowed. "None of this makes any sense. Missing him hurts like hell."

He wheeled into a McDonald's parking lot, parked, and then pivoted in his seat. "Come here," he said.

I fell into his arms, and he hugged me until I cried myself empty. He handed me wads of old coffee shop napkins to wipe my tears.

"Thanks." My heart overflowed with pain and gratitude as a gust of humid air dried my face. I stared up at the underside of the palm fronds rustling in an endless tropical whisper.

"It's okay to cry. You needed to get it out of your system." He tucked my seatbelt back into its slot. "Let's get back to my place."

We held hands until he parked the Jeep at the bungalow. Shadows hid the front porch. I hoped that was all the darkness concealed.

"Here. Take the keys." He heaved the box of documents up the steps to his house. I unlocked the door. "Light switch is just inside."

Light flooded his living room. The box thudded onto the floor.

"I'll be back in a minute. I need to use your bathroom," I said.

"Sure. You know where it is."

Inside his tiny bathroom, I washed my face, grimacing in the mirror at my red-rimmed eyes and swollen nose. So much for the attraction factor. Jazz sat on the living room floor when I returned, the box of papers spread around him, and his cellphone beside him on the carpet with a Google window visible. "What are you doing?"

He paged through the documents. "I got you a pair of cut-off sweats and T-shirt to sleep in." He gestured to the clothes on the sofa.

"Thanks." I sank down beside him on the floor. "What's this?" I asked again.

"Sorting." Seven piles of documents sat stacked on the floor. "So far I've seen documents from four companies and three people."

"How do you know these initials are people?"

"The language is different. See here? It refers to individual accounts. These say corporate or business accounts."

"Good catch," I said.

"That's not all. Seems like a couple of them overlap. We'll have to figure out what to do with those." He handed me a bottle of water from the table. "You look like you could use this."

"Do you always pay your debts in pot?" I uncapped the bottle and drank thirstily.

Jazz rubbed his raspy jawline. "You have to know how to handle Frankie. Payment depends on the type of job and the urgency. I figured I had to pull out all the stops to get a rush on this."

I touched his arm, more grateful than I could express. "Thanks. I'll pay you back."

"It's fine," Jazz assured me.

The air between us coalesced. I diverted my attention to the files on the floor until my heart returned to a steady rhythm. Picking up a sheaf of paper, I studied the first set of documents. "Oh good. No initials. These are from a company called Exton. I've never heard of them." There were memos to and from shipping and receiving divisions. Orders for products with item numbers but no names. "Whoever this company is, they order a ton of merchandise from China. This is for over a million dollars."

"What is it? What did they order?" He peered at the papers.

"I don't know. It doesn't say. Can we search for this company?"

He typed into his cellphone. "Let's see what we find."

"Thanks." He didn't have to help me, but I was glad he was.

"Don't thank me yet. This says the place is in Tampa, but it gives a post office box in Fort Myers. No street address."

"Yeah, look at this. All of the bills and orders list the company's post office box. Then where do they ship all this merchandise? The post office isn't taking it." I bent over the next pile. "Try this one. I know this one from the office. Dorminy Holdings."

He shifted the papers in the DH stack. "Same thing. No actual address."

An unwelcome buzzing began in the back of my mind, a warning bell clanging on low volume. Something about these companies had interested Dad. There had to be a reason. If only I could ask him…

Throat tightening, I shoved the thought away. "Do you have a notebook? Something to write on?"

"Yeah, I might." Opening a kitchen drawer, Jazz removed a single subject notebook and two pencils. He set his trumpet inside its case to give us space to work. I knelt beside the table so I could reach the piles on the floor.

In the notebook I wrote down the names of the companies and their addresses, adding details about what they bought and sold. "None of these have a street address. That's weird."

"Yeah. If they're ordering this much stuff, where's it going?" He tapped one of the invoices. "This sounds like machinery—some kind of pipe bending machine. They'd have to have a warehouse, right?"

"What if these companies and the orders are fake?"

"What do you mean?"

Shrugging, I said, "I'm not sure yet, but my Dad sometimes talked about things people asked him to do—things he wouldn't—like setting up fake companies to hide the owners."

"Why would they create companies that don't exist?"

"Why do you think?"

He shook his head. "Never mind. Stupid question. Because whatever they're doing is massively illegal."

"Right." I collected a new stack of papers from the floor to review. "What's in those other piles? The ones with the people's names?"

It didn't take long to search the names on the internet and come up with a new set of post office boxes. No pictures or social media accounts for any of them other than stock photos of people who looked too efficient to be real; no company website more than a page or two-deep with the same post office boxes we'd found. The contact buttons led to a similar form to fill out with a promise someone would contact us within two business days.

"This is a big pile of nothing," he murmured, dejected.

Very neat. Very clean. Completely fake.

"Maybe. Maybe not," I said.

Tendrils of dread crept into my chest, working into knots until one big tangle of unrest consumed me. My parents had talked about situations like this, where other law firms got into big trouble because of the things they'd done. My father had lectured me, up and down, over the shady dealings I should never get involved in once I started my own practice.

These were shell companies, operating in the dark with no real purpose other than to move lots of bad money around the globe. A big no-no in the lawyer world. What we had amounted to fake names and businesses making fake deals to cover up ill-gotten gains.

We needed the "why."

The creepy fisherman had collected this information for Dad and then he had given it to me. Since Mom remained in custody, there hadn't been anyone else to take the flash drive. Made sense, but the drive was a ticking time bomb waiting to blow us to bits. The fisherman said this might prove my mother wasn't guilty of murder. But was she guilty of something else?

Chills rushed over my skin, and ice burrowed into my veins. If this stack of documents constituted a threat, and Mom knew about these companies, she'd be lying beside my father in the morgue, not sitting in jail.

Jazz pushed against my shoulder. "Earth to Lily."

"Sorry. Trying to work this out in my brain."

"If anyone can, it's you. You're the almost-lawyer. I'm just an observer."

"Yeah, right, Mr. Inspector. You figured out a ton of this already. It's like these people who own these companies are made up names. M. Holden, R. Donovan, and K. T. Sunick. Initials and last names."

Jazz handed me a short stack of paper. "Except for these. There's overlap. Sunick and Dorminy Holdings. And Holden and Exton."

"But these aren't real people, right?" An unnamed worry poked at the back of my mind.

"What is it?" he asked.

"I've seen a lot of these agreements at my parents' office, and they're more filled out than these. See this here? There is no legal counsel listed. No cover letter from their attorney. Any big business with this kind of money is going to hire a lawyer." The documents included asset lists for two of the companies. Both listed millions of dollars in cash, although maybe the amounts were bogus. "Just because it's on paper doesn't mean it's real."

He yawned. "I thought you could do it yourself—start a corporation. Find an internet site or something."

"Yeah. If you're running a small business. Not like this." I squinted at the corner of the page at an illegible note. "There are taxes to pay, forms to file that need an attorney. Some of this is international."

"Spoken like the child of a lawyer," he remarked.

My eyes felt sandy; I had a hard time focusing. "Yeah, I know. My family is a blessing and a curse. This one is difficult to read." I handed him the page and then scrubbed my face with my hands to get the blood flowing.

"I can't make this out either," he said.

"There's enough in these files to keep us guessing for a month. No matter what else we find, this secret investigation means one thing—Dad suspected someone at the office."

"That's shit scary." Jazz handled the paperwork as if it might bite him.

I leaned back against the couch. My brain function reduced to a zombie-crawl. "I wonder where he got all these files?"

"I guess you're eating at The Whale tomorrow night." Jazz rested against the couch next to me. His fingers lifted my hand from my leg. "We'll have to cancel practice. I wonder if Sun Runner's will let us postpone our audition?"

"No," I said, gripping his hand and squeezing until his gaze met mine. "We can't give up the spot. We'll never get a chance like this again. How long have we dreamed of getting a foot in that door? Mara, Cecilia, and Paul would never forgive me. Plus, we have the other guys on the hook to help out." We'd gone all out, inviting some friends to step in and double parts to make us sound bigger. Right now, I couldn't handle losing anything else in my life. The threat of tears clustered in my throat. "If we get the job, we'd make enough money to pay everyone, plus buy a new laptop and audio console."

His eyebrows rose. "Hey, it's okay. I told them what happened. They get it."

"No. The audition is next week. I'll be ready." I swallowed the tears. I wouldn't mess this up for my bandmates. I wouldn't.

"Okay." He laced his fingers through mine.

Fervor drained away, leaving me tired and unsure of our next move. "Thanks for this and for hooking me up with your gamer friend. I don't know what I'd have done without you today."

"Whatever you decide to do, I'm here to back you up. The band too. You say play, and we'll play." He brushed the hair back behind my ear, his fingers lingering on my temple. "You're wiped out. I can tell by your eyes. Why don't you try and get some sleep?"

"I am." Emotionally, mentally, and physically spent. I was running on my last spark.

Belle wouldn't make it home until tomorrow morning. If I stayed with him, I wouldn't have to be alone wondering who might be waiting outside my door.

Still, I'd never slept over at a guy's house—in particular not one I kissed on the beach. I didn't want him to get the wrong idea. I wasn't throwing myself at him or anything. But I needed someone tonight, even if he slept in the next room. We were friends. Dad would understand...

Stop. If I thought about him now, I'd lose the iron grip holding my heart together. Instead, I asked, "You're sure it's okay for me to crash here?"

"Yes. Nobody's home at your place. I'd lay awake all night wondering if you're okay."

My heart ached in thanks. "Do you have an extra pillow?"

After we made up the pull-out couch, I swished some mouthwash in my mouth and then snuggled into his borrowed T-shirt and sweats. With Jazz's scent wafting from the pillow, I burrowed beneath the quilt, unconscious the moment I shut my eyes.

Chapter Six

My sister's silver BMW sat in the driveway when I got home after Jazz insisted on taking me for pancakes at the IHOP. For a split second, I thought *Mom will have nowhere to park*, but my error punched me in the stomach. I doubted she would come home today. Her black Porsche Cayenne had spent the night in the parking garage. She loved her flashy SUV. Maybe I could bring the car home later, even if she couldn't be here too.

"Good luck," Jazz said as he helped me carry the box of printouts into the garage. "Let me know if you need back up."

I waved as he drove away.

My heart hurt as I stood in the driveway with my purse and his borrowed sweatshirt clutched in my arms. Belle had been frighteningly silent. She didn't text me when she arrived to find my car was in the garage and the house empty. Dread multiplied with each step. Even the palm trees on either side of the driveway rustled and whispered as if discussing the secrets lurking inside the house. Maybe I should have let Jazz stay to run interference. Fueled by uncertainty and anger, I stepped inside the garage to face the next catastrophe—my sister.

A sob slipped from my lips as my eyes adjusted to the gloom. Dad's workbench sat to the right of the door, his tools where he had left them. I returned his hammer to the wall pegs and leaned against his bench as my anger bled away in a wave of sorrow. His car was missing from its spot as well, parked in the space next to Mom's in the office parking garage—unless they impounded his Mercedes. Right at this moment, some investigator might be ripping through his car for more evidence against my mother.

Suppressing the threat of resurgent tears, I hurried through the echoing garage into the mud room and shut the door behind me. No chance of making it to my bedroom without her seeing me if she lurked in the kitchen or dining room. I'd rather take a shower and change before

Hurricane Annabelle made landfall.

I slipped out of my sneakers and braced myself as I entered the main part of the house. All was silent except for the ticking of the grandfather clock. A rich brown scent wafted through the house like incense. I sniffed. She'd made coffee. That was a good sign.

But she hadn't texted to bitch, and her avoidance worried me. A silent sister scared me more than a screaming one. The creepy fisherman on the pier had pointed me in the right direction. Now my sister needed to hear the story. The tale might sound crazy, but what about the last twenty-four hours wasn't insane?

Better to get it over with.

"Hello?" I followed the smell of coffee and bacon into the kitchen. Belle sat on one of the counter stools, looking younger than her twenty-six years in a ponytail, sweatpants, and an old, faded T-shirt from her high school days. Her makeup-free face was drawn and tired.

"Where were you?" she asked, staring into her coffee cup.

A plate with a half-eaten slice of toast sat on the counter next to the butter dish. Her auburn hair had gotten long in the months since I'd last seen her. Neon pink polish covered the nails on her bare feet. Her gaze shifted from her coffee to me, and the resemblance to my father caught me off guard. The strong bridge of nose in contrast to my somewhat upturned one. The defined cheekbones.

"I stayed at a friend's house. I didn't want to be alone." I plopped down making sure to leave a stool between us. Years of her fists in my hair had taught me well. We'd been oil and vinegar from the moment my parents brought me home from the hospital. I'd never understood her animosity toward me—never wanted to believe what she said about my parents' fighting. As I got older, I pretended I didn't care.

The corner of her mouth snaked up a fraction. "Of course, you didn't. Make sure you think about yourself first. That's what you're best at."

"Don't be a bitch," I snapped.

"This isn't bitch. You haven't seen bitch." She brushed stray hair behind her ear and nailed me to my spot with her gaze. Someday Annabelle Harmony would be a fierce courtroom advocate. "Have you seen Mom?"

Exhaustion pressed me into the seat. "Not since the office."

"You didn't go to the jail?" Her fists clenched. "To see if she was okay?"

"They told me to go home, Belle. More than once." I couldn't tell her I didn't want to talk to my mother when they'd taken her away, and I'd believed she might have killed my dad.

"And you listened?" She dropped her spoon into her mug with a clank. "You should've gone with her."

I ripped the hair tie out of my bedraggled ponytail, losing several strands in the process. "You weren't there. You didn't see him die." The memory caught in my throat as the image of my father's blood-streaked face slammed into my brain and took my breath.

She tugged her lip into her teeth, bit then released. Tears glistened on her lashes. Who knew? Somewhere under that hard, crunchy outer shell, a heart beat. "I'm trying to understand how this happened. How did you not see the person who did this? You were there."

Her tone tossed accusations she didn't have the guts to say straight out. "I was in the partner's office, dropping off her filing. If someone else was there, they'd have to pass her office. But no one did. I would have seen them."

"You sure you weren't playing your little video games?"

My skin flushed with embarrassment. "What are you talking about?

"I saw you watching some guy stream when I was here for Christmas. Every chance you got." My sister sneered. "What a waste."

"I wasn't streaming yesterday. I was working."

She pursed her lips. "Sure you were."

I leapt out of my chair and stalked to the windows in the breakfast nook. My temper might blow if I didn't move. What did she know? Not as much as I did. How dare she make assumptions.

Stomping back into the kitchen, I ignored her and whipped open the refrigerator door. I stared inside as if the answers to the questions of the universe might be hidden behind the milk. The information on the thumb drive sat fresh in my mind. I wanted to get back to my room and make notes before I forgot important details. My suspicions about Mom would be put to rest once I had more information. Maybe not enough to get her out of jail, but enough to believe she was innocent.

At least my partner-in-crime had kept the drive. A third party, who had nothing to do with my parents, their firm, or their family kept the simple, but menacing rectangle of plastic safe.

Quiet footfalls announced she'd followed me. "You don't seem too upset about Dad," I said without lifting my gaze.

She yanked me around by my arm, and her eyes narrowed dangerously. "Go to hell. You don't think I've been crying? Take a look at the inside of my car. At the tissues." Her head tilted to the side. "Crying's not going to help us now." Her gaze raked over me as if I were something offensive. "The funeral director will be here in an hour. I suggest you pretend to be a human being when she gets here." She set her cup into the sink and stomped down the hall to her bedroom.

Why did people keep walking away from me? Belle, Stephens, the creep on the pier. As if always on the outskirts of the circle, why did no one bother to hang around and help me deal?

Doubts dangled without answers as I carried the box of files from the garage into the breakfast nook and unloaded the copies and a thick manila envelope. My hands stilled. I didn't have the strength to dwell on the questions swirling in my mind or the files. Instead, I poured a cup of coffee. Careful to not slosh the contents, I carried the cup toward my room and the shower I needed to clear my head. If my sister wanted to take the lead on the arrangements, at least I could support her in front of the person she called. We had decisions to make for Dad—even if we hated each other's guts.

Chapter Seven

I sat stoically beside my fuming sister at the dining room table while the funeral director discussed the details of the service. I tuned the woman out, my emotions swinging in wild arcs of highs and lows. If I could pretend we were talking about someone else—not my father—discussing flowers and music would be easier. Except I couldn't pretend. Every time I glanced up his empty chair stunned me. Ironically, my sister and I had spent few nights at this table as a family, yet here we were at the same table making choices about how to honor him. When she demanded a viewing open to the public, I balked but relented. I had no desire to stand in a funeral home for hours accepting the condolences of people who'd come to gawk—to see the family of the lawyer killed by his wife.

My sister insisted we had nothing to hide. I kept my mouth shut when she picked out the casket with an ivory lining, white lilies, and pink and yellow roses. She added a bouquet of red roses from my mother without a card, also her choice.

I bit holes in my tongue to keep from screaming.

As soon as the door shut behind the woman, my sister unsheathed her claws. "It'd be nice if you showed some class. Don't you think Dad deserves a proper funeral? Those people need a chance to pay their respects."

"Who are 'those people.'" I air-quoted for emphasis. How could someone who scored a near perfect grade on her SATs be so socially stupid? "You don't live here. You don't know anything. They don't care if Dad's dead. Not really. They'll want to see what they can find out about Mom. You realize these people are gonna stand there and talk about us?"

"Gonna, is not a word," she snapped. "What are you? Four?"

"Whatever, Belle." Turning on my heel, I stomped to the kitchen. "Whatever. We're not having a funeral until Mom's out of trouble. You can make all the plans you want. They don't mean a thing."

"You don't know if we can wait that long," she said. "They'll finish with the investigation soon. Once the autopsy is over, they'll let him go."

The fight drained out of me, but not my bone-deep resolve. "I'll wait for Mom. I don't care what you do."

I rummaged around in the cabinets and came up with a Kind Bar. Someone needed to go to the grocery store. Probably me. My sister sat at the dining room table going over the funeral director's notes. I did my best to ignore the rustling and shifting of papers. *Enough.* Belle could figure the funeral out on her own.

"What's this?" she called from the other room. When I didn't answer, she stormed into the kitchen holding a brown manila envelope and a sheaf of color pictures. "Lily? What's this?"

"What? Where did you get that?" My heart stopped because *I knew.* The envelope of photos came from the fisherman's drive. Blood drained from my face. In the top picture, Mom was locked in a heated embrace—but not with my father.

Patrick Malvern, my parent's other partner, gripped her by the upper arms while my mother shifted her wine glass to the side as if trying not to spill the dark liquid. Her eyes were closed.

The kiss was passionate, vile, disgusting.

"Oh my god," I whispered.

"Where did you get this?" The photo quivered in her hand.

I stared, unable to speak. Jazz and I had been so wrapped up in the business paper trail, we'd never bothered to look inside the envelope.

"Answer me! Where the hell did you get this?" Her voice fractured like thin ice.

My knees softened. Weak, I leaned against the counter. There was nothing to do but tell her the truth. "Those are Dad's. He hired an investigator before he died."

Her features froze, and her hands trembled crinkling the envelope. "Dad did this?"

Nodding, I sighed. "The investigator gave them to me. Last night. That's where I was. The information was on a flash drive this guy had. He followed me to Fort Myers Pier. I...I went to a friend's house to print them."

"Whose house?" she asked, eyes narrowed to furious slits.

"No one you know. It doesn't matter." My defenses bristled. "We need to figure out what this means."

She tossed the pictures onto the counter as if they burned her fingers. "This is disgusting. You need to get in touch with the investigator. Right now."

"I can't—I mean, not yet." I didn't need her tagging along on my meeting with the fisherman. Maybe if I gave her the job of making sense of the other information on the drive, I could ditch her. She was the almost-lawyer after all.

But with the stubborn set of her chin and don't mess with me attitude? My chances of meeting with the fisherman without her were slim.

Her gaze grew distant as if she considered a dark portal where portents of the future swirled in sinister waters. "Lily, this is motive. This could be enough for the court to convict Mom of Dad's murder."

When she put it like that, what choice did I have but to include my sister in the horrible truth?

I swallowed the lump clogging my throat. "There's more, besides the pictures. I have documents. Files. Lots of stuff I haven't read yet."

She stared at me, saying nothing. How could I reach her? An ocean of resentment had brewed between us growing up. At one time she'd been decent, when I was nine and she was graduating from high school. The spotlight had shown on her, illuminating her accomplishments. Then, she'd disappeared into college and retreated from our life to become someone else, a stranger.

Now we were broken.

I stuck my hands out in supplication. "I need your help, Belle. I don't know what to do next."

Her features softened—the tiniest bit.

"I know you hate me. I get it. But we have to help Mom." We had to function, as the only Harmonys left, without killing each other. Our future, bleak as it was, sucked. Mom *would* be home soon. We'd make sure she got home.

My challenge went unanswered, and Belle's dismissal cut me. How hard would it have been for her to say she didn't hate me? That she was sorry for ignoring me?

"You believe what this guy gave you?" She sounded skeptical and retrieved the picture from the counter. Her jaw set as she stared at our mother's infidelity.

I left her question unanswered and stepped into the dining room. She followed as I lifted the flaps on the box of papers and removed the notes I'd made on the different companies and the people with the mysterious initialed first names. "These are not Dad's regular clients, but I recognized one of the business names from the mail yesterday at the office. Dorminy Holdings. There wasn't a file in Monica's office or on the computer, but a continuance for some kind of hearing was in the mail."

She folded her hands in front of her. "Can you get anymore vague?"

"I didn't read it." I glared and tried to maintain my cool. "Dad wanted me to watch for it. I did. I was going to give it to him. Are you going to help or not?"

My sister took a deep breath and sank into a chair. If nothing else, I'd attracted her interest. I dove in while I had most of her attention.

"This is what I figured out so far." I planned to omit Jazz's and Frankie's involvement in deciphering the drive. She might not like it if others had seen these documents—people like a couple of gamers. "All of these companies are fake. I searched them on the internet. They have post office boxes, but no addresses. Their websites are nothing but a front page."

She went through the first stack of paper, studying each document for several moments. "Why did Dad want this information? These companies are shells, and I can't find anything that says he was the one who created them. They can't engage in legitimate business practices with all this subterfuge. Have you researched the off-shore companies they're doing business with?"

"No. I didn't get that far."

"We need to do that." My sister shifted into lawyer mode. She bent over the documents, checking the arrangement for order, her fingers sorting the pages into neat piles.

"I don't know anything else. I just got the paperwork last night. But…I might have a way to get some of the answers we need."

"How?" She pinned me with her gaze.

Squirming on the inside, I cleared my throat and said, "The investigator who took the pictures told me to meet him tonight."

She pinched the bridge of her nose. "Tell me again how you got this. Start from the beginning. Sit." She poured a fresh cup of coffee for each of us. I obeyed as she set a legal pad and a pen on the table. "Okay. Spill it."

"I remembered details of Dad's office, the way the glass had fallen. None of it made sense, but I thought my recollections could be important enough to get Mom out. I called the detective, and he agreed to meet with me at the coffee house at Times Square."

She toyed with her pen, her gaze far away. "I don't like you meeting with him alone." I wished I could hear her thoughts and understand her frown. "What did he say?"

"He told me to mind my own business." Anger bled into my

voice.

Her eyes widened as she paled. "He what?"

The memory hurt almost as much as my mother's absence. "He didn't want to hear about the roof or the gun. He told me they would handle it, and I should go home."

She didn't say anything for several minutes. "Okay, the cop is an ass. How did you get this drive?"

"I was...upset. I walked out on the pier in the dark after the detective told me to get lost. I wanted to be alone." She gave me a 'how stupid are you' eyeroll. "I know, I know. I just wanted to clear my thoughts. I walked past a guy fishing and then hung out at the end of the pier for a bit. When I tried to leave, he stopped me."

"The guy fishing? What did he say?"

"He said I had a big problem. He knew my name." Unease washed over me. "The guy said whoever did this...would come for me next. He said Dad hired him, but he didn't say why. The flash drive was meant for Dad."

Her brows drew down in concentration, deepening the shadows beneath her lashes. Except for Dad's nose, she and Mom favored each other in coloring, with their auburn-blonde hair and hazel eyes—and facial expressions. I'd inherited my father's easy tan, crazy wavy hair, and love of the ocean.

"Dad had to know about Mom and..."

"Patrick."

She nodded once, her features schooled and unreadable. "I know him as Attorney Malvern. He started at the firm after I left for school. I met him once or twice." She drew a lazy doodle on the edge of the page, another trait she and our mother shared.

"He's quiet in the office and doesn't handle court cases like Dad. I guess he's more of a paperwork lawyer. Wills, trusts, real estate sales, that kind of thing. I don't know much about him because he keeps to himself."

"Not completely to himself." She scowled. "We need to find out what this bastard has to do with Dad's death."

Nausea churned in my gut. Mom cheated. So what if they went to counseling? Didn't everyone go through a rough spot now and then? Not like some of my friends' parents who lived in the same house but didn't say two words to each other. We were a family. We had grill night in the warmer seasons and game nights in the winter. They went on vacation together. Held hands. Flirted.

Our happy family had been a ruse, some great fake my mother perpetuated to avoid suspicion while she cheated on Dad. Had he found out? Maybe that was what their recent arguments were about—Patrick.

"I wonder how long this has been going on." The sentence hitched in her throat. Whatever she felt toward Mom, anger or sadness, the reality was our father was dead.

Like my sister, grief flared beneath the surface of every breath I took. I cuddled my hands to the gray, stoneware coffee cup, absorbing the warmth. "Does it matter? The investigator told me something on the drive might be dangerous. What should we do with what we know?"

"Where's the drive now?"

"It's safe with a neutral party." A tremor of fear rushed through my veins. I hoped Jazz was right—keeping the drive with him had been the best course of action. If the people the fisherman warned me about watched our every move, he could be in danger too.

"With your friend?"

My back stiffened at her tone. "Yeah."

She jerked the elastic from her hair and freshened her ponytail. "So, when do I meet this friend who did all this printing for us?"

"Look, that doesn't matter. I have to go tonight to meet this guy. He said he'd be having dinner at The Whale."

"You're going out to dinner with the guy who took this picture?" Her caustic tone dripped with accusations. "Dad dies, and you're sleeping over with friends and making dinner dates. Glad to see you're real broken up."

Furious tears threatened, and I blinked them away. Show no weakness in front of my sister. But, oh god did she know the exact words to shred me. "You don't understand. The fisherman told me he would be having dinner there tonight. I'm going to meet up with him again at the restaurant."

"Oh, I understand, but you're not going by yourself."

"I invited my *friend*."

Her left eyebrow rose in a skeptical arc. "Your *friend* has a name?"

I cleared my throat, swallowing the rest of my upset. "Jazz."

"The video gamer?" She smirked when I nodded. "Why am I not surprised."

My spine stiffened. "He also plays trumpet in my band and goes to college on his own dime. His parents kicked him out when he was a senior in high school. Stop being freaking stuck up."

"Hmph. What do you know?"

"Nothing. That's my point. Belle, we're different people—you and me. You have to deal with it and stop judging me and my friends. Get over yourself, already." The years she had on me might as well be a lifetime. Our interests, our commitment to our family couldn't be more different.

"Call him. Tell him I'll go instead. Your friend might scare this guy off."

I wanted to protest, but she was right.

She rubbed her hands over her weary face. For the moment, I stemmed the flow of her criticism. "There's so much here to go through. I need to absorb all this material and get in touch with Liz Monroe. I'm going to ask her to take Mom's case."

"I left a message earlier. She hasn't called me back. Do you think something happened to her too?"

"Maybe she'll call me." Her superior tone reminded me of one more thing I hated about her.

"Why? Because you're more important than I am?"

She retreated, her hands up. "All right. That was a shit thing to say."

I planted my hands on my hips. "I don't think you should tell her about what we have," I said. "Not yet. We don't know what it means."

After a moment, she relented. "You might be right. This fisherman might be full of shit." Even as she said it, her expression told me she didn't believe the contents of the flash drive were unimportant in our father's death.

"I'm sorry I talked to the cops," I told her.

"I'm sorry I was a bitch."

"Was?"

"Am a bitch." She laughed.

Chapter Eight

After my sister and I declared a truce, I flopped on the couch in the family room, my laptop perched on my bandaged knees. Belle went into our parents' bedroom to search for anything Dad might have kept at home. Their bedroom door was a threshold I wasn't ready to cross. I lived here every day with our mom and dad, and in my mind, that made the room their sanctuary, a barrier I couldn't traverse even after I heard my sister's quiet weeping on the other side of the door.

I couldn't cry again, alone or with her, and she wouldn't want me to intrude on her grief.

The fisherman and his ominous message frightened me, and I needed to think, not cry. Tonight, I would ask him how he got that picture of my mother—if Belle didn't slug him first. Then we'd make some sense of the flash drive and the hundreds of documents he'd collected.

Wondering if my parents could somehow be involved in these sham companies scared me the most. As long as the fisherman told us the truth up front, without his vague riddles, maybe we'd get the answers we needed.

I sat up on the couch with the computer across my lap and called Jazz to break it to him my pushy, pissy sister was going in his place.

"You okay?" he asked when he answered.

"Yeah. I'm fine. My sister is here."

"How'd that go?"

"About as expected," I said with a sigh. He knew about my contentious relationship with her. "She wants to go tonight."

"Okay. Should I meet you there?"

With a grimace, I said, "I think we should go by ourselves. She doesn't want to scare this guy off."

"You think I'm that intimidating?" he scoffed.

Laughing, I said, "It's not that. If he bails, we might not get another chance."

"You know, it might be a good idea for you to introduce me to her."

"I will. I promise. Just not tonight."

He went quiet for a moment.

"You still there?"

"Yeah. Please be careful. And text me when it's over, okay?"

Warmth spread across my face, and I was grateful he couldn't see me blush. "I will. Talk later."

He cared. There was no doubt in my mind. But what kind of care—friends or something more? Maybe when this was over and my mother out of trouble, I'd have the chance to find out what his intentions were.

I jumped when the doorbell rang. Sighing, I set my computer aside on a couch cushion. Since I'd gotten home, we'd received three floral arrangements and a deli platter from my father's favorite judge. My parents were successful, respected litigators in the area with a lot of professional friends and acquaintances. Did any of them know my mother had cheated on my dad with his partner?

Relief rushed through my body when I opened the door. Liz stood on the porch.

"Lily. I'm so sorry. I was in the air when you called." She wore sharp pressed, camel-colored slacks and a black silk T-shirt. The narrow tips of her black pumps peeked out from under the pant cuffs, and a wide black clasp secured her hair at her nape. She looked clean and pressed even with Gulf humidity. "I just can't believe it. I came as soon as I could."

I invited her in and accepted her hug. "Thanks so much." Relief sapped my resolve to keep the tears in check. She hadn't ignored my calls after all.

Her chin trembled as she released me. "Come on. You guys are family." I moved aside to let her into the house. She took in the stone fireplace and Spanish tile floors. "This is a great place. I told your mom how much I liked it when they had their holiday party."

I nodded, remembering the wall to wall people. I'd spent most of the night hiding in my room watching Jazz stream, even though Dad had wanted to introduce me to people as his "heir." "Let's sit in the kitchen. This way." I set her up at the table in the breakfast nook overlooking the pool. "I'll go get my sister."

Down the hall, I rapped lightly on my parents' door. "Hey. Liz is here." At Belle's muffled reply, I went to the kitchen to allow her time to drag herself together.

"Do you want coffee? Or water or anything?" I asked from in

front of the fridge.

"A bottle of water would be great."

I set the bottle on the table and took a seat across from her. Sunlight streamed in the windows, warming the tile beneath my bare toes.

She reached into her briefcase and removed a legal pad and a small digital recorder, setting both on the table. I'd removed all traces of the investigator's work and our notes. Those were safely tucked between my mattress and box spring, with the paper box hidden in the laundry room. Probably overkill, but I couldn't shake the feeling I had to protect the information, even if we didn't know what it meant.

Right now, I didn't know who to trust. Hopefully, the fisherman would fill in the blanks.

"Thank you." She uncapped the bottle and drank. "I haven't stopped since I landed."

"Did you talk to my mother yet?" I asked, afraid to know how Mom fared.

She took a swallow and then set the bottle to the side on a wicker coaster. "Yes. Briefly. She's okay."

"Where is she?" I asked.

Liz patted my arm. "In the county holding facility. Your mother is one of the toughest attorneys in this state. She's going to be okay."

My sister came in and shook the lawyer's manicured hand. When Belle graduated in the spring, instead of only adding her name to the letterhead, she'd be taking the firm over if we didn't get Mom out of trouble. She could lose her license to practice law. For the first time, the ripples of my mother's imprisonment spread beyond the immediate crisis.

"I'm going to record this session." Liz clicked on the recorder as my sister took her seat with a notebook in her hand. "Lily, I'd like to start with you." Sympathy gleamed in her eyes. "I can't imagine how difficult this is for you. For both of you. But I need you to tell me everything. Could you take me through yesterday morning?"

When I finished, she clicked off the recorder and tapped her nails on the tabletop. "Okay. I've met this detective when I went to discuss bail for your Mom. He's the arresting officer. He seems pretty sure of himself."

"Yeah. He wouldn't listen to me. I told him I remembered more information, and he told me to mind my own business."

"You talked to him again? When was this?"

Retelling the coffee shop meeting, I left out my conversation with the fisherman.

"As your attorney, and from this moment on, I am representing the both of you as well as your mother. I'm going to advise you not to speak with the police again. About anything. If you suspect you have important information about the case, call me. I'll decide how and if we use it." She added to her pages of notes. "Okay. Anything else since then?" The lawyer shifted her line of questioning to Belle.

"No." My sister's gaze locked with mine.

Relief washed over me. As we'd discussed, Belle kept the damning photos quiet. Good. Liz's office sat next to Patrick's. The last thing we needed was a war breaking out between them.

"Okay, on to Annabelle. I know you were at school when this happened. Do you have anything else to add? When was the last time you spoke to your father?" Liz adjusted her glasses and leaned forward.

"About a month ago? I think, maybe. We talked for a little while, but he was on his way to a hearing." Her eyes gleamed with tears, and her voice fell to a whisper. "I should have called him again. I didn't think it would be the last time I talked to him." Belle swallowed hard.

Liz made note of the conversation as the clock in the hall chimed two. "Nothing out of the ordinary?"

My sister sighed. "No."

"What about your mother? When did you speak to her last?"

"Mom and I text almost every day."

This shocked me. Mom never mentioned my sister outside of general conversation as if she were a distant planet revolving around our family in a lost galaxy.

"Okay." Liz leaned forward. "Those texts. Anything odd?"

"No. Just regular day-to-day stuff."

"I'm going to advise you not to delete those texts. If there is a subpoena for electronic communications, it would be better if we were up front with those, especially if they show your mom as stable, acting normal in the days leading up to the shooting." She picked up the digital recorder and noted the timestamp on her legal pad. "I should probably get a copy of those now."

"I can email them to you," my sister offered.

"Perfect."

"What about the investigation?" I asked. "Aren't there ways to prove Mom didn't fire the gun?"

Liz smiled. "Absolutely. Gunshot residue tests are being done as we speak, and they don't take long. I believe the evidence is what will free your mother—maybe as early as tonight." Her eyebrows drew down in concern. "But I'm afraid of what will happen as a result of the bad press."

"You mean at the firm." We shared a glance that told me Belle was worried as well.

"Yes. I'm concerned about what your parents' clients will believe about what they've seen and heard in the news reports. I'm driving to the office now to start making phone calls. I'll put out as many fires as I can." She set her pen down. "Not now, but in a week or so, I need you to come in and help me go through your father's files. Until your mom is back on her feet, we need to make sure important dates aren't missed." Her full attention shifted to me. "You've been working for him since Monica left, right?"

"Yes." Deep in my gut grief twisted a dull knife. Poor Monica. She'd worked for my dad for years. Dad's death would hit her hard. Someone should call her and see how she was doing.

"Good. At least you'll have some basic client knowledge for your father's practice. That will help me tremendously. Excuse me for a moment." She glanced at her phone as a text chimed. "Ahhh… I've been summoned to judge's chambers. I have to handle this. It might be good news."

I let out a hopeful breath as she gathered her notes and the recorder into her briefcase.

"Thank you." Belle said.

"It's going to be okay. You both know how to find me." She smiled. "And I should have your mother out on bail by dinner."

"Really?" I blurted out.

Relief cleared some of the exhaustion from my sister's gaze. "That's wonderful. Can we pick her up?"

Liz smoothed the wrinkles in her shirt. "I have to be there when she is released. I'll drop her off later. Give me your cellphone number. I'll text you when we're on the way."

I walked her to the door. "Thank you," I told her with hope in my heart. At least Mom would be home. Some part of normal would fall back into our lives.

Liz gave me a quick squeeze. "You stay strong. Your mom needs you."

When she left, I joined my sister at the table. She'd lit Mom's blackberry candle on the stove. The familiar scent calmed me. "You didn't tell her about the pictures. Or the files."

She drew on her notebook. "I've been thinking about the fisherman, and I think you're right about this. Why would Dad hire a private investigator to check into those companies? And to follow Mom around?"

"Yeah, that's freaking odd." Outside, the pool sparkled in

abundant afternoon sunshine. I never appreciated how simple my life had been, which made my next thought cut deep. "Because he didn't trust his partners. Or Mom."

"Yeah. Exactly. From what she said to us today, I'm assuming Liz didn't know anything."

"So now what? Mom's going to be home tonight. How do we keep this from her?" Part of me didn't want to. I wanted to pass these insane conspiracy theories off, discarding them into some dark closet corner. But I couldn't do that. The photographs made my mother appear more guilty than innocent.

"We should. For now. We don't know enough about what's going on to bring her into the conversation—mainly between her and Patrick."

Our situation sucked from so many angles, and stress bounced around in my brain like a ping pong ball in a bird cage. "I'm worried about whoever did this will freak out when Mom is released. Right now, they think they got away with it." I rubbed my sweaty palms on my shorts to dry them. "You know what we have to do?"

"What?" Belle asked.

I didn't want to go back, to see the blood.

"Lily? What do we have to do?"

I started as if shaken from a nightmare. "Go to Dad's office. If there's information on why he decided to hire the investigator, that's where it will be. I want to know everything I can before we go to dinner tonight."

"You're right," she agreed after a drawn-out moment. "If Dad didn't trust the people he worked with, we sure can't. We need to go through his things before Mom comes home. Besides, Liz is out dealing with her case. She won't be there."

I grabbed my car keys off the counter. "Let's go."

~ * ~

We parked in the garage not far from my parents' side-by-side cars. The police hadn't taken the Porsche after all. That was a small blessing. We'd brought my mother's spare keys to bring her car home. After, we'd repeat the trip to transfer my father's Mercedes to the house. No police cars sat outside the building—another good sign.

My sister shouldered a big tote bag for the files we hoped to find. "We should look in Mom's office. Maybe there's a hint of what's going on between Patrick and her."

"We could check his office too." I pointed toward the empty parking spot. "His car's not here, and I have keys." Florida heat blasted into the car, wilting me the moment I exited.

"Then we better get moving. We're running out of time."

"I know," I said. When Liz texted us, we'd have to get back to the house for my mother's homecoming.

We rode the elevator to the top floor. Outside the office suite, everything appeared normal. I unlocked the glass doors and coded out the security system while Belle studied the cameras nestled in the corners. "Too bad these weren't on in the offices too. Cameras would fix this mess in a hurry."

At the office, I showed her the door. "I was in here. In the back corner of the room, filing. I had headphones on, listening to music."

She surveyed the office, the distance to the door, and the length of the hallway leading to our father's office. "Okay. I can see how you'd have a hard time knowing anything was wrong."

"Thanks," I told her, relieved she released the guilt chokehold. For every bit she forgave me, I forgave myself by eighths and sixteenths. "Should we start in Dad's office?"

"I guess so," she said hesitantly.

I didn't want to go in there either. But the cops weren't digging for the truth. The detective had his murderer, at least until they released Mom. If we wanted to know who killed Dad any time soon, we were the ones who had to dig.

A sudden knock on the office suite doors startled us. I peered out of Liz's office toward the glass doors at the front of the firm. Jazz waved back.

"Who the hell is he?" Splotches of angry color livened Belle's cheeks.

"My friend." I smiled despite the heaviness of our situation.

"Did you send out invitations?" she asked.

I threw her a nasty glare, and she waved me off as I marched up to the glass, let him in, then relocked the door. "How did you know where I was?"

He pecked my cheek and smiled sheepishly. "I had Frankie ping your phone."

"What! He can do that?" My impression of the pot-smoking hacker jumped ten pegs.

"Pinging without a warrant is illegal," Belle informed, her hands planted on her hips.

He let the comment slide off and stuffed his hands into his pockets. "I'm Jason Sumner. You can call me Jazz."

She folded her arms across her chest. "I can also call the cops and haul your ass out. What are you doing here?"

He sighed. "Helping," Jazz said.

I stifled a giggle as my sister's expression darkened.

"Guys, let's move out of view, okay?" I shuffled them back toward Monica's office. "I wouldn't have those files if it weren't for him. He has skills."

Jazz bowed like she was royalty. Her lips drew back from her teeth as if she wanted to bite him.

"And I have friends with better skills. What are you doing in here?" He glanced around the office suite and grimaced at the ceiling speakers. "Nice plants but the piped-in instrumental has to go."

I was so thrilled to see him, I wanted to hug him. "Trying to find a connection between the documents and what happened to Dad."

"Wait a minute." My sister worked out the details. "This is the video gamer?"

"You have a problem with gamers? I'll have you know I have a 4.2 KD in *Call of Duty*." A challenging gleam appeared in his eyes.

"What the hell is that supposed to mean?"

"That he's good. Belle, please. The other attorneys could show up at any moment. We're running out of time." I needed to bring everyone back on track.

He took a step into Belle's space. "Excuse me, I'm better than good. That's semi-pro."

"Gaming is not a profession," she said.

"Whatever."

She hmphed in her throat. "Okay. Let's get this over with." With a finger aimed at me she said, "We'll discuss the illegal pinging later."

I threw up my hands. "It's illegal. So is stealing files from law offices. Get over it!"

They followed me down the hall to my father's office. The earlier police presence was evident, but nothing indicated we couldn't enter, no matter what our attorney said. Black powder dusted the doorframe and handle. How many times had I entered this door in my life? Some of those prints belonged to me. Would I land in the suspect pool next?

"We need to open this without adding a print," my sister cautioned.

"They're done here," I countered her argument with one of my own. "They believe Mom did it." Even though I assumed this to be true, I used the bottom of my T-shirt to grasp the door handle, preparing myself for what awaited us on the other side of the door.

Plywood and plastic covered the gaping hole where the glass door used to be. Glittering shards of glass littered the desk, chairs, couch, and floor. But worst was the stain where my father had died—a visceral reminder of the way his gaze had fixed on me for those seconds, like he wanted to tell me something. If we'd only had a few minutes more…so I could tell him how much I loved him.

A wave of pain overwhelmed me; I couldn't drag air into my lungs. My body collapsed against the doorframe. Jazz squeezed my hand, and I tore my gaze from the blood, instead focusing on Dad's packed bookshelves, a safer view.

"His laptop is here." Belle sniffed and wiped her tears on the back of her hand. Someone had set the computer back on the desk.

The image of the office when I'd found Mom and Dad swam into focus. "When I came in, after the shots, the laptop was on the floor, upside down. Like a tent."

"He might have something on there," Jazz said. "Can you take it?"

"This room isn't sealed." My sister scanned the area as if searching for no trespassing signs or bright yellow caution tape. "They haven't told us we *can't* be in here, and they didn't take the computer, so…"

"*Ignorantia juris non excusat,*" I told her. "Ignorance excuses not."

When Jazz raised his eyebrows, I shrugged. "You have no idea how many times I heard that growing up. Mostly when I did something I shouldn't."

He smirked. "Harsh to have lawyer parents. Bet you didn't get away with anything."

"Not much," I admitted.

She closed the screen and tucked the laptop into her tote bag.

Entering the office took an act of will. I crossed to the filing cabinets then drew my notes out of my pocket. The names of the companies the fisherman had researched didn't appear in the cabinet. Nothing. "There aren't any matches in here for these people or the companies." I closed the last file drawer. "I don't get it."

"What about this drawer?" He jiggled the handle on my father's desk. "It's locked."

On the backside of the desk, a single file drawer took up the right side. I tugged on the handle. "I don't have a key for this."

Belle searched the rest of the drawers, shifting pens and supplies, but placing them back where they were. "Maybe it's here somewhere." We searched in vain for a key.

"I don't see anything," I said.

Jazz settled on the floor in front of the desk and peered into the keyhole. "This is an old desk," he murmured.

"It's an antique," she warned. "Don't scratch it."

Ignoring my sister, I asked, "Is the age important?"

"So, the lock is old too and easily picked." From the pen drawer, he removed a hefty paper clip and a thin metal letter opener. "Give me a minute."

He didn't need the minute. The drawer popped free in less than thirty seconds.

"Look at this!" My heart hammered my chest. Files on the companies from the fisherman's drive, as well as files on Patrick, Liz, and...

"There's a file on Mom." My sister withdrew the jacket from the drawer. Her hands trembled as she lifted the cover.

"What's in it?" I asked her as her phone buzzed with a text.

She fumbled then read the screen. "Uh-oh. It's Liz. She's picking up Mom now. I need something bigger than this tote bag for all of this."

Jazz squeezed my arm. "Your mother's getting out?"

I nodded. "On bail."

"That's awesome."

"Yes, it is," I agreed. "But we have to get home before she does."

After rummaging in Dad's closet, she produced a faded, navy-blue gym bag big enough for the trove of files.

"What's with the bag?"

"Take it. All of it." My sister shoved the gym bag at me. "We need to get this material out of here before someone else does." She slipped the files on Patrick, Mom, and Liz into her tote.

"Do you think Liz knows about these files?" We stared at each other for a full minute. "The person who did this is going to want the flash drive and all these files," I said. "Where are we going to hide this stuff?"

"Later," Belle told me. "We'll figure it out once we know what we've got."

"Uh, do you have a security system in your house?" The way he asked made the hair on the back of my neck stand up.

"Yes."

"Make sure you use it." His warning echoed in the office. "I don't like the feel of any of this."

Belle hefted the gym bag on her shoulder. I lifted the tote bag with Dad's laptop then paused to be with my father's memory. His familiar scent wafted through the space, a mix of sandalwood and spice, but even his cologne had been tinged with the unmistakable tang of blood.

Jazz's fingers brushed against mine. "You okay?"

"No." I lifted my chin. "But I will be when we get out of here."

We loaded the bags into my car. My sister slid into the Porsche with a wave in our direction and roared out of the garage. I lingered for a moment alone with my friend and co-investigator, the one person who "got" me.

"Thanks for coming, partner." I smiled at him.

"Ah, now I'm *your* partner. So you still love me even though I illegally pinged your phone?"

"You can ping me anytime."

He opened his arms, and I slid into his embrace. "You're not alone, Lil. I want you to remember, I'm here."

"Thank you." Gratitude pushed the grief threatening to swamp me back into the corners of my heart.

His arms tensed. "You remember the night on the beach?" Before I could react, he dipped his head and kissed me on the lips, then drew back a fraction to gaze at me.

Not trusting my voice or lack of breath to answer, I nodded.

"I think about that night a lot." His eyes sparkled.

"Do you?" I whispered.

"Yeah. Do you?"

Breathing? What was breathing?

"Yes."

He kissed me again then released me. His scent blanketed me in visions of sand and safety. "Good," he said as he walked away.

When I slid behind the wheel of my car, the trembling in my body had nothing to do with my father's murder or secret files and everything to do with memories of being with Jazz.

Chapter Nine

"What should we say to her?" my sister murmured when a car parked in the driveway. We stood side-by-side at the living room window as my mother climbed from Liz's SUV.

"I don't know." I'd been obsessing over the same question on the drive home from the law offices, wondering about the contents of the hidden files. The gym bag and tote bag were buried in the bottom of Belle's closet.

We'd lost a father, but Mom lost the man she'd been married to for twenty-eight years. Add in the accusations against her, and I didn't have an answer for my sister.

Mom walked in the front door, followed by Liz. I'd never seen my mother outside of the house without makeup, without her hair perfect, and her clothes impeccable. The woman who stepped into the foyer was a shadow of my mother—a distant, ghostly cousin who'd been stripped of her freedom, but also her persona. Her clothes had been covered with blood the last time I saw her. I didn't know this woman with limp hair, tired eyes, and dressed in a prison-gray T-shirt and pair of ill-fitting sweatpants. She scared the crap out of me.

"Girls," she said, her words thick with emotion.

Without a word, I slid my arms around her waist, and my sister added her arms to our knot. We stood for several minutes, a tangled web of grief and despair. Fragile in my embrace, Mom no longer embodied the formidable attorney who had ruled our house and the legal office for years.

Liz cleared her throat. "You ladies will be okay?"

Mom nodded without glancing up or speaking. The door closed as Liz let herself out. After several minutes, we parted. Mom clung to one of each of our hands as if we were buoys in the sea of uncertainty.

"I'm so sorry," she said.

"You didn't do anything, Mom." Frustration and the truth about her and Patrick strained my response.

My sister brushed her hand down Mom's arm. "Are you all right?"

When she smiled, the creases at the corners of her eyes were more prominent than I remembered. "I could use a hot shower and my own clothes. I'm tired."

"I'll make you tea," I offered.

She touched my hair, the side of my face. Whatever I said to the detective on that awful morning wouldn't come between us. "Thank you. I need to get some things…out of the bedroom. I'm going to stay in the guest room for a while."

A tear escaped. I wiped it away so she wouldn't see me cry. Of course, she couldn't stay in the room my father had woken up in yesterday. I couldn't bear to step inside.

"Are you hungry?" my sister asked. "Do you need dinner?"

Mom breathed in and sighed. "The tea's enough. Thank you, girls."

She retreated to her bedroom. After a minute, the closing click of a door echoed in the hall. My sister swore under her breath, but I caught most of the colorful content. Mom might be home, but far from free, not with the memories and implications of what happened looming over her.

"We have the laptop and those files. We need to get to work." The pressure of time weighed on me like a bomb I needed to defuse. She'd never survive another night in prison—forget about the years it would take off her life if they found her guilty.

"You make the tea," my sister directed. "I'm going to put together a tray. I bet she'll eat some crackers and fruit if we put it in front of her."

By the time Mom emerged from the shower, we had cobbled together a light feast of halved strawberries, cheddar, grapes, and whole wheat crackers. Mom sank down at the table next to the pool, staring at the water cascading over the rocks at the edge.

"I made you tea."

She laced her hands around the cup. "I missed you guys." To my sister, she said, "I'm sorry you had to leave school. Your semester must be almost over."

"I have it worked out. Don't worry."

I stared at my sister, suspicion bubbling in my mind. Her quick reply and tone told me she lied. There was no way she'd done anything more than gather her belongings into the car and drive south.

Mom picked up a tiny slice of cheddar and nibbled the corner.

"Have you talked to anyone about the funeral?"

"Yes," I murmured. "We have the details if you want to look them over."

Tears coursed down her cheeks unbidden. "Maybe tomorrow."

"Okay." I passed her a pile of napkins.

Belle sat beside her. "What happened? Can you tell us?"

She drew a tremulous breath and wiped her face with a napkin. Her voice steadied as she began her story. "I don't know. I was in my office—the door stood open between our adjoining offices. We had coffee together, and we were talking about an upcoming case Dad would litigate. The case would be a huge undertaking. We decided to work together on it." She paused and blew her nose. "I went back to my desk to read through my email. I remember I sent an answer back to Judge Mundey. That's when I heard the first sound. Like an explosion. It hurt my ears like a sudden decompression. I jumped up, terrified at first, thinking I should run, but the wind gusted in the office from your father's room, and I went to the door."

She tried to pick up the tea, but the liquid sloshed. Her gaze met mine, then my sister's as she set the cup down. "There was someone there, dressed in black. With a ski mask on. I'm sure it was a man—by his height and build. He had a gun pointed at your father. Dad stood behind his desk with his gun in his hand, behind his back. He held up his other hand, like to stop the man in black. He saw me standing there, just for a second—" She broke off.

"Did the person you saw in the office see you?" Belle asked.

"I'm sure he knew I was there," she said. "I screamed for your dad."

"What did Dad do?" I asked.

"He tried to make his way around the desk, toward the front. As soon as he made a move with the gun, the man shot him. Dad fired back as he fell." She pressed her hands to her mouth, her face a mask of agony. When she recovered, she continued, "The man went out on the balcony. I ran to your father and took the gun out of his hand. He tried to sit up, to go after the person, but he couldn't."

"Then I came in?"

Mom focused on me. "Yes. Girls, I'm sorry."

"There's nothing you could have done. He could have killed you too," I told her. This fact troubled me. The killer had left a witness.

Mom pushed the snack plate away. "Thank you both for this. I need to lie down. I didn't sleep much last night." She gave us both a hug before disappearing down the hallway to the guest room beside mine.

In the kitchen, I covered the tray in plastic wrap and tucked it into the refrigerator. "She's telling the truth."

My sister's eyes widened. "How do you know?"

"Her body language. The way she spoke in detail, not omitting facts. Her voice was steady. She made eye contact."

With a proud smile, she said, "You're going to make a great lawyer someday."

"Or a criminal profiler. Kind of the same thing."

She chuckled as she washed the teacup and set it to dry. "I have to write the details down while they're fresh. In my room. Not out here."

I retrieved a pen from my desk and the box of files before pausing at the door to the guest room. My mother lay curled on top of the bedspread. A bottle of sleeping pills sat on the table. I set my box down and covered her with a blanket. She didn't move, lost in her pharmaceutical slumber. After what had happened, she deserved a dreamless night.

Belle sat on the bed in her room, her hair tied up in a messy knot at her nape. She'd changed out of her jeans and sweatshirt. I smirked at the pajama pants. Tiny images of Edgar Allan Poe's likeness dotted the fabric. She glanced up as I dumped the box of materials on the floor.

"Oh, good." Her gaze met mine. "How's Mom?"

"Asleep. She took something. She'll be out until tomorrow."

The corner of her mouth veered down a notch. "Hopefully she only took one."

"Would you blame her if she didn't?"

"Not a bit." She tapped her pen on the tablet. "So, I wrote down Mom's statement. How about reading this over to make sure I didn't miss anything?"

I picked up the tablet, scanning her precise writing. "This is accurate. Why did he leave Mom in the office? He didn't try to hurt her."

"I thought about that too. Distraction maybe? Hoping she'd be blamed? The cops treated her like she was guilty."

A light flashed outside the window. My pulse spiked. "Belle. The motion lights just came on out back."

"*What?*"

We shrank back into the corner of the room. The light shut off and kicked back on several times. "Is the security system on?" I whispered.

"I don't know! I don't live here, remember?"

I couldn't recall resetting it after Mom came home. "Stay here."

"Where are you going?"

"To lock the door," I snapped back.

"What if he's on the other side?"

"Who? The man in black?" I feigned annoyance to hide my terror. She was right. The guy could be wandering through the family room right now. "Wait. I have the password to check the security cameras." I stuck up an index finger. "Hang on."

"Are you calling 9-1-1?"

"No, just wait a minute. Okay?" My fingers flew over the screen. I brought up the rear cameras and rewound the feed by five minutes, then fast-forwarded. I inhaled a relieved breath. "Raccoon. See?"

"Jesus. Let's lock the damn doors."

With the house alarm enabled and every door and window checked for locked, we returned to her room and sank down on the floor, surrounded by papers.

"We need to know who this man in black is and what he wanted from Dad."

"He wanted him dead," I said, pain blooming in my chest. I'd done a good job of containing my emotions, but my mother's recollection—what she'd gone through seeing my father shot—hurt worse than my own sorrow.

"You all right? You're shaking."

"Nothing about this is all right." I wrapped my hair into a ponytail. "Let's get to work. I need something to stay busy or I'll lose my mind."

"Tell me about it. We need to figure out the motive."

The files from Dad's desk waited as I gathered the courage to open them. My hand lingered on the file with Mom's name written on the tab in his handwriting. Inside were copies of documents she had prepared for different cases, travel itineraries for conferences she'd attended. Dad had circled a set of dates on one of the trips—a conference in Washington D.C. last spring.

"Anything there?" Belle hadn't touched the file as if she didn't want to be tainted by more truths about our mother.

"Nothing leaps out at me. He made notes on this conference paperwork. Circled dates. That's about it." I set the file aside, located my notes on the first company, and opened the corresponding file. The folder contained handwritten pages and printouts similar to what I'd amassed, plus a few faded newspaper clippings. "Check this out. Newspaper notices of incorporation for a couple of different companies." I suspected my father had written the date of publication on each snippet.

"These aren't client files," she noted. "They're arranged more like a scrapbook. Why would he hang on to memorabilia? Why collect it in the first place?"

"Good question." All the file jackets contained similar items.

"Dad must have figured out something wasn't right about these companies. I wonder what tipped him off."

"Do you think Mom knows?"

"I don't know. Why did he keep them locked up? What does this have to do with the firm?"

Her gaze met mine as she folded her legs beneath her. "He didn't want her to know what he was doing."

"Right," I said. "And sometime later he hired the fisherman… Oh no! We're supposed to be at The Whale in a half hour!"

"Guess I better change out of my jammies." She scrambled off the floor.

"Thanks."

"For what?"

"Helping with this. Believing I'm not crazy." I meant it, every word. I didn't want to meet the fisherman alone.

"I don't hate you, Lily. I know we didn't get along…it's old news. Okay?"

That's an odd thing to say. Instead of pressing her and dissolving this tenuous partnership we'd forged, I agreed to her terms. For now. "I'll meet you at the car."

Chapter Ten

"Did you reset the alarm?" I asked Belle when she slid onto the passenger seat.

"Yeah. I checked on Mom too. She's still out, but I left a note just in case. I told her we went to get something to eat." She checked her makeup in the visor mirror.

"Well, it's sort of true."

The drive took twenty minutes to reach the restaurant. At eight-thirty, the horizon glowed with a faint strip of orange, and purple clouds edged with gold hovered above the ocean. The restaurants and bars up and down Estero Boulevard were gearing up for a night of post-sunset watching debauchery. Tourists wandered on both sides of the road, clustering at the crosswalks like vibrant birds.

Music pulsed in the air, a mix of Jimmy Buffet, pop, and reggae. A humid breeze washed over the Gulf, loosening strands of hair from the knot at the base of my neck to whisp about my face. I'd worn longer shorts than usual, my favorite floral tank, and strappy brown sandals. Belle had chosen a dark blue tank dress. The skirt landed at mid-thigh, and she paired it with silver leather flip flops that gleamed against her tan. We looked the part of a couple of girls out for a night of dinner, dancing, and guy-hunting.

"You have any idea where he'll be?" She scanned the throngs of people from behind her sunglasses.

"No," I said playing with my napkin. "He said he'd be here, eating crab cakes and drinking beer. Nothing else." Truth was, I didn't know if I could pick the fisherman out of a crowd. The night and no lighting hadn't been favorable for getting a good look at him. And he'd kept his face concealed. I expected he would find me before I could find him.

"A beer? You know how many men are drinking beer in here?" She blew out a breath.

"He said Key West Ale was his favorite."

"I hope this isn't a monumental waste of time."

"Me too."

It took fifteen minutes to get a seat on the packed upper deck. Tourists and locals vied for one of the best views of the sunset-streaked sky. We huddled under an umbrella as the strings of white lights bobbed in the breeze above us. She ordered a Sunset Rum Punch, and I settled for an iced tea.

Condensation pooled beneath her frothy drink. I licked my lips.

"Don't worry. Your day will come," she said with a smirk as she drank.

We watched the crowds. As I sipped my tea and pretended to admire the view, I didn't notice anyone who I suspected was the fisherman. "What if he's inside?" I asked as our grouper salads arrived. If we missed this opportunity to talk to him, how would I ever find him again?

I poked at the blackened fish and tender greens. This was always my favorite meal, but today it tasted like elementary school paste clogging the back of my throat.

"Relax," my sister said. "There's nothing to do but wait."

When the dishes were cleared well after nine o'clock, we nursed our final drinks, and the waitress tried to shuffle us on our way. "Maybe he changed his mind," I said.

"We can't hang out here much longer."

"I'm going to run to the ladies' room before we leave."

"Okay, I'll wait here and fight off the server."

The indoor seating was less packed than the upper deck. I made my way to the back of the room where the bathrooms were located, scanning the tables for someone familiar. It had been dark on the pier, and his face had been shadowed. Any of the mid-fifties men in the restaurant could be him.

But when I exited the bathroom into the dim hallway, a man stood leaning against the wall. He wore a dark baseball cap pulled low, khaki shorts, and a teal polo. A beard occluded his features, but I recognized the tattoo on his arm and the Marines emblem on his cap. Adrenaline arced my pulse into the red zone. It was him—the fisherman.

He lifted a bottle of Key West Ale and took a long swig.

"Ah...hi," I stammered.

Without glancing in my direction, he slipped a hand into his pocket and withdrew a slip of paper which he dropped to the floor.

I rushed to pick the paper up as he walked away.

Back on the roof, Belle had abandoned our table. She leaned on the railing of the deck, watching the activity on the street below. I startled her when I touched her arm.

"You were gone a long time," she said.

"I saw him. Downstairs. He gave me this." I unfolded the paper. "It says: *The pier. Ten minutes.*"

"He was here?"

I nodded. "Yep."

"We better get moving. We'll have to hurry."

In the car, I locked the doors even though the fisherman was long gone.

"Did he scare you? What did he say to you?"

"Nothing. He dropped the note and walked away." I maneuvered through the heavy evening traffic, making my way to the north end of Estero Boulevard. I parked in front of a men's clothing store next to the coffee café, the only spot available. Ahead, the pier jutted over the ocean. "You ready?"

She breathed in as if working up her nerve. "Yes. Let's find out what's going on."

We strolled toward the pier, stopping to gaze over the side like normal people on an evening jaunt. A moist breeze churned off the Gulf, blowing strands of my hair into my mouth. I tugged them away, my focus forward. We'd made it to Rudy's Treasure Chest on the pier when the screaming started. Belle and I locked gazes as my dread blossomed.

"Lily, wait!" she yelled as I took off.

Running down the pier, I sprinted toward the fishing platform.

People clustered around the rail, pointing to the water. Before I reached the edge, I guessed exactly what I'd find. A spot of teal floated face-down on the tranquil waters illuminated by the pier lights. The fading orange of sunset stained the water around the dead fisherman.

~ * ~

We huddled in the car and watched the emergency crews retrieve the fisherman's body from the water. My sister wept silently, her head resting against the window. I couldn't cry. My fears and emotions formed a complicated lump of incredulity, drying my eyes and freezing my stomach into a block of ice. How did someone kill the fisherman in the middle of the pier without anyone seeing, not five minutes after he met me in the restaurant?

Only a professional killer could commit murder without getting caught, not once but twice.

"He's dead because of me," I whispered in the space between us. "Someone had to be following him."

"He's dead because of Dad," she corrected me. "He did a job for

Dad."

"Now two people are dead because of it." I gripped her hand. "Could they be following us too?"

She didn't answer for several seconds. "And all of our work is on my bedroom floor, and Mom's home alone."

We stared at each other. Belle's face was pale with angry fear. The shadows menaced with shifting darkness, and the memories of conquered childhood terrors rose like ghosts from the ground. My gaze swept over the crowds, scanning faces and body language, searching for someone searching for us. "Maybe we should take this to the police."

"Hmph. Do you think they'll believe us?"

"Probably not. I'm not sure I believe it."

She jabbed a finger toward the pier where the rescue crews loaded up the body. "They killed him. Like they killed Dad!"

"But who are *they*? Why? What do *they* want?" *They* could be anyone, no one. The nameless horrors were the new monster hiding in my closet, waiting for me to turn my back to the door.

She wiped her eyes with the back of her hand. "Let's get out of here."

A sudden worry for my mother filled my chest. "Could Mom be in danger?"

"I think *we're* in danger. We have a decision to make. Drop this and go on living or pursue it and take a swim in the Gulf."

I drove over Matanzas Pass Bridge, the docks along the intercoastal waterway glinting in the deepening dusk. My emotions churned with the intensity of hurricane whipped waves. "I'm scared," I confessed. "Someone doesn't want this scheme or scam or whatever it is to be revealed. Whoever set up these bogus companies is most likely the person who killed Dad and the fisherman."

"Or who hired someone to do it."

This new possibility chilled me to the core. I lowered the air conditioning as I tapped the steering wheel at a red light on Summerlin. Every time the car stopped my pulse spiked. Out on the street, I was exposed, an easy target. The information we'd accumulated may have made us expendable and next on the hit list. We were all in harm's way.

Belle touched my arm, an unexpected offer of comfort. "Let's see what they say about this on the news. They'll give his name. Maybe knowing who he is will get us some answers."

"So what's our next move? What about Liz? Do we need to tell her?"

As usual, my sister took her time answering, considering possibilities before she offered her opinions. We'd driven on from the light, toward Sanibel and our house on Shenandoah Circle. Our community had a gate and guard—an extra layer of security. Plus, the alarm system in the house was top notch. Except none of it took the edge off my fear. Every bush hid a set of watching eyes, every shadow a lurking horror.

We'd rounded the corner toward our street when Belle finally spoke. "If Dad hid information from Mom, I don't think we can tell her yet." She pressed her fingers to her forehead. "What if the partners are involved? We need to hack into Dad's laptop."

I struggled with the implications of the people my father trusted turning on him. "But telling Mom, finding out what she knows, could help get her out of trouble," I reminded her. "If the cops investigate the fisherman, they might discover what he knew."

"And get us into tons more trouble with the cops. What about Patrick? He's in those pictures with Mom. Can you imagine what Stephens would do if he saw those pictures? His head would explode."

"Now that's something I'd like to see," I said. "He's a total jerk."

"You're right about that, but Mom's the one who has the answers. She's the one we have to talk to."

The image of their embrace sickened me, burning through a bit of my fear. *How could she?*

"Mom needs to tell us what the kiss was about," Belle continued. "We can tell her Dad had the picture and say we came across it when we went to find Liz's contact information."

"She's smarter than that." I parked in the driveway. "Mom will see through us."

"Maybe not. She's not thinking straight right now. Hitting her with this will throw her."

"It sounds cruel when you say it like we believe she's a suspect." I shut off the engine and gripped my keys in my hand, pressing the edges into my palm.

"Any crueler than her cheating on Dad?"

My shoulders slouched. "No. I guess not."

Inside, we checked the house again, trying windows and doors, resetting the alarm system.

"I'm exhausted. I'm gonna make sure Mom's okay and try to get some sleep. There's no way we're getting anything from her tonight." Belle kicked off her flip flops on the way to the hallway.

"What about the files?" Tired or not, the hallway clock counted time like a relentless drum major the week before finals. Mom might be home, but our questions remained unanswered, and Dad's killer still walked free. "And the laptop?"

Belle stopped, leaned against the wall, and blinked her bloodshot eyes. "I'll box the files up and bury them and the laptop in my closet for now. Night."

My sister shuffled into her room, the weight of what we'd learned riding on her shoulders, hunching her forward. I carried the same burden as if my family's future sat on my back. Finding the murderer. Saving Mom from jail. Solving the mystery that had gotten the fisherman killed.

Truthfully, finding out what Dad had on his laptop scared me almost as much as the person who killed him.

My stomach grumbled. I sent most of my dinner salad to the trash. Hunger drove me to the kitchen where I removed the plate of snacks from the refrigerator along with one of my father's precious Longboard beers. Ever since we'd been to Hawaii, he preferred the island beer over all other. Never much of a clandestine, high school drinker, I figured if my mother could medicate herself, so could I.

In my room I switched on my television and connected to Twitch. Jazz popped up in his late-night stream. I smiled at his Hawaiian shirt and shades. He was doing well, with almost twenty subscribers watching his feed.

What would Jazz think of our night's investigation? I wanted to tell him about the fisherman, about the teal shirt floating in the Gulf, but not now. Not with his potential sponsors online, and his deals close and ready for ink. My disaster wasn't a distraction he needed. But the slight hint of smile ghosting his lips told me he knew I'd signed on.

I settled in with a pile of pillows behind my back to watch him play, thankful for the mindlessness, the sweet strawberries between my teeth, and the beer.

Chapter Eleven

Mom exited the guest room the next morning, dressed in khaki capris and a dark blue sleeveless blouse—a stark contrast to the sad, plain woman who arrived home last night. She poured coffee into her bright blue mug and joined me at the breakfast table. Makeup concealed the dark patches beneath her eyes.

"Did you sleep?"

"Some," she said. "How about you?"

I lifted a shoulder. "A little better with you and Belle in the house."

She nodded once, blinking back tears as she glanced at the empty chair across from hers. Clearing her throat, she asked, "Do you want to come with us to the funeral home?"

"I think I'll hang here," I said, unable to vocalize the volume of emotions his death spawned. They didn't need me for this.

Belle and Mom left just after nine to go to the funeral home, leaving me to wander around the backyard and sort through my fears. I added chlorine to the pool and picked weeds from the flower beds to keep my hands busy while my brain wheeled from one terrible outcome to the next. We hadn't heard from Liz yet, and I hoped she'd been able to calm the firm's clients. What if Mom lost her law license over this?

Missing Dad hurt like nothing I'd ever experienced, but I was old enough to know we had so much more left to lose. This house. My college and Belle's last year of law school. Not to mention the bad publicity for the firm.

And, if the tests didn't prove Mom innocent, she could go to prison.

Chores done and alone, I jumped into the pool then swam with strong strokes, punishing my muscles to erase the pain in my mind and heart. The cool water slipped by as I completed lap after lap, the sun warming my back. Later, I floated, face to the sky, eyes closed, as the sun danced on the backs of my eyelids.

If only this was real, this sense of peace and tranquility. If only my father were here.

Thoughts of him drove me from the water and chased me into the shower where I sobbed against the tile until exhausted. For a long time after, I sat in a chair by my bedroom window wrapped in my bathrobe, listening to the soothing tinkle of pool water splashing on stone. I wondered how Mom was handling the funeral planning and if she agreed with our choices.

I hoped my obdurate sister was being patient and kind.

Frustrated, I removed my saxophone from its case and worked through warmups, limbering my fingers and my lips. It felt like forever since I'd played. I ran through the set we needed to play for the Sun Runner's audition next week—jazz standards like *Fly Me to the Moon* with a couple of beachy covers thrown in for good measure. With the music pouring from my horn, I went to that place in my soul where only the next note and the next measure mattered. Satisfied with my practice, I dressed in jean shorts and a tank covered with tiny sunflowers then went outside to sit in the sun.

Half an hour later, the door leading from the garage to the kitchen slammed. I hurried inside stunned by Belle's appearance. "What happened?"

"They won't release his body." My sister's red-rimmed eyes spoke of the tears she'd shed on the way home. "The coroner's office is holding Dad pending further investigation."

I drew in a sharp breath. "What investigation?"

Mom sighed. "Let's go sit and talk this through." We went outside, and my mother sank into a shaded chair. "We don't know. I called Liz. She's going to find out what she can."

Belle and I shared a frightened look. "I'm going to get some iced tea. Do you want some, Mom?"

My mother brushed a hand over her hair. "Thanks. Tea would be nice."

"I'll help you," Belle offered.

In the kitchen, away from my mother's hearing, we huddled in the corner. "What is that about?"

"It can't be good." She wove a vicious string of swearing and kicked the corner of the cabinet. "What could they want? This has to be about more than the shooting." She took a glass from the cupboard and retrieved the iced tea pitcher from the fridge. "What if you call the detective? Maybe he'll tell you."

Stephens didn't like me. I had the impression he didn't trust me either. "You want me to act like I don't know anything?"

She lifted a shoulder as she carried Mom's iced tea from the counter. "It might be the one way to find out."

I sighed, dreading what she asked me to do. "Okay. I'll go call him."

In my room, I located the detective's card. There was a very real possibility he could hang up on me or refuse to take my call, but I dialed anyway. After being shuffled around several departments, the detective answered on the other end. "This is Stephens."

Swallowing, I dove into the speech I'd practiced as I dialed, except my oration sounded more compelling inside my brain than out. "Uh…this is Lily Harmony. Why won't they let us bury my father?" My voice cracked in just the right places, without trying when I thought of my father lying in some cold, dark morgue.

"Miss Harmony. I'm sorry. But this is an ongoing investigation," he said wearily. "I can't discuss this with you. You have an attorney, yes?"

"Yes." I bit my lip to keep the words I wanted to say in check. Maybe my sister's vulgarity was rubbing off on me.

"Then work through your attorney to get the information you want."

"Did my father do something wrong?" I blurted.

There was a pause on the detective's end. "I'm sorry, Lily. I truly am. You and your sister are victims as well. But I can't answer your questions. Please. Let us do our jobs." The line went dead.

I resisted the urge to fling the phone across the room. This conversation confirmed everything I suspected. The detective's view of murder suspects remained narrow. The one way to shake him loose from his beliefs was to slap him with the truth.

But what was the truth? And how did I find it?

I hid my anger and smiled at my mother when I returned to the patio with a dish of sliced pineapple, adding to the chips and homemade salsa my sister had brought out.

"You girls don't have to wait on me." Mom paled and the dark circles bleeding through the coverup under her eyes worried me more than Stephens's evasiveness. I'd never seen my mother fragile.

I made a face and snagged a slice of pineapple, careful not to meet Belle's probing gaze. "What are you talking about? This is mine."

My mother laughed, the loveliest sound in the world.

We talked about school and summer, chatting like we'd done a million times, as if we could pretend Dad had gone to work while the girls hung out. The fantasy worked until my mother mentioned my upcoming graduation. Her expression shattered, and she excused herself to the guest room.

"I've never seen her so beat down before." I slumped in my chair, a sudden exhaustion softening my spine.

"This crap has got to stop." She bit into a tortilla chip, catching the crumbs in her palm. "Did you get in touch with the cop?"

"Yeah. It didn't go well." When I told her what happened, crimson stained her cheeks.

"What a jackass. We need a new angle, like who filed the incorporation papers for these companies. Then we'd have something else to research."

I chewed on the end of my pen, working out the tangles in my logic. "What about the advertisements themselves? They had to advertise before they could file the paperwork." Since Monica's departure, I'd placed a few ads for the firm. It was standard procedure.

"You're right," she said. "There has to be a money trail back to whoever paid for them. How can we find that out? The newspaper isn't going to tell us."

I smiled. "No, but I know someone who might be able to bypass the paper."

Chapter Twelve

Jazz met us at the coffee house. I hugged him publicly, happy with the recent uptick in our relationship. He nodded toward my sister and slipped beside me in the order line. Iced lattes in hand, we strolled away from the pier toward the bathhouse and crowds of witnesses. Safety in numbers, they said, whoever *they* were. Probably not people like me, who'd seen two people die in the span of days.

We hung out on the bathhouse deck and sat on the concrete bench in front of a pair of pelican statues, our feet propped up on the blue metal railing. On the beach below us, parents struggled to de-sand their kids while power boats raced offshore, dancing in the surf near the end of the pier.

A gorgeous Fort Myers day.

Muggy air glided over the water while I sipped icy caramel. I had no desire to wander out on the pier, even though tourists and strolling locals crowded the area. All those prying eyes hadn't helped the fisherman. The icy chill in my bones told me if whoever had killed him and my father wanted me out of the way, I'd be history.

And, as morbid and dark as my thoughts ran, they gave me an idea. Dad had hired him, and my father had been a fastidious record keeper. Somewhere, we'd find a name for the dead man. A phone number. Maybe knowing more about the fisherman would help us find out why Dad had employed his services. I nudged my sister.

"Hmm?" She licked whipped cream off her straw.

"I wonder if Dad kept a record of the fisherman's contact information. Maybe it's on the laptop. Or his cellphone."

"The news didn't give his name in the story I read online. That will make figuring out his number tough." She met my gaze as if acknowledging our conversation was out of place for a summer beach day.

"I read it too. His throat was cut. They're calling the attack a robbery. He died without identification on him, and I didn't see an actual obituary yet."

"Maybe the killer took his wallet," Jazz suggested.

"Someone should be missing him," she said. "A wife? A family?"

"I don't know. But he had to have one—a name I mean—an identity. And an obituary when they learn who he is. Maybe it's a lead we can follow." *Or another dead end.* "Dad had to pay this guy."

Jazz brushed the condensation off his cup, his fingers spraying me with drops. He dodged my swats. "I have my connection checking the Florida obits for someone who matches your fisherman. But if he didn't live around here, we might not see it. He could be from Tampa. Or Miami."

He had a point. Just because the fisherman sought me out and worked for my father didn't mean he had a residence in Fort Myers. "Or nowhere," I grumped. If Dad tried to be discrete, chances were the man was not local. "But we had another idea, one that might require some more of Frankie's specialized skills."

Belle leaned forward. "In Florida, a company has to advertise their choice of a fictious name if they aren't a corporation, like in newspaper classifieds. Some of these are corporations, so there won't be a record. But a couple of them are just fake storefronts. Those are the ones we might be able to track."

"Okay. So we attack the newspapers to find a name. I'll get my connection on board." He pitched his straw and lid into the trash can.

I stared out at the ocean, wishing the answers would ride in on the waves and drop at my feet like sand dollars. "Do think your *connection* can hack the newspapers?"

"Probably. But the price would be super *high*."

I rolled my eyes at his pot pun.

"What do you mean…hack? Who are you talking about?" Belle's tone came across less than happy.

Jazz pressed his temples like she'd given him a migraine. "Really? You question my methods after the pinging incident?"

She glared from him to me.

"We need to know, Belle. My friend has his sources. Leave it at that." The less she knew about the boys' involvement, the better.

"Wait a minute." Her face brightened. "I have an idea."

"So, you *do* want us to hack into the paper?" he asked over the top of his cup as he crunched ice.

I stifled a laugh at his hopeful tone.

My sister rolled her neck, stretching. "I remember one of the corporations—Morrell Industrial—filed recently, maybe two months ago. If we call the paper and complain about a misprint, maybe we can get some more information—like who paid for the advertisement."

"Pretty slick." I had to admit, this was the best idea we'd come up with, even if there was the chance the newspaper would shut us down. If it didn't work, our next call would be to Frankie. I glanced at the clock on my phone. "It's four-thirty. Better do this fast before they close. We need a phone they can't trace back to us."

Jazz bumped me with his elbow. "There's an old-fashioned payphone down at the other end of Estero."

We both stared in shock.

"What?" he asked with a smug smile. "We used to go to the Royal Scoop and crank call our friends from it. Best quarters we spent all night."

I threw my empty coffee cup into the trash. "I'm feeling like a post-caffeine sundae. How about you guys?"

~ * ~

We left the cars parked and strolled down Estero Boulevard past the bright blue umbrella tables at The Whale and the tourist trap T-shirt shops. Traffic picked up as locals hurried home from work and visitors jostled for parking spots in front of the restaurants.

Perfect. No one would notice us.

I hoped.

I waited in line to place our orders at the Royal Scoop, nerves humming like a live wire, while Jazz and Belle did their thing at the payphone. With the phone to her ear, my conniving sister tapped her flipflop on the sidewalk. I stifled a grin. The poor clerk on the other end of the line. When Belle set her mind to something, look out. She'd get what she wanted or threaten legal action, citing the exact statute they had violated.

They met me at one of the picnic tables after the call, their faces plastered with smiles as we dug into sundaes. Carmel sauce leaked down the side of my cup. I licked my sticky fingers as palm fronds danced in the sea breeze. The ocean called from behind the shops, its constant whisper brushing the sand.

"That was easy." Digging her spoon into her double chocolate and catching the dripping fudge on her tongue, she smacked her lips with pleasure then explained, "When I told them they misprinted the Morrell company name and my customer threatened to sue because of it—which of course also made them liable—they were more than willing to read the application back to me word for word."

"The suspense is killing me. Who placed the ad?"

Triumphant, she slapped her palm onto the table. "You're not going to believe it. Monica Foster."

"What?" My voice climbed an octave. "Monica Foster? Dad's secretary Monica? Recently pregnant, Monica?"

My sister shoveled ice cream on her victory lap. "Yes. It lists the owners of Morrell Industrial as Dorminy Holdings—we've heard that one before—and Atlantic Trading Partners. These companies all circle back in on one another." She wiped a spot of fudge from the table with her napkin.

"No people?" Jazz asked in between strawberry mouthfuls. "More fake names aren't gonna help us. How do you spell it?"

"D-O-R-M-I-N-Y," she told him as he removed his cellphone from his back pocket.

"Yeah," I agreed, deflated. "Try the other one. We already know Dorminy is a dead end," I emphasized with a swipe of my spoon. "If Monica filed the paperwork, Dad had to know about this, right? Dorminy is the name he asked me about—if any mail concerning them had arrived. But Atlantic and Morrell are new. Maybe we'll get something there?"

Jazz searched for the name. "Uh, no. Atlantic is another post office box. This one is in Ocala. We're screwed on this end."

My sister's smile faded. "There's got to be another way through all of the duplicity. This could be layers deep."

"We need to find out who owns these companies," I said. The overwhelming task loomed above us like a Gulf squall about to dump. "Otherwise, we're never going to get anywhere."

"You're sure there was nothing else about these companies at Dad's office?"

"Other than those secret files? No. Not in the past couple of weeks. If anything came in on the company, Monica must have taken care of it before she left."

"Where would she put the file?" Belle wondered aloud.

"I bet the file's not in your father's office," Jazz said. "It's in hers."

"I never checked for a hidden drawer in her office. Dad had one, maybe she did too. Do you think Monica's been filing these motions and the paperwork without Dad's knowledge?"

"There's one way to find out," she said.

"We have to go back to the law firm?" Jazz lamented, rolling his eyes. "Are you trying to get us in trouble?" he teased.

"I'm afraid so." I twined my fingers in his, grateful for his support. "You have a stream coming up, don't you?"

He groaned. "Yeah. And I have a new sponsor checking me out.

I can't go with you. You think you can sign on while you're digging through the files?"

"Sure."

"Streaming? You're doing it for a job?" Belle raised a single eyebrow.

"College textbooks are expensive," he said.

My temper flared. "We'll discuss it later." How dare she question what he did. Why did he have to justify his work to her? He made more money as a streamer than most people made in their minimum wage, day jobs. With another sponsor in the wings, his income would go way up.

Her mouth closed in a tight line. No comeback?

What a change. Before this happened, my sister had been absent from my life for most of my turbulent teenaged years. I wouldn't stand for her superiority act now. No way.

Jazz stood and drew me into the comfort of his arms. If I hadn't resisted this for so long, we could have been more before Dad died. I think Dad would have liked him. Grief lunged for my throat. *Stop.* Accept this new togetherness. See where it goes.

I hugged him back, wishing my dad *had* gotten to meet him.

"You text me later. When you get back. Make sure, okay?"

I met Jazz's lips with mine. "I will. Good luck tonight."

He gave me one last squeeze before jogging back down the street to his car.

"What's going on between the two of you?"

At this moment, with our lives in turmoil, I didn't need her condescending attitude or questions about who I chose to be involved with. "Your opinion of what someone should or shouldn't do with their time should be kept quiet. We've been friends for a long time. We're close."

"So I see," she remarked. "What does he think about you leaving for Boston in a couple of months?"

The question stopped me in my tracks. Leaving for Boston seemed like a distant dream meant for someone else who lived a normal life. Someone whose father hadn't been murdered in the next room.

"Boston's over," I told her. "I'm not leaving Mom. Not now. I'll go to school here." *And not for law, either.* But that was an argument for a different time.

"You're going to give up Boston College? Dad would flip."

"Dad's not here!" I yelled.

People stopped on the street to stare. "Shut up," she snarled, grabbing my elbow and muscling me toward the other side of the street.

I was crying too much to pay attention to where she led me. I found myself on the beach in front of an orange and lime green condo complex. Towels fluttered from the balcony railings like vibrant flags and music wafted over the wind. She didn't stop until the ocean covered our shins.

The water lapped against my legs while I sobbed, my body shaking with tremors. She hugged me with her right arm, and I didn't shrug the contact away. We stood on the beach in silence, watching the water foam over the sand. Offshore, the last few beachgoers swam and splashed. A man on a Jet Ski roared up to the beach, parked, and then headed for one of the beach bars.

"I'm sorry. My inner bitch needed another lesson in shut-the-hell-up."

I bit my lip and nodded once.

"You didn't deserve that. Neither did he. He's a good guy." She gave a deep-throated laugh. "Hell, he plays video games for a living. I work myself to death to get a degree, so I can work myself to death to make partner in ten years. Who's the smart one?"

I inhaled a long, shaky breath, tasting the sea. "I'm glad you came home."

She slipped her arm from my shoulders and heaved out a sigh, her gaze fixed on the darkening horizon. "You're not the only one questioning her career path."

My jaw dropped. "But Belle! You're almost done." She had a few months. A semester, no more, before she graduated with a law degree.

The sunlight glinted off the water and made her eyes glow amber. "Then what? Kick Liz or Patrick out of their office so I can become part of the firm?"

"You know who I'd vote for," I snarled, imagining armed guards escorting Patrick from the building. Preferably in handcuffs.

Her brows drew down. "Agreed. But wills and trusts. They're subjects that don't interest me."

"You don't have to be a firm lawyer like Mom and Dad. You can do other things."

"A Harmony is built for one thing. If I don't finish law school, I can't be pressured."

What had she gone through as the oldest sibling—the first heir apparent to Harmony Law? I'd never considered how Mom and Dad might have pressured Belle into becoming a lawyer, similar to what I experienced in my senior year. The grooming. The expectations.

Except, like my sister, I wanted no part of the firm. But I didn't know if I could live with disappointing my father.

"What do you want to do?" I asked her after a moment.

"I like interior design. You know, setting up houses, spending other people's money to decorate."

I couldn't tell if she was serious. "No way." Then again, her room at home resembled something in a fancy house magazine. I'd always thought her bedroom was cool because of what she bought, not a particular skill. "I like to paint. I've been painting since junior high."

"I know. I've spied on you a time or two. Is that your work on the mantle? Next to Dad's picture?"

"Yes."

"It's good. Really good. Maybe you should major in art. Or music. I used to love to listen to you play when you were a kid." She kicked at a wave and showered our legs with water. "But the truth? I'm thinking about applying to the FBI."

"An agent? You really want to be an agent?"

A wry smile brushed across her mouth. "Ironic, huh? I told Mom a couple of months ago. That's what we've been talking about. The *right* time to tell Dad."

I kicked at an incoming wave like punishing it could take the place of every evil in my life. "We're a mess."

"Very true. I can't help but wonder what Dad would've said when I told him. You know? How he would have reacted." She covered her mouth with her hand for a moment, composing herself. "I hope he would have been proud."

"I am." I breathed in a shaky breath. "You feel like searching a law office?"

Belle tugged off her flipflops as we slipped over the sand. "It's three o'clock now. Chances are we might run into someone."

"Are you kidding? The only person hanging around will be the security guard. The partners are never in the office after three."

~ * ~

Except, they were.

"There's Liz's car," I whispered even though no one was around to hear me. We parked on the other side of the garage, but with a clear line of sight to the elevators. "That's her Jaguar SUV. His black Lexus is over there by the exit ramp."

"What are they doing here so late?"

"With Mom and Dad both out, maybe they're trying to pick up the slack?"

We stared at each other, and I imagined my reaction matched her skeptical expression.

She took out her phone and surfed through her apps. "Might as well get comfortable. We can't do anything with them in the office."

"You think this is a stake-out?" I asked. "Aren't you getting ahead of this whole FBI agent thing?"

"You have a better name for it?" She tilted her chin defiantly. "Agent Belle Harmony? Kind of has a nice ring to it."

I rolled my eyes.

An hour and a half later, my full bladder matched the pressure in my temples. At last the stairwell door opened and first Patrick, then Liz appeared. We crouched low in the car as they chatted beside the Jaguar. A curse exploded from my throat when my parents' co-workers embraced in a possessive kiss. I snapped photos with my cellphone as fast as I could.

"Wow, Lil. You're getting good at this detective biz. I'll have to start calling you Inspector Harmony."

"No. That's *your* title." I thumbed through the pictures. I'd gotten some excellent incriminating evidence. "Did you see that?"

"Yeah. The cheater is cheating on Mom with her lawyer."

"What the hell is going on here?" My question hung in the car like a restless spirit searching for an anchor in unfamiliar territory.

Belle slid her phone into her pocket and removed the keys from the ignition. "When we get our hands on the files, we might have some of those answers."

We dashed up the three flights of stairs to the sixth floor. The hallway outside of the office was quiet. "Do the partners have their own secretaries?"

"Yeah," I said. "The firm hired a woman to take care of Patrick's clients right after the holidays. Carol something. She's in the office next to Patrick's. But the mail comes across Monica's desk first."

Belle's lips drew down as she apparently deduced what I already thought. "Does his office adjoin with hers?"

"Yep. But I'm hoping what we need is in Monica's filing cabinets and we won't have to go in his office." I unlocked the office door and punched in my father's personal security code. "What the heck?" The panel blinked back as if I inputted the wrong number. I tried it again with the same result.

"What's wrong?"

"Someone changed Dad's security code." Panic bloomed in my chest. I tried it one last time to no avail. The alarm counted down from sixty.

"Do you know Mom's?"

"I'm not sure of it," I admitted.

"Then you better go find the files in a hurry!"

I fought the urge to run down the hall in view of the cameras, opting to make it appear as if I was supposed to be here. After strolling into Monica's office, I rushed into the file room, a countdown clock clanging in my brain. A drawer I'd never noticed in the farthest cabinet back, marked COPIES, leapt out at me. If she hid something in this office, the drawer glared as the obvious place to look.

I had the drawer open before my feet slid to a stop. My fingers flew over the tabs. Dorminy and several others I now recognized were clustered together at the back. I yanked the files from the drawer and stuffed them under my shirt. On the way out, I picked up two plants from Monica's desk.

"What are those for?"

"Cover. An excuse. Pretend like we're supposed to be here." I strolled past the blinking keypad without a care in the world.

We fled to the parking garage as the alarm system tripped.

"They're going to see us on the cameras," she groaned. "Who the hell changed the code?"

"Would the police do that?"

Her lips twisted in a frown. "I doubt it. Besides, the partners were just in there. They didn't set it off."

"So what? It doesn't matter. We have every right to be there. We are watering Monica's plants so they don't die." My family still owned the firm, regardless of the accusations against my mother.

We dove into the car and drove out of the parking garage with Monica's plants between my feet. It took a couple of miles before my pulse settled back into a reasonable rhythm and I could process a thought. I removed the files from under my shirt and laid them on my lap. "I hope this was worth it."

"It has to be. Let's go home. I've had enough for one day."

Except we weren't done just yet. A police car sat in the driveway, blocking our path to the garage door.

"How could they hear about the alarm so quick?" I tapped my fingers on the dashboard. "Do you think the security company called them?"

"I don't think they could. If the security company called the cops, they'd go to the office. Not the house. This is something else." She picked up her purse from the passenger side floor. "Stick the files under the seat. Come on."

I carried the plants toward the house and into the garage bay. My sister soundlessly opened the door leading to the kitchen. She pressed a finger to her lips. Leaning forward, I listened beside her.

Muted conversation came from the family room. I gestured with my head in the direction, and she nodded. We couldn't hide where we'd been forever. Sooner or later, Mom would know we'd been at the office—if she didn't already know thanks to the tripped alarm.

We stepped into the kitchen. A deep, rumbling voice sounded from the family room. "No way," I whispered.

"Who is it?" she mouthed.

"The detective."

"Son of a bitch." She straightened her back and strode into the family room.

I followed with my armful of houseplants.

He sat on one of the couches with a cup of coffee in front of him on the table as if my mother had invited the bastard over for a social visit. A true gentleman, he rose from his seat before sitting back down. "Annabelle. Lily."

I set the plants on the coffee table. Mom's cheeks were tear-streaked, but she smiled. "Mom? What's wrong?"

"Maybe I can answer," he offered. "The tests done at the crime scene show your mother did not fire a gun at the time of your father's death. She had no gun powder residue on her hands. The bullet did not come from your father's gun. The charges have been dropped."

Belle let out a squeal as I enveloped my mother in a hug. We laughed and cried at the same time. When we composed ourselves and sat beside her, the detective got down to business.

"This means the investigation remains active. We're hunting for your father's killer. Evidence concludes your father fired the second shot. Lily, I'm sorry I had to dismiss you and your concerns. Until these tests came back, I had to maintain a measure of distance."

I nodded at his apology though my opinion of him being a total jerk remained intact. Mom gripped my hand in a tight squeeze. The relief on her face lightened my heart, even if a murderer lurked in the shadows.

"We've begun examining other areas. Clients, individuals who might have held a grudge. We're vetting your father's staff, including his secretary, although I understand she is on maternity leave." He checked his notes. "I'll need to get her contact information."

"Yes," my mother said. "That won't be a problem."

"You don't have any other staff? No temp taking her place on a regular basis?"

I raised a hand. "Just me." This gave me an idea. "Which is why I went to the office tonight. I left piles of mail on the floor in Monica's office and forgot to water her plants. I went to pick them up, but Dad's alarm code didn't work."

"Is that why the alarm company called me?" Mom asked.

"I used the same code I've always had—the one Dad used—50103. The keypad rejected it. I ran in and tried to get the mail up, but the alarm went off. I guess we sort of panicked." I shared a guilty grin with Belle that had more meaning than the repentant detective could possibly understand.

He pursed his lips and shifted his attention to my mother. "Maybe you should check on the code with the security company. Odd it didn't work."

She gripped his hand. "I will. Thank you, Detective."

"Please call me if you need anything. I'll keep you informed of our progress as much as I'm able." The slight tilt of his lips told me he suspected my sister and I setting off the alarm hadn't been a coincidence.

Did I have 'I'm guilty' stamped on my forehead?

"Miss Harmony. Can I have a moment with you?"

I avoided my sister's questioning gaze as I followed him to the front door, my pulse spiking in half time.

"I am sorry," he said. "But I have to ask if you are aware of any information which might help in your father's case." He slipped his hands into his jacket pockets and studied me appraisingly. "I know you were digging into something. This isn't safe or smart. There are a hundred reasons why someone would murder a man like your father. Revenge is one that comes to mind. You don't want a bad guy transferring his anger onto you or your sister. This family deserves some closure. Some peace."

My throat choked up, and I couldn't answer around my indignation.

"I just want you and your family to be safe."

Yeah. Right. The detective wanted us out of his hair. Playing with my emotions wouldn't stop me from unraveling this mystery—not with him dragging his feet. "Are they going to let us have the funeral?"

"Yes," he said. "I'm going to authorize the release first thing in the morning." He removed a fresh card and pen from his pocket before jotting down a phone number. "Here. My cellphone is on the back—don't call through the switchboard. It takes too long to reach me." His eyes narrowed, and I sucked in a breath, as it became evident just how scary the detective could be. "If you stumble upon something, call me. I'll help you. I mean it. Don't play investigator. Whoever killed your father is still out there. Don't forget how dangerous this guy is."

With trembling fingers, I took the card—but I still didn't like him or his tactics. Yet I needed him to think I'd heard and taken his warning. "Thank you. For this. For my mom."

He hesitated then said, "For what it's worth, I never believed she was guilty. But I had to do my job."

"I understand."

The door closed behind him, and I walked back into the family room. They stared at me as I entered. "What was the third degree about?" Belle asked.

"He wanted to apologize. To me, personally."

"Well he should," she griped. "He's been a total jackass. Even if he is kind of cute."

"Annabelle!" Mom cried.

"Mom. I'm twenty-six years old."

We burst into nervous laughter.

"You're right. We need to celebrate," Mom said, then she sobered. "I know we're dealing with a lot, but I need this tonight. Tomorrow, we'll do what needs to be done."

My sister whipped out her phone. "Should we order food?"

Mom nodded. "Let's get something good. We need one night to just be okay."

I wrapped my arms around her. No matter what I'd seen in those pictures, my parents had loved each other. And she was right. Tomorrow there would be time enough to plot our next move.

~ * ~

After I retrieved the files from beneath the car seat, I retreated to my room. I laid the stack of files on my desk, itching to get a closer look at what was inside. A light rap at my door told me my sister was ready to search them as well. She blew out a huge breath. "I don't know what I feel right now. I'm just numb."

"Me too."

Belle flopped onto my bed and kicked her flip flops away. "What did he really say to you?"

"Basically, he was sorry, but he knows I'm up to something. He said not to dig around in this mess. It's not safe."

"I wonder what he knows." She swished her mouth to the side and stared up at the slow-turning ceiling fan, her expression thoughtful.

"I have no idea."

"Did you open any of them yet?"

"Not yet. I was about to. Let's start with Dorminy first. The name keeps coming up." Inside the file were the documents that set up the final shell corporation, the copies of the cashier's checks sent to the State of Florida, and receipts for filing fees. "Hey! These were signed by Patrick, not Dad."

"So why did Monica file the fictitious names? Why didn't he use his own secretary?" Belle got up to stand over my shoulder. "Check out the dates. These were done in March."

"The advertisements ran in April. Patrick hired his new secretary in January. Maybe she didn't know how to do the filings yet?" I flipped over a page. "Look at this!"

"This is signed by Dad," she whispered, narrowing her focus on the signature. "But wait. It's not his handwriting." She unpinned a postcard from the bulletin board behind my desk—one my father had sent me from a business trip to San Francisco. She laid the card beside the signature. "See the loops in the "William" are different."

"No, he didn't sign this," I agreed, a blend of horror and relief clashing in my chest.

"Okay. So, who signed it, and why did Monica secretly file it outside of Dad's files?" She homed in on the documents, studying them closely. "Let me go over these."

I relented to her opinion. As almost a lawyer compared to my almost a high school graduate status, who was more qualified to make the judgments?

"What about an address for the company? Anything besides a post office box?" Moving over so I stood beside her, I allowed her better viewing.

"Doesn't look like it," she said, as she flipped through the paperwork. "No, wait. Maybe. Look at this." She handed me a copy of the check used for the filing. "The check lists a street address in addition to the post office box."

"The zip code isn't Fort Myers."

"No. It's on Sanibel Island. Boulder Drive."

"Odd place to set up a new corporation," I noted.

"Right? It's not like they can build a big company building. Sanibel is environmentally protected. Where's your computer? Can you map this location? Maybe we can see a street view."

Lifting my laptop from its bag on the floor, I set it next to the files on my desk and powered up. She handed me the copy of the check, tapping her toe as we waited for the screen to wake. Once in the map program, I switched to street view and zoomed in on the address, locating the building matching the location. A charming yellow beach house on Boulder Drive with a green metal roof and a wide front porch appeared on the screen. Palm and citrus trees crowded the front lawn, offering privacy to anyone who ventured outside.

"It's not a business address," she said. "It's a house."

"Yeah. I wonder who lives there?"

Her eyes gleamed. "Want to take a ride?"

"Absolutely. But Mom needs us here, remember? She just ordered food from Alfredo's." If we left now, claiming to go to the beach, she'd be suspicious. Mom was too smart to not pick up on our behavior.

Belle let out an exasperated sigh. I didn't want to wait either. "Tomorrow. We'll leave as soon as we can."

"I have to check my assignments. They've got to be piling up." Since the school heard about Dad's death, my teachers had given me tons of leeway with less than two weeks left before graduation. Right now, I didn't feel like going through the ceremony without Dad there. "What about you? Do you have work to do for your classes?"

"I've got it covered."

I didn't like the peculiar emotion drifting over her face, the evasiveness. Something was amiss. More wrong than my sister doubting if she wanted to practice law for a career.

We didn't say anything for a moment. I wondered if she would confide in me. After all this time, would she tell me what went on in her life? We had dismissed our common dislike in the search for the truth, but with Mom freed, Belle could bridge the years-long gap between us. I didn't know anything about her life in Georgia. Did she have a boyfriend? A best friend? A job?

The doorbell rang, interrupting my thoughts.

"Food's here," she said.

Ahhhhh…you don't want to tell me. Eventually, the truth will come out. It's a matter of time.

Mom had the bags on the kitchen counter when we got there. "Mom! Did you order dinner or a buffet?" I asked, laughing.

"I guess I overdid it. I wanted to make sure we all had something we liked." She opened containers of Greek salad covered with Kalamata olives and crumbled feta cheese and linguine with oil and broccoli. I inhaled the fragrance of garlic and parmesan. Not deli trays and donated casseroles tonight. Divine.

"There's nothing like Alfredo's," I said.

She smiled. "It's your Dad's favorite." Her lips trembled, and she pressed a hand to her mouth. "I'm sorry. I didn't think."

"Dad loved this. He would want us to celebrate your homecoming." Belle hugged Mom.

My gaze met my sister's over my mother's shoulder. I had dozens of questions for my mother. About the holding company and Monica's involvement, and why she'd been kissing Patrick who had moved on to kiss Liz. But those could wait until tomorrow or the next day when we had time to process today.

Blinking away tears, my sister released her.

We sat beside the pool, eating, laughing, and ignoring the moment when we'd have to give up this fragile peace to deal with burying my father. When we finished, Belle and I stored the leftovers in the refrigerator. Mom poured a glass of white wine for the three of us. I appreciated her treating me as an adult.

"I'm going to go to the office tomorrow. I'll call the security company and find out what happened to Dad's code."

"Thanks," I said. "I have more mail to pick up. I was afraid the alarm would get us in trouble."

She patted my hand. "We'll get it done. I'm going to need your help going through Dad's calendar. He had a couple of big cases coming up in the next month. I'll have to get those continued."

"When are we going to have the funeral?" my sister asked.

Mom inhaled and blew the long breath out as if gathering herself. "Toward the end of the week. Maybe Thursday? I'll have to talk to the funeral home now that we can move forward."

"Mom, his office…" I started.

"I know. I'll have someone take care of it too."

Good. I never wanted to see the stain again.

Mom gazed at Belle. The profound sadness I saw in that look tore wounds in my heart I'd hoped were healing. "His office is yours if you want it. Now you're nearly finished with school. You can start working for me while you study for the Bar Exam. I could use an extra set of hands." Apparently, Mom had forgotten their conversations about the FBI.

My sister pressed her lips together for a moment before answering. "Sure. Thanks."

What had she wanted to say? *Remember our chats about not being a lawyer?* Something was up with Belle. There was an issue at school. My gut told me so.

Chapter Thirteen

The following morning, Mom left for the office after eight. I didn't care what she said. She wasn't ready to go back there, but what choice did she have? Harmony Law needed a Harmony in the office. Someone to make sure clients were happy.

As soon as her car cleared the end of the street, we hopped in my Audi and drove off in the opposite direction with the sunroof open. Sanibel Island sat just off the coast of Florida, tethered by a narrow highway. I wondered what it would have been like to visit Sanibel in the 1950s, when the only way to the pristine shores had been a chugging ferry boat. The romantic in me liked the idea. The practical part was happy to crest the causeway and land on the other side in minutes.

When I was a kid, we often visited Sanibel's beautiful coast and serene preserves. My dad piloted his boat past the lighthouse because it was my favorite landmark. I'd lean against the rail and watch the pelicans and ospreys dive into the water searching for a fresh fish meal.

Belle gazed out the window without speaking as we followed the best lead we had to find out who owned these companies and why did someone—my wager was on Patrick—forge my father's signature. My heart thumped like a bongo player in a reggae band as I considered the possibilities. I had never liked him. Although shrewd and rarely kind, he'd never been outright mean. He was the type of person who was at least nice to your face.

So, why had our mother kissed him?

"I'm sorry I can't talk about school," Belle said out of nowhere as we made a right off the Sanibel Causeway onto Periwinkle. The GPS told me I'd taken the correct path.

"I didn't ask," I reminded her. If she wanted me to know, she'd tell me. Otherwise, I'd wait until she wasn't paying attention and figure it out on my own.

"That's not what I mean. I can't talk about school because I haven't been there in six months. I quit just before the end of the fall term."

I darted into a small parking lot next to a laundromat and slammed on the brakes. "You quit?"

She tugged her lower lip into her teeth and nodded.

"Oh my God," I murmured. "How did you hide it from us?"

"I don't come home much," she said. "I figured if I wasn't around, I wouldn't have to lie."

Before Dad's death, the last time I'd seen my sister was just after the new year before she went back to school. Almost six months ago. With the distraction of Christmas, her secret had gone undiscovered.

Stunned, I asked, "What have you been doing?"

"Working. I got a job at a computer firm. We handle data security. It's okay, but not what I want to do with my life."

"Do you know what you want to do?"

She smiled. "Yes. I wasn't kidding about joining the FBI."

I smacked the steering wheel. "That's freaking amazing."

"You think so?" She sounded pleased at my approval.

"I do. You're a natural at this. You understand the legalese. And if you work with data, you'll be a guaranteed in."

Belle leaned against the headrest. "I've got to tell Mom the truth. She doesn't know I quit. I planned on coming home at the end of the term and breaking the news." She squinted against the brassy sunshine baking the interior. "I've already applied to the FBI. They're going through my application. Running the background checks and such. Then I have to wait for an opening if the take me."

"Maybe you better wait before you tell her."

"I don't have a lot of time. I've submitted the application, but the background checks take a while. She's going to find out pretty soon when they contact her."

"Is this case going to be a problem for you? Isn't Mom's arrest going to cause red flags in your application?"

"I'll be fine," she said as I eased back into traffic. "She's been cleared."

What would my father have said when he learned his daughter gave up a chance to work in the family firm for a job where she enforced the law, not defended it? Eventually, he would have accepted her decision, I was sure. But he'd have made a hell of a row until then.

Just like he would have when I told them I planned to change my major to music.

"Are you still living in Georgia?" She could live anywhere with a cellphone and no contact.

"Yes. But I'm in Atlanta now. I rented a small apartment, and I like living in the city. There's always a lot to do."

I took in a deep breath, and the words tumbled from my lips. "It's amazing. I don't blame you one bit. I don't want to be a lawyer either. I want to study music."

Her grin lit up her face. "We're big disappointments, you and me."

"Seems like it." I guided the car toward our destination and followed the GPS to Boulder Drive. We drove past several houses until the navigation told us our destination was on the right. "There it is. The yellow one. No car in the driveway."

"No. But there's a garage out back."

At ground level, the palms and plants in the yard appeared taller. The foliage obscured the view of the front of the house.

"There's a mailbox." I drove into the driveway and parked.

"What are you doing?"

"Pretending we're lost. There's a name on the mailbox." I squinted but couldn't make out the name. "Stay here."

"Lily!"

But I was already out of the car and on my way to the box. I pretended to search my phone. Instead, I took pictures of the name on the side of the mailbox. Patrick Malvern.

Gotcha.

I hurried back to the car, excitement buzzing in my veins. We found the connection we hoped for. "It's his house. Patrick's. I don't get it. He's got a condo on the beach. What's he doing with this bungalow?"

"Maybe it's an investment and not where he lives. Let's get out of here before someone notices."

We drove down the street and merged back onto West Gulf Drive. The endless stream of traffic made me feel better. Safety in numbers. Chances were Patrick hadn't been home, so he didn't see us snooping. "What do we do now? We know he's involved. He's running this fake business out of his house, and Monica covered for him."

"What is the business? I want to know." She cranked the air conditioning up a notch and fanned her flushed face with her hand. "If he went to all this trouble to hide his involvement in the shell companies, there has to be a reason. Something is going on that's not quite legal. He wouldn't want his name associated with dirty deals and risk his law license."

"I wonder if that's why he forged Dad's name on the paperwork?"

"Maybe."

I had to ask the question haunting me. "Do you think he killed Dad? He just doesn't seem the aggressive type."

"I don't know. Does murder have a type? But I have a gut-feeling he's involved. Someone who goes to these lengths to hide his involvement in a shell corporation isn't going to walk into his partner's office and shoot him in cold blood. But he could have hired someone to do his dirty work."

My brain hurt thinking about all the ifs and possibilities. "We need to talk to Mom," I said, my chest aching with sadness. The last thing I wanted to do was add to her pain.

"I know. We're at a dead end otherwise." She squeezed my hand. "Let's wait until after the funeral, okay? We can talk to her this weekend."

She was right. We needed to get through this as a family. We couldn't ask the questions that needed to be asked until we were finished. "Okay. This weekend."

Chapter Fourteen

I shivered at the graveside despite the morning heat in my plain black dress and sandals. Belle's arm never left my mother's waist as they received the last condolences of the group who gathered to pay their respects to my father. I recognized judges, other lawyers, friends, and people from our neighborhood. Monica had sent a floral arrangement and her regrets, blaming the twins for her absence. Liz was there, as well as Patrick. He gave Mom a chaste peck on the cheek before disappearing to find a seat.

Beside me, Jazz swore under his breath.

"Tell me about it," I growled. We glanced at each other from behind our dark sunglasses. I wanted to strangle the lawyer with my bare hands.

"He's got a lot of nerve," Jazz said.

The priest began the graveside prayers, and my mind drifted away on the familiar comfort of the words until Jazz's fingers brushed mine. I gripped his hand. He was dressed in dark pants, loafers, and shirt and tie. I'd never seen him in anything but his best T-shirt and shorts. While he was handsome, he looked too much like a lawyer for my tastes.

I was so done with the law.

My aunt stood beside her husband and son, wiping away tears with a ruined tissue. Aunt Claire had been my father's only sibling. So much like Dad—the same dark eyes, stiff-straight posture, and raven hair.

Pain tore through me as fresh and sharp as a new blade. I had to turn away to focus forward. The beauty of the flowers covering the casket drew my attention from the fresh hurt—the layers of roses, lilies, and carnations a bandage on my breaking heart. Would I ever remove the sight of my dying father from my memories of him? He'd made time to coach my softball team and taught me to swim in the backyard pool when I was six. Then there were the concerts, the trips, the quiet conversations at sunset. There had to be some way to retrieve those moments, to strip off the bloody taint.

Maybe finding his killer would free me.

After the service, we remained at the casket while the last of the mourners disappeared into their cars. Mom laid her hand on the side of the casket. I followed her lead, surprised at the warmth of the metal. My last chance to be connected to him. My last goodbye.

She touched Jazz's shoulder. "Thank you for coming. Your being here means a lot to Lily."

"You're welcome, Mrs. Harmony. I'm very sorry for your loss."

Mom inclined her head in thanks. "Are you ready, Lily?" She squeezed my wrist.

"I guess so." The broken grief in my chest burned. I imagined the shards of my heart slipping through vital organs, cutting me from the inside out. I took a cleansing breath and lifted my gaze to the blue, cloudless sky.

His hand wove around mine, steadying me, bringing me back to the present. My sister separated roses from the bouquet until she had an armful. Mom and I gathered blossoms from the casket and the arrangements beside the grave until we filled the back of the limousine with flowers.

"It will be nice to keep these around the house for a few days," she said with a sad smile.

The one good thing about waiting for the police to release his body was we had some time to come to terms with Dad's death. But today dawned raw. Saying goodbye hurt beyond anything I ever experienced, and knowing I'd never see him again carved a hole in my world I'd never be able to fill. But maybe I'd learn to live on the outside of the sharp edges without slicing myself open.

Jazz slid into the seat next to me in the limo. I would never be able to thank him for this. He'd been there since the first day. I glanced at his profile as he watched the street scene speed by. How had I gotten this lucky?

I sighed, worrying about what Mom would say when she figured out he played video games for a living. Or worse, that I had no intention of being a lawyer.

The limo took us to Alfredo's where a room had been reserved for us and Aunt Claire's family. More than a year had passed since we'd seen Aunt Claire and Uncle Jack. They lived in Portland, Maine. It was cold and snowed there, and I determined at a young age I'd never visit. Aunt Claire taught elementary school, and Uncle Jack sold real estate. They rarely left the north except in the summers, which made no sense because July would be the one month I would venture outside if I lived there. Our blistering Florida summers kept them away. In other words, we never saw them.

"Lily," Aunt Claire said, drawing me into a cozy, floral-scented hug. She approached me when I was off by myself. "I'm sorry you had to go through this, honey."

"Thank you, Aunt Claire. Thanks for coming. I know this isn't a good time for you." School semesters in Florida might be ending mid-May, but she often taught her kids until late June because of their horrid weather.

"I loved William with all my heart. He was my big brother and all the family I had left. It didn't matter we lived a thousand miles away. We texted each other most days—random stuff. Nothing important, but we stayed connected. I keep glancing at my phone waiting to hear from him. I keep wanting to text him." She stopped, choked by grief, and tugged on the single strand of pearls at her pale throat.

"I didn't know," I said, surprised again at the silent family communication that occurred beneath the waves of our lives. To me, our connections to Aunt Claire were infrequent birthday and Christmas cards. I never suspected she and Dad were close.

She glanced at my mother, the pain in her eyes transforming into a hardened emotion I could only describe as distaste. "I know. I'm sorry. I wish I got to see more of you and Belle when you were growing up."

I tucked the obvious animosity between Aunt Claire and Mom into a back corner of my mind. Very interesting. Something to discuss with my sister later.

"Maybe we can see each other more."

"I'd like to. Are you still planning to go to school in Boston? You won't be far from us. Maybe you could come up on the weekends?"

"Yes, I'm going to college this fall." Even though I wasn't being honest with her or myself, I opted not to mention Boston and the thousand miles between Fort Myers and there. "That would be great."

"What does your boyfriend think about you leaving the area?"

The term stunned me for a moment. Was Jazz my boyfriend? We'd been dancing around the edges. Was I ready to step all the way in?

"He knows. We'll work it out."

"I hope so. You two are cute together." She gave me a loving squeeze and rejoined her family.

"Is she your aunt?" he asked when he returned from the restroom. "I hung around the desserts to give you guys space."

"Thanks. She's my Aunt Claire from Maine. We don't see them much." A surprising wash of regret settled on my heart. What had I missed out on, not knowing them?

"You couldn't get me to go to Maine on a bet," he remarked.

"It's supposed to be beautiful." For some reason I needed to defend my aunt's choice of residence.

"So is the Arctic Circle. But you wouldn't catch me there either."

We carried plates over to the buffet laden with my father's favorites.

My throat closed. He would have loved this spread. Chicken parmigiana, linguine with broccoli, orecchiette with sausage. All of it made my stomach heave.

Jazz nudged my arm. "What's been going on in the case? I haven't heard from you much the past few days."

"I'm sorry. It's been busy with Mom home and," I gestured around us, "preparing for this. Now that she's no longer a suspect, she's been working a ton to figure out what Dad had on his case load. There are some big trials coming up."

"Criminal cases?" He nibbled on a garlic breadstick.

"No. Dad didn't take criminal cases. There's some big land case, I guess. A real estate deal that went bad. Mom's figuring out what must be done before the civil trial. With Dad's secretary on leave, getting it sorted out has been a challenge."

"Monica? The one who popped out the kids is the one who filed the funky paperwork, right?"

I stiffened, my suspicions rearing up like a cobra. Monica sat on the mountain peak of the people I no longer trusted. "I think she's been helping from home while she's on leave." Across the room, my mother accepted countless hugs and condolences. At least she was holding herself together.

"You don't think that's a problem?" He wrinkled his nose.

"It is." If Monica had access to the files, she could cover up for Patrick. Maybe even destroy the information we needed to prove what Dad's partner had done. "Watch out," I told him as Mom made eye contact. "Mother incoming."

"I'll behave," he said with a smirk.

My foot nudged his. "You'd better."

She strode over to where we stood. "Thank you again for being here today. I'm sorry we didn't get to meet before this, Jason. I didn't know Lily was seeing someone." She smiled but let the last statement drop like the accusation she intended.

"Well, I'm in the band with her...and we've been friends," he said as a way of explaining the relationship I had trouble defining.

"And now?" Mom pressed as we wandered toward the buffet

plates.

"Mom," I said, a not too subtle warning in my tone.

"Sorry. I can't help myself." She smiled at him with real affection, a gesture that told me even though she didn't know much about him, she liked him. "You're welcome to come back to the house later."

"Um, thanks. But I have work this afternoon. Some other time?"

Her brows shot up, and my back twitched as she bit on the lead-in he'd offered. "Oh? Where do you work?"

"Mom, this isn't an inquisition." No way would I let her grill him—today of all days. She'd find out what he did on my terms, if at all.

She sighed. "Again. Sorry." She picked up a plate. Her hand trembled. "Your Dad loved their Chicken Scampi."

A stab of pain hit me in the gut. Dad would never have the chance to eat here again. The incredible lunch on my plate smelled as appetizing as a pile of moss-covered stones. This would be my last meal from Alfredo's for a long time.

Jazz must have noticed my distress because he caught my elbow in his fingers. "Come on. Let's find a place to eat out of the spotlight." To my mother, he said, "Do you want to eat with us, Mrs. Harmony?"

My body tensed then relaxed as she excused herself to find Belle.

We settled into a corner table. Under his coaxing, I picked at my food, realizing as I made my way across the plate how ravenous I was. I cleared the food and filled another small plate at the dessert table.

He pointed to the slab of cheesecake on my plate. "See? I knew you were hungry."

"More than I knew."

"You don't have to tell your mom what I do." He sobered, and his tone told me he'd been hurt. "Older people don't understand streaming is an actual thing. It's a new gig. I get it."

"What you do didn't exist a couple of years ago; it's a real job. I need her to understand you're not hanging out in your mother's basement playing D&D."

He laughed. "I started there, so…"

I smacked him in the bicep. "Stop it."

Leaning over, he kissed me. "I don't want to." His eyes gleamed with meaning.

"You two should just go get a room."

Food lodged in my throat as Belle dropped onto the empty chair at our table with a plate of cake and a cup of coffee. "What'd I miss?" Her inquiring gaze met Jazz's.

I glared. "Nothing? Why?" I shoveled cheesecake into mouth to avoid saying something really nasty.

"I thought it was something," he quipped and nudged my elbow.

The lump of cake cleared my tonsils. "And you have horrible timing."

"Ha! It's my superpower." She took a swig of coffee. "I saw you and Aunt Claire chatting. What was that about?"

I crumpled my napkin and tossed it on the cake plate. "I'm not sure. She sort of mentioned she and Mom don't get along too well. Like Mom's the reason we didn't see her much. Did you know they didn't like each other?"

"No." My sister drew the tines of her fork through the icing on her cake. "I wonder why?"

"You always find out family dirt at times like these." Jazz picked apart a brownie until it left little brown tufts on his plate. "When my grandfather died, we found out he had a mistress and another family. Not a good time."

"I bet that was ugly." She laughed.

"Yep."

"What time are you streaming?" I changed the subject.

"Around four. If you're busy, don't worry about it. Kellison Controllers hasn't sent me anything. I'm thinking they're a pass for sponsorship."

The disappointment in his voice tugged at my heart. I wanted this for him. So much.

"There will be another one," I assured him. Hollow words when he needed this one so badly.

An endorsement from Kellison would have meant the difference between making ten thousand a year streaming and a hundred thousand. Plus, it would have meant even more opportunities for the eSport company.

"I know. I just hoped this was the one." He tried not to appear dejected. It didn't work.

I placed the wadded napkin on my empty plate. "This party is winding down. You want to drive back to the house with me? The limo is waiting for us."

"Nah. Too flashy for me. Frankie's going to pick me up. He's got some new hardware to help with my stream speed. We're going to hook it up before I have to go live." Jazz drew me up and into his arms. I nestled my head on his shoulder, my new favorite place in the world. His words brushed against my hair, sending shivers down my back. "I'll see you later, okay?"

"Yes. Good luck tonight." With one final squeeze of my fingers, he left.

"He's a nice guy," my sister commented as we gathered our things to leave.

"He is," I agreed.

"Did Mom ask questions yet?"

"Like a rabid dog on a bloody steak," I grumbled.

"What did you tell her?"

I sighed, exhausted, both mentally and physically. "Not enough. She'll want more soon." The reveal was coming. About Dad, the case, Jazz, college. Truth lingered off the coast of our family, spinning like a tempest.

"Not before we get the chance to ask *our* questions," she said. Spine straight, chin up. Belle at her determined best.

In fact, she sounded angry. I wondered why, but this was not the time to ask. The last thing we needed was to throw gasoline on the embers of suspicion floating around our parents. I had enough misery for one day. "I think Mom's outside." I gathered my cellphone and purse.

"She's ready to go," my sister noted.

Outside, the afternoon sunshine blinded me. My mother chatted with Uncle Jack in front of the restaurant. Aunt Claire sat in their rental car with the air conditioner on and the windows up.

"Awkward," Belle commented as Jack hugged our mother.

I dropped my sunglasses on my nose. "When do you want to ask her these questions?"

"Sooner than later. Let's see what tonight brings." There was the irritated tone again grating beneath the surface of her calm.

"Did something happen, Belle?" I couldn't resist poking the bear.

She shook her head. "I'm just tired of being lied to."

Chapter Fifteen

After we got back, I hid in my bedroom and slipped under the sea green comforter in my underwear, my dress and shoes clumped in a pile on the sand-colored carpet. I sought quiet time with my dad's memory—sobbing into my pillows until they were damp. I needed to get this agony out of my system. This time alone with him was a gift to me before the next heartbreak struck.

Disaster would. I knew it.

There was work to do, hard, gut-wrenching work that would require us taking sides against our mother. We needed to show her those pictures and demand an explanation. Belle wouldn't wait long. I had to be strong enough to back her up when the time came.

On the white wicker table beside the bed, my phone blipped alerting me to Jazz's stream. I flicked on the flat panel television on the far wall and brought up his game. His image in the corner made me smile. His public gaming persona wore dark sunglasses, spiked hair, and his favorite Mario Kart T-shirt. Nothing like the guy who I hung out with earlier dressed in his Sunday best, who'd been with me at my father's grave this morning. Watching Jazz work calmed me and cleared my mind. After about a half hour, I went into my bathroom, showered, and then dressed in shorts and a white tank top.

Time to make an appearance.

My sister sat in the family room, propped up on one side of the brown leather sectional. An apple scented candle burned on the mantle, and CSI reruns played on the television with the sound off. She tapped on her phone with headphones on. The epitome of multitasking.

I waved into her line of sight. She uncovered one ear.

"Are you paying attention to this?" I hooked a thumb toward the screen.

"Yeah, why?"

"I didn't know you could read lips." I collapsed on the sofa beside her.

"I've seen them all. I know what's going to happen."

Of course, she had. "How do you want to do this?"

She shut off the television with the remote. "It's time. We need to show her the picture. She can't refute hard evidence. If we say something like 'odd that Patrick left so fast,' she could explain away his exit. I don't want to give her an out. I want the truth, and I want it the first time."

"You're angry about this." Her scarcely masked fury stunned me.

"Aren't you? She messed around on Dad. There's no date on the picture, and your fisherman friend isn't around to fill in the blanks. The kiss could've been two years ago or last week. Maybe Patrick's not the only guy she's been with. There's no way to know unless she tells us the truth." She set the remote on the coffee table next to a book of Ansel Adams's black and white prints. "By the way, did your friends find anything about the obituary?"

"No," I said. "Last I heard, the news said they still hadn't identified him. That doesn't make any sense. Isn't someone looking for him? Like his family?"

She scowled at the ceiling and dragged her fingers through her hair, combing out the tangles. "They must be looking in the wrong place. Maybe the cops are waiting for DNA to come in. Remember we talked about him not being from around here? I bet he's not a local."

A man with no name, hired by my dad. Dead because he talked to me. "What if Mom lies to us? I don't like thinking about asking her these questions. She could deny everything." Butterflies with razor-sharp beaks took flight in my stomach. "Is she home?"

"She went to the grocery store. She'll be back soon."

I might hate the idea of ambushing Mom with what we knew, but no easy way existed to bring up her infidelity.

~ * ~

When Mom got home, Belle and I were preparing dinner, a meal I had no intention of eating. She seemed stunned for a moment, taking in the salad, grilled lemon-garlic chicken, and early squash. A simple meal—in direct contrast to what we planned to do. Our conversation had complicated written all over it.

"Wow! You girls are way ahead of me. I picked up a rotisserie chicken, but we can eat that tomorrow."

I helped her unpack the groceries and put everything away while my sister set the table in the breakfast nook. She opened one of the windows, and influx of scorching air licked my skin. In that way we were similar; we liked to listen to the tinkling of the pool while we ate, no matter how blistering the temperature outside.

We sat to eat, and I poured a glass of iced tea wishing for something stronger. Belle's steady stream of small talk grated on my nerves—I think I preferred the sullen sister than the nervous, chatty one. I half-choked on a strawberry chunk when she nudged me under the table.

"Are you going to keep the law office open?" Belle asked.

Mom's eyebrows drew down in confusion. She chewed and swallowed before answering. "Of course. Why?"

Belle prodded me with her gaze. "Um…I didn't know if one of the partners would want to buy you out," I said, then sipped tea to cover my nervous mouth.

"That's an odd thing to say. Where's this coming from?"

I winced. Mom and the detective had taken the same class on deflection. Answer a question with a question. Shrugging, I tried to play it cool, imagining my sister wanted to pick up the salad bowl and dump it over my head. "I don't know. Liz didn't stay long at lunch today after the funeral. Weird, right?"

Mom spun her glass in her fingertips. "I'm sure she was busy on a weekday. Court is in session. And she's holding the office together for me." The twist of her lips told me Liz's quick getaway and Patrick's absence at lunch bothered my mother as well. Good. A segue to the next questions appeared.

"Mom, do you like them? I mean Liz is okay. But Patrick always seems kind of…"

"An asshole?" Belle piped in for the save with her favorite label.

"Kind of," I echoed.

"First," Mom said, leveling a death stare over the table, "watch your mouth. Second, Patrick is an exceptionally good lawyer with a sharp eye for real estate. He's saved your father and I multiple times when called in to consult. We're indebted to him."

"How much?" Belle asked.

Mom went still. "What do you mean?"

My sister leaned forward in her chair, dropping to a whisper as she said, "How much do you owe him, Mom?"

"Belle…" I waded into the fracas.

"I don't like your tone." Mom snatched her dish from the table.

"And I don't like that you screwed around on Dad." Belle's fork clattered to her dish.

The plate wobbled in Mom's hands. This interview had gone off the rails.

Heart thudding, I removed the envelope with the picture from under my chair and pinched the clasp. Mom said nothing as I slid my finger under the flap and removed the photo of her embrace with Patrick.

Her color drained. "Where did you get these?"

"Does it matter?" I tossed the photo across the table at her like a grenade. "Why?"

She backed away from the photo until her spine hit the granite counter. The white plate fell from her hands and shattered on the tile sending bits of salad into the corners of the room.

"Did William know?" she whispered, but the question didn't seem to be directed at us. Neither of us answered her as the clock ticked in the hall. "Did your father know?" Tears collected beneath her lashes.

"We don't know. He hired an investigator, and the man took this picture." She hadn't denied having an affair. We'd been prepared for all kinds of excuses but not her quiet acceptance that we knew what she'd done.

Mom sank down onto the chair, ignoring the mess on the floor. Her shoulders drooped. "I'm sorry," she said. The banked tears ran down her cheeks. "I never meant for this to happen."

"Well it did." My sister jabbed her finger at the picture. "We want to know why you did this. We deserve an answer."

"We attended a conference." Mom's words came flat and toneless. "We didn't go together. We ran into each other after one of the sessions and decided to grab dinner." Her eyes glazed as if she paced through the night in her mind. "I had too much wine. I'm not sure what happened. One minute we were sitting in a restaurant, and the next I was waking up in my hotel room alone. But I knew…" She straightened her shoulders and breathed deep. "Something had happened, but I didn't know what. I remembered going to dinner with Patrick, but he wasn't in my room when I woke up. I suspected—but I couldn't prove he'd done anything or that he'd even been in the room. How could I accuse him? No one would believe me."

"He *drugged* you?" Belle's fingers clenched into fists. "And you didn't fire his ass?"

Mom bit her lip before she answered. "I thought so. Because I don't remember." She blotted the corners of eyes on a napkin. "He…must have. I can't prove it."

Fury tightened my chest. No physical evidence didn't mean she imagined it.

"So what!" Shoving her plate away, my sister leapt up to stand in front of the window. "He deserved getting fired. He should be arrested." She wrapped her arms around herself.

If she'd been drugged, I had no reason to doubt our mother. I breathed to control my anger and glowered at the picture, suspicions growing in my mind. Maybe the kiss, the affair, weren't real—the whole thing had a feeling of being staged somehow. "When was this taken?

"This spring. Beginning of March." Mom pressed a hand to her mouth. "We were in Washington D.C. for a conference on real estate environmental issues."

The conference. Dad had conference documents in the file he compiled on Mom. Those notes made me wonder what he knew and what he only suspected.

My sister went still. "A real estate conference?" Agony laced her words.

Mom nodded. "I was there for a few days. This happened on the last night. Patrick and I never spoke about it." She shuddered.

"You should've told Dad." Belle's voice cracked like brittle ice.

Mom cringed at my sister's accusation. "I couldn't. Patrick never said anything. He acted like nothing happened. We never spoke after that about anything except business. I couldn't remember and had no proof. Your dad and I...we were having some issues. If I said anything, your dad would have thought..." She drew in a shaky breath. "We were in counseling. I don't know if Dad would have believed me. I wanted our problems to smooth out, for us to be happy."

"I heard you fighting," I said.

"I know. I'm so sorry, honey," she said, her words laced with regret. "That's when we decided we needed to do something before it was too late. We were working so hard to get our marriage back on track."

Belle returned to the table, her face splotchy and red. "What about these pictures?" She removed several shots of Patrick and laid them in front of Mom while I cleared away the dinner plates.

Now that we'd learned the pictures had been taken at the conference, they made more sense. In two of the pictures, Patrick had been engaged in conversation with other attorneys. In another, he sat across the table from a man in a dark suit.

"See this here," I said. "Do you see how Patrick's sitting? He's leaning back from this guy, like he doesn't like him." I handed the picture to my mother. "Do you know him?"

"No. There were hundreds of lawyers there, plus other attendees. Surveyors. Title clerks. Real estate agents. He could be anyone."

"This guy is familiar somehow," Belle murmured, tapping a finger on the photograph. "We need to figure out who he is."

"How did you get this?" Mom's lawyer-tone had returned—

inquisitive and strong.

"Mom, there's something we need to show you." I hurried to retrieve our notes and the files.

I set the box on the dining room table to give us more space while Belle cleaned up the broken plate. Mom wore a haunted expression as if waiting for a python to appear from the depths of the box. Dark, puffy circles framed her eyes. Honestly, if the weatherman told me a Category 5 barreled straight for us, it wouldn't have surprised me.

She watched without comment. We spread out our notes and the files we'd taken from Dad's office then added the fisherman's information. Mom removed her glasses from her shorts pocket to study the documents. The air conditioning whirred in the background while we awaited her thoughts.

"Where did you get all of this?" she asked again.

I couldn't tell her where without telling her the how. "The night Dad died, I remembered some things from the office—things I thought would help you. I called the detective, and he met me at the coffee house by the pier. He didn't think what I had to say mattered. After he left, I went out onto the pier to be alone."

"In the dark?" Mom asked, her tone threaded with parental concern.

"Yes. I was out there, and this guy approached me. He knew things about what happened. He said Dad hired him to look into something. He wanted me to have the information."

"Why would he do that?" Her nose scrunched in concentration.

"We've been trying to figure it out," my sister said.

Mom lifted some of the documents for closer examination, nodding now and then, clicking her tongue at others. "I recognize some of these from the files Dad shared with me on the real estate case. We need to talk to the man who gave you these. Do you know where he is?"

"We can't talk to him. He's dead," Belle said.

My nose wrinkled in disgust. Tact was not my sister's forte. At least she could try and soften the blow.

Mom's attention whipped in her direction. "What do you mean?"

I interrupted to continue, "I had a meeting set up with him again. He told me to come to The Whale. We did," I said, hoping my sister going with me made some of this sound not as horrible. "He told us to meet him on the pier." A shiver rushed through me. I'd never forget the teal spot floating in the water. "But when we got there, he was dead. Someone stabbed him and threw him into the water."

Her jaw tightened, and her skin blanched. "You don't know his name?"

"Nope. The paper hasn't released a name. They said the man had no identification on him."

Mom pinched the bridge of her nose. "Did you mention any of this to Detective Stephens?"

"No. We didn't need to say anything because you were released." Belle paused, leveling her gaze on our mother. "Mom. I have to ask you this. Did Dad think you were having an affair? Was there any reason for this guy to take your picture? It doesn't match anything else in the file."

"No," Mom said, gripping my sister's hands. "It wasn't an affair. I swear I never cheated on Dad. Not willingly."

Belle bit her lip before she replied, "If this guy Dad hired wasn't following you, what was he doing in Washington?"

Ah ha. The puzzle piece clicked into place. "He was following Patrick," I said. The real estate case Dad was working on. Patrick specialized in real estate. For some reason, the two details tangled together. I just didn't know how.

"I bet you're right." Belle stalked away from the files and stared out the window at the pool. Her emotions read across her face in the tightness of her jaw and the flush of color creeping up her neck, a novel of conflict and betrayal. "Dad's death and the fisherman's involvement has something to do with these companies. Patrick may be running this one out of his house on Sanibel."

"How do you know?" Mom's eyes widened.

I smirked at my sister, happy we'd done as much digging as we had. We had Mom back, and we weren't in the dark. "We've been investigating. We found an address. The house belongs to Patrick."

"Your investigation stops this second." She held out her hands in a pleading gesture as if she expected we'd ignore her request. "Girls, if this is true, not only did this investigator die because of a case at the office, but so did your dad. This is dangerous. We need to turn this over to the police."

My sister spun on her heels. "Turn what over, Mom? What do we have? Some theories? A couple of suspicious coincidences?" She shook her head. "They'll do nothing. Just like before."

"What do you propose?" Mom removed her glasses and pinched the bridge of her nose again.

The gleam in Belle's eyes told me she'd been thinking about how to proceed for some time. "We keep digging. You're taking over the real estate case. We need to know what it's about—how Patrick might be connected."

Mom pressed her knuckles to her lips.

"We need to know, Mom," I said.

"Ganging up on me isn't going to change anything. I can't break attorney-client privilege," Mom said.

I stared at her in disbelief. "Really? At a time like this? What about Dad? If we're right, they killed him for this. Something to do with this case. We'll never find out unless we know more." Tears threatened. I didn't want to cry. Not when my sister was calculated and calm. But the loss was too great, the stress too much.

"We need something to take to the police. More than our notebook sketches and a couple of cobbled together databases." My sister swept her hand over the files.

"Girls, it's complicated. You know I want the person who did this caught." Mom tugged her lip in her teeth before she said to me, "Your security code didn't work the other day."

"It didn't, and I used Dad's code. I set off the alarm."

She removed and toyed with her glasses, folding and unfolding the earpieces. "I called the company. They said the system owner deleted the code."

"Who's the owner?"

"Your father." Fear filtered into her words.

"But that's impossible," Belle whispered, all bravado evaporated. "It was *his* code!"

Dad had been dead when the code changed. *Not possible.* Just like my mother kissing another man and my father's partner forging his signature on documents Monica later filed. The world had tilted, inexorably, off its axis. For the first time, the bigger picture shifted into focus. This went beyond a case, beyond a single act of law office treason.

A strange and frightening sensation coursed through my body. The sick thrill of someone lurking in the corners of my safe place. Like I'd seen too many horror flicks and couldn't turn off the lights. "Mom, what's going on?"

Her ashen face flushed. She clenched her teeth—one of her *lawyer tells*—a trick of her body language told me she teetered on the edge of losing it. "We'd better figure that out." She shoved back her chair then hurried out of the room.

"What just happened?" my sister asked. "Did she just tell us someone at the firm impersonated Dad after he died to revoke the security code?"

I nodded, my heart galloping in my chest. "Yes." Monica, although somehow involved in this mess, hadn't been at the office. That left the other lawyers in the firm. My mother's attorney and her one-night stand. The guilty circle around those two kept shrinking. "What's worse, Liz and Patrick are romantically involved. Should we tell her?"

"Not yet. She's been through enough."

"Yeah. I agree." We didn't need to pile more suffering on her today.

"Are you beginning to think one of those losers didn't want us to find those files?" She paced across the room and back.

"Exactly. Maybe they didn't know where they were. What's going to happen when they discover we took them?"

Her gaze cooled to sub-Arctic-level as if she were preparing herself for the harsh truth she planned to speak. "They already know, Lily. Face it. They rewind the security footage in the hall and know we were up to something. If Patrick knew where Monica kept the Dorminy file, all he had to do was open the correct drawer."

"We should have taken pictures of the file contents, then left the originals there in the drawer." Or maybe I could get Frankie to log in and delete the video footage. Maybe Patrick hadn't seen it yet.

She shrugged as if a pack of murdering thugs weren't out to get us. "With the clock ticking to zero, neither of us thought about our options."

"Mom needs to talk to Monica. Get the truth out of her."

"Agreed," she said as Mom returned to the dining room carrying a cardboard box. She set it on the table with a resigned thump, her hand lingering on the lid. Belle peered at the labels on the top of the box. "What's in the box?"

"If I'm going to lose my license, I might as well go all the way. These are copies of the files on the real estate case. There's something in here. I'm sure of it now." She reached into the box while I cleared away our notes then removed a stack of folders. "As of this moment, you are both employees of the Harmony Law Firm, helping me to prepare this case. We'll do the paperwork to make it official." She arranged the folders to make the tabs visible. "This is what Dad had on the defendant. Our client is an environmental protection advocacy group. They are trying to prevent the sale of a piece of wetland property south of here."

"Where?" my sister asked.

Mom massaged her temple. "Near the Everglades. I have to look up the address in the file. Dad told me about the case though. The owners wanted to sell the land, but an injunction filed by our client stopped the transaction." She removed a second, smaller stack of files. "This is on the defendants. The owner of the property and the buyers."

"Why did the group you represent want to stop the sale?" I asked, accepting the files from her.

"From what I've had time to read, there are certain species of animals and birds on this land which are protected. The financing package put together by the interested parties included developing the land, building roads, and setting up home and business sites. They are a subsidiary company, with three other companies coming into the sale as angel partners. F & S Consulting, Summit Realty Group, and Dorminy Holdings."

"Dorminy!" I exclaimed.

"What about them?" Mom asked.

My smug sister leaned back in her chair as if she knew all the answers. "That's the company in which Patrick is involved. The one where the mail goes to his Sanibel Island house."

Our mother went very still. "Oh my God. How did this happen? He's manipulated this so the case falls apart with compromised counsel. If the judge ever became aware of the involvement of our office in both sides of the dispute..."

"What happens if it does get sold?"

Mom rubbed her eyes. "There's a good chance the land will get developed. The environmental group doesn't have a lot of resources to fight with. On the other side, the buyers have lots of reserves."

I didn't believe it. We'd known Patrick was up to something and yet another road led back to him. The holding company, drugging my mother, changing the security codes.

The killer had to be him.

She sank onto a chair.

Belle touched her arm, her expression tight with concern. "Mom?"

"He did this. All of this. Patrick. The picture, the conference..."

"He would have blackmailed you," my sister said, her jaw set. Belle wasn't about to stand down. Neither was I.

Mom stared at the box as if it might leap off the table and attack us.

I hooked a thumb toward the bedrooms. "Go get your laptop. We need to start at the beginning."

Chapter Sixteen

By midnight, we had created multiple spreadsheets, diagrams, organizational chains, and documents detailing what we knew about Patrick from his first day of employment at the Harmony Firm, to his involvement in Dorminy Holdings and the real estate case my father was working on when he died. Mom filled in the blanks with details from the case files. She'd left two messages for Monica to call her.

When we finished, we had a clearer view, but questions left gaping holes in what we tried to prove—that Patrick was a murderer.

Belle bit on the end of her pencil, staring at the white board we propped up against the dining room wall. "Patrick has been with the firm for six years. He got his law degree at Georgetown and his undergraduate degree at Fordham in New York."

"He had impeccable credentials," Mom said. "He came with outstanding references."

My sister snorted as if none of his previous history mattered and continued her run-down of his past. "Before he applied for the job with you and Dad, he worked for two years at the Florida State Environmental Protection office as a legal consultant." She paged through his personnel file on her computer. "He worked in land acquisition. How convenient."

Mom nodded. "If I remember, he handled issues where cases came up about protected areas. People trying to build where they shouldn't. He had a good record."

"Has he abandoned his former values?" Belle wondered.

"Why did he leave?" I asked. "Sounds like it was a really good job."

"He told us he wanted a position with more regular hours instead of being on call, traveling up and down the state. Life on the road would get old," Mom commented as she thumbed through a thick file.

I chewed on the back of my finger before blowing out a frustrated breath. "If we make a list of what we don't know, it'll be as long as my arm."

"We know he doesn't stay at the house on Sanibel. The hurricane shutters were down over the windows, and the grass needed mowing," Belle noted.

"He has a condo on one of the golf courses around here. Why is where he lives important?"

"I don't know," I admitted. "If he has another address, maybe we could connect him back to another of these companies if he used the address to set it up. Maybe he also owns one of the others."

"He went to a lot of trouble to hide his identity," my sister reasoned. "I bet he figured Dad would catch on before the case went to trial. That's why he—" She broke off and averted her gaze until her emotions were in check. "Other than his involvement being a conflict of interest in the firm, what difference did his participation in the case make? Patrick could have just told Dad."

"Because Dad would have recused himself from the plaintiff's side." I tapped the enter key just for something to do. "The case would have been delayed until another attorney and firm were brought in."

"There's something else here we're not seeing." Mom studied the board, her arms folded, glasses perched on the end of her nose.

Belle regarded her for a moment. "Mom, I don't want to be a lawyer."

Mom smiled without shifting her attention from the board. "I know."

"What?"

"The provost at school called me the day you dropped out. We're old friends from our undergraduate years. I figured you'd tell me when you got around to it."

Her face was stricken. "Did Dad know?"

She smiled at Belle. "Yes. He was proud of you for doing what you wanted with your life, not what you thought you were expected to do."

My sister deflated as if she'd been holding her breath for a year. In many ways she had been. "Son of a bitch," she murmured as my mother gathered her in an embrace.

"Can we get back on task?" Mom yawned when they separated. "Or maybe we need to start over in the morning with a fresh pot of coffee."

My body reacted to the promise of sleep like I'd been given an injection of melatonin.

She checked the locks on the sliding doors and closed the blinds. "Get something to cover everything. I have an awful feeling about what's happening here, and I don't think the danger is past. We need to keep this quiet and out of sight until we know more."

In the hall closet, I found an old tablecloth and covered our work before excusing myself to sit by the pool. Outside, a heavy, humid darkness pressed against my skin. The palms swished and dipped in the late-night breeze. A frond fluttered to the ground at the edge of the yard, setting off the motion sensing lights, and I jumped at the sudden brightness. Lightning outlined the clouds over the distant Gulf.

This was the kind of night I'd always loved; one where I'd sit out under the covered patio until the fat drops of rain marched in from the Gulf to land in our backyard. But my sanctuary no longer felt secure, and my Dad wasn't here to chase the shadows away. Even near the house, inside our gated, guarded community, my senses remained wary. On edge.

Would Patrick figure out we were on to him? It was only a matter of time until he discovered the missing files. I'd seen two dead bodies in the past week. Proof enough we needed to be careful.

I retreated to my bedroom and closed my curtains. After I snuggled into my bed with the quilt up to my nose, I texted Jazz.

Hey?
Hey yourself
Sorry I've been quiet family stuff
Figured didn't want to pest
You never pest
He sent me a winking face.
I smiled at the screen. *A lot going on...*
Wanna tell me?
Can I see you tomorrow?
Sure

We settled on morning doughnuts on the beach—a habit we established before we knew our friendship would lead to investigation associates and occasional kissing. Breakfast at the beach with him would bring a comforting sense of normalcy.

I needed normal. I needed him.

~ * ~

I sat up straight.

The motion lights outside my window flicked on, illuminating my room through the slit at the edge of the shade. After jumping out of bed, I scrunched into the corner between the closet and my bedroom door to hide. My pulse raced as the light went out. Another palm frond? Or raccoon?

Did the light wake me or had it been a sound?

I breathed in and out, slow and shaky, counting the exhales until I hit thirty.

The light flicked on. *Shit.*

Motionless, I stared at the window. One minute elapsed, two. The light stayed on—that meant whatever triggered the lights still moved outside. My phone rested beside the bed, on the charger. Inching my way out of the corner, I grasped the phone by my fingertips as a dark shadow slid past the bright gap. This was no palm frond.

Not breathing, I sidestepped the door and flattened to the wall. The figure hesitated a moment before continuing by. I thanked my lucky stars I'd pulled the opaque shades down last night. I dimmed my phone screen and accessed the security app, selecting the camera on the back corner of the house, nearest to my room.

Tears welled in my eyes as I bit down on my lip and tasted blood. I smothered my whimper with my hand. On the phone screen, a person skulked the edges of the house, glancing up at the cameras on each of the corners like they were surveying where our security began and ended. The intruder wore some kind of mask and a baseball cap low on his brow. Never touching a door or window, he simply walked and watched.

I switched cameras as the figure neared the far back of the house. My blood chilled when the intruder took out a cellphone and recorded the layout of my house.

Enough. I hit the panic alarm for the cops. The figure crashed over a patio chair as every exterior light burst on, as well as a horrific whooping siren guaranteed to wake up my mother, Belle, and every other person within half a mile.

The figure ran through the backyard toward the street. There they leapt into a small car obscured by the darkness and drove away toward the main road.

Across the hall, a door whipped open and smashed into the wall. "Lily! Belle!"

In the hall, I met Mom as she shrugged into a robe.

My sister brandished a handgun.

"Where did you get that?" I asked.

"I have a permit." She shifted her gaze toward our mother. "I want to work for the FBI."

"We'll talk about it later." Mom spied the security app on my phone. "You hit the panic alarm?"

"Yes." I told them about the person outside my room and rewound the footage from the security system. "He's gone. I hit the silent alarm too. To the police."

Mom dragged a shaking hand over her bedraggled hair. "They'll be here any minute. Go change."

In my room, I took her advice to put on more than a braless tank and shorts. The bank of windows facing the pool had gone dark behind the shades. Normally, the wide panes of glass channeled the morning sunshine into my room. Now I wished they were boarded over to protect me from the outside.

My father wasn't here to tell me everything would be fine. I hated the weakness, the vulnerability. And I hated the reality that the same person who killed my father might also want me and his family dead.

Dressed and ready, we waited in the living room when the police arrived. The patrolman took my statement, since I'd been the one who had seen the prowler. To my mother he said, "Ma'am, can I get the name and contact for your security company?"

"Certainly." She wrote the information from memory.

Luckily, my sister had put away her gun. I didn't think I could stand any more excitement at the moment.

"Did you see the car?" the patrolman asked me.

"On the security feed. It was small. Like a Honda? Or maybe a sedan."

"Bet you don't see many Hondas in this neighborhood," the patrolman said, glancing around our living room. "I'll check with the security gate."

I narrowed my glare on him. Mom wouldn't like his dig any more than I did.

"Did you check the grounds?" The annoyance in her tone dripped like acid.

Nothing like a condescending remark about how we lived to set her off. Maybe that's where I got my defensiveness. I'd worried my friends would think the same things as the cop.

"Um, yes. We did. There are a few footprints around the pool. Whoever sneaked around stepped in a soft spot from the sprinkler system. We have a team checking to see if we can get a useable print. It might tell us if this person was male or female."

"Thank you," Mom told him without warmth.

"If you see or hear anything else, please let us know." He checked me over as if sizing up my prowess. "You scared him off."

"Yeah. Go me," I replied.

The police officer shrugged then left.

"Someone's paying attention to what we're doing." A ghost of fear danced in my sister's eyes before she reined in her emotions.

Mom double-checked the locks and reset the alarm twice.

"Unfortunately. We have to continue as if nothing is wrong. No one outside this house can know what's happening." She zeroed in on me.

"You know it's too late for secrets," I told her. "We wouldn't be this far without my friends helping."

She held up a finger. "Need to know. You both work for me now. They don't. I have to maintain confidentiality."

Back in bed, I alternated staring at my ceiling and the windows and waiting for the next intrusion from either human or critter. I couldn't settle my pulse or my racing mind after the work we'd done trying to tie up the loose ends we untangled.

Patrick stood in the epicenter of my father's murder—I was sure. And yeah, I suspected his death had something to do with the real estate case. Did he want to buy the land and something Dad had done had prevented Patrick from completing his plan? Could his evil actions be about the money—lots of it?

Determined to not glance at the windows, I flopped on my side and willed my mind to relax. I concentrated on the inside of my eyelids, the dark shield against my thoughts. Sleep tugged on me, but I startled awake each time I drifted, until my eyes popped open and sleep fled.

Wait a minute.

What if this mess wasn't about the deal but the actual piece of land? Mom had mentioned Patrick left his career at the state where he dealt in environmental protection. Was there something special about the land?

I climbed out of bed and padded down the silent hallway. In the dining room, I dimmed the light over the dining room table and searched through the files for the contract to purchase the land. According to the contract, the land was just over four hundred acres. An aerial photo of the property revealed a single dirt road connecting the land to a two-lane paved road. The narrow path bordered a swampy tract that led to the Everglades National Park—in the middle of freaking nowhere. An envelope contained additional surveys from a lower altitude. A narrow canal snaked through the property, maybe big enough for a rowboat or small motorboat.

Ugh. There had to be alligators in there. And big slimy snakes. I shuddered, imagining a scene out of *Jumanji*.

My gaze shifted to the other pictures, most showing intense green treetops and dense undergrowth. What was so important about this isolated chunk of land? You couldn't build a Starbucks and expect to get any customers in this century.

One of the photos caught my attention. Maybe my exhaustion or the late hour had muddled my brain. Or the scare, or my dry, sandy eyes.

Then I saw it. A slice of angular gray against the green treetops. Long, thin, definitely not natural. Within a few moments, I figured out what the object was.

A plane's wing sticking out of the jungle overgrowth.

But whose plane and how did it end up in such dense foliage? I went to my computer and ran a search for plane crashes in the area. Nothing. Someone should be searching for this plane and the pilot.

Using my phone for a magnifying glass, I focused on the plane. The wing didn't appear commercial jet-sized, but it wasn't a small private plane either. I'd been on my father's Cessna enough times to know. This was a middle-sized plane. Maybe like two propellers. The kind often used for cargo.

I frowned at the image, my brain caught in a spiraling tailspin. Cargo? This plane could be why Patrick wanted the land.

In southern Florida, the only lost cargo worth two lives would be drugs. I'd seen stories over the years of someone stumbling across a downed plane full of marijuana or worse contraband. Stolen planes full of bullet holes, some with dead pilots, some abandoned on landing.

Maybe when Patrick did the aerial survey of the property, he saw the plane. Didn't they use drones for taking overheads? If he had more footage of the property, it would be on his computer somewhere. Or his phone.

My heart soared. This evidence gave us motive.

If we were able to prove this plane contained something valuable, we'd know Patrick had a reason to make sure this court case never went through. If he was trying to buy the land from the owner, and Dad's case would have prevented the sale, Patrick might have gone to extreme measures to make sure the owner sold the property.

Might, maybe, possibly. No hard evidence from our investigation tied back to Patrick—just a ton of speculation. At least not enough to make the detective skip his afternoon coffee to hear me out.

But if we could get the drone survey or pictures of the wreckage…then we'd have something. His phone or laptop might hold the key to tie Patrick to my father's murder.

Fortunately, I knew just the hacker to help me find the truth.

Chapter Seventeen

After a sleepless night, I met Jazz outside the coffee house with two iced mocha coffees in hand. He wore palm tree board shorts and a bright blue sleeveless T-shirt, a getup fit for an afternoon lifeguard shift. My rumpled tank top said I slept in my clothes—in case I had to run for my life—which was basically true. Since the anxiety of last night, I couldn't be bothered to change. But seeing my disheveled appearance reflected in his eyes sent a shiver over my body, even though the temperature was already in the mid-eighties. The flood of fear returned.

"You all right? Your mom? Belle?" He gripped my hand and drew me into an embrace. His voice rumbled in his chest, and I listened to his steady heartbeat. "What happened?"

After I told him, relief coursed through me as if the ordeal had been someone else's. "We're okay. Just shook up." Still I clung to him. He had to know how much I'd been through the night before by the trembling.

Slipping his arms to my waist, he took a half-step back to focus on my face. "Did you bring the security video?"

"Yeah." I offered him my cellphone. "It's on here."

"Good. Frankie will give it a try, but he's not promising anything."

I'd already resigned myself to a negative outcome. "I know. I'm more interested in finding out more about the property." I took his hand and led him toward the beach, a result of my sudden aversion to standing in one place too long.

I scanned the crowds, watching for Patrick, expecting him to jump out from behind a palm tree. Since palm tree trunks were thin, this wasn't likely. The image I'd drawn in my mind of him lurking made me giggle.

"What's so funny?" Jazz asked.

"Nothing. Just jumpy and punchy." I brushed the hair off my

cheek. "I'm seeing ghosts."

His arms tightened around my waist. "We're okay. Lots of witnesses."

The fact witnesses hadn't helped the fisherman sat on my tongue, but I kept the comment to myself.

Strolling the busy street full of people walking dogs, making deliveries, and jogging, we proceeded toward the entrance to the beach. No one seemed out of place. The normal ebb and flow of Fort Myers Beach life whirled by. Parents, kids, retirees. No guys in black masks. No Patrick doppelgangers.

"What's wrong?" Jazz asked, his gaze following the path mine had taken.

"Nothing," I lied. I didn't want him to worry.

"We're going to figure this out, Lil. We're getting closer."

"I know." My gaze caught on a middle-aged man sitting on a bench to our left. I'd seen him before when I parked my car. He'd been drinking coffee, leaning against the rail, and staring out into the Gulf. A newspaper had replaced the coffee cup.

"Lily? What's wrong?"

"In the store. Now. No questions." We hurried into the nearest T-shirt and flip flop establishment. I drifted deep into the store and shuffled through the merchandise and kept my sunglasses over my eyes. Lifting a bright orange shirt from the rack, I asked, "How's this?"

"Lily, what the heck are you up to?"

At that moment, the guy ambled in front of the display window as if interested in beach shoes. His line of vision shifted inside, and I *knew* the creep searched for me.

"We're being followed." I whipped out my cellphone. "Hold this shirt up in front of you. Hurry!"

Jazz complied, and I snapped a picture to catch my tail behind him as the man peered inside.

"Got him." I grabbed the shirt and hung it back on the rack.

"Where is he?" His fingers dug into my bicep.

"My left, your right. Let's walk out the door we came in and go right." My plan was to walk toward the pier but hang a left behind the restaurants. The narrow stretch of beach behind the eateries to the parking lot would conceal our escape. We'd be hidden if my stalker tried to double back and find us.

We made our way toward the door. "Ready when you are," he said.

Our guy had vanished. Jazz took my hand. We hurried to the right, past the outdoor restaurants and in the direction of the pier. We almost succeeded.

Instead of passing by and doubling back, the man had made a circuit of the complex. I expected him to show up behind us, but he appeared in front of us.

"Kiss me," I demanded.

With a loud whoop, Jazz swept me up into his arms and spun me. I let out a giggle before he planted me back on the ground and kissed me. I forgot about stalkers and planes as my mind spun and my body leaned into his. He smelled of the ocean, and his hair tickled the sides of my face.

The memory of sand and his lips on my throat washed away the fear and devoured my pain. I returned his kisses until his hands were in my hair. Drowsy with the sensations coursing through my body, I drew away, and his lips nuzzled the underside of my throat.

My gaze locked on our shadow. The man stood at the end of the street, pretending not to watch our spontaneous make-out session.

"Run," I whispered.

"To be continued..."

We bolted for the pier past startled people waiting in line for ice cream and French fries. Hurrying along the left side of the pier to the beach, I kicked off my flip flops and drove my legs into a sprint. The parking lot served four restaurants and the shopping district. A plentiful number of cars hid our flight.

I pounded up the steps to the lot, spinning back the way we'd come in time to see the man halfway down the pier. He spotted me at the same moment.

"Go!" I yelled, digging into my shorts pocket for the car keys.

Jazz slid onto the passenger seat as I slammed the driver's door. Gunning the engine, we zipped past the shocked attendant and dove into the traffic flow.

~ * ~

My pulse finally dropped back to normal as we rushed through the office to the safety of our gamer's inner sanctum. We'd driven around for half an hour, in and out of alleys and parking garages, until satisfied we weren't being followed.

Our stalker could be someone who worked for Patrick. Another hired gun, like the fisherman had been. He might be trying to find out what we'd done with the files. Fear shivered over my skin. The stalker could be the same person I'd seen on the security feed outside my bedroom.

When we walked in, Frankie was digging behind the wall of monitors, zip tying cables and plugs into a neat bundle.

"Hey," Jazz called. "You alive back there?"

Frankie took a zip tie out of his mouth and waved a hand. "Be a couple of minutes, unless you want to give me a hand."

I took in his attire. Today, he wore a black sleeveless turtleneck over khaki shorts with a pair of bright green Pumas, no socks, and hot pink gauges.

If only I could be as fearless.

I took a seat while they leaned behind the monitors and tied cables. Gah, the inner sanctum was cold. I wrapped my arms around myself, wishing I'd picked up a sweatshirt on the way out. The air conditioning blasted at freezer volume I suspected kept the electronics cool. Maybe the temperature explained the not-so-Floridian turtleneck in today's wardrobe.

When they completed the job and he had dusted off his shorts, Frankie asked, "What's up?"

"Other than getting chased through Fort Myers by some guy? Not a lot," I said.

His eyebrows shot up. "No kidding? I need to hang with you two more."

"I got a picture of the man."

He laughed when I showed him my phone. "I like her. She brings me interesting shit to do."

Jazz snorted. "Interesting? Someone tried to break into her house last night. We have a security feed too."

"Cool! Email it to me." He rattled off an email address.

In moments, the dark figure appeared on the giant LED panels on the wall beside the picture of the man who'd been watching us by the pier. A shudder wracked my spine.

"You have any idea who this guy is?" Frankie asked.

"No. None."

"Maybe we can do something with the picture. The guy at the beach looks like he might be in his thirties." As we watched, the man's face swam in and out of focus until it sharpened.

My hopes plummeted. Even clear, the man had been a half a block away, and the shot from inside the store had picked up a glare. "It's hard to see his features."

"Yeah, sucks. That's about the best I can do with it. Let's watch the video feed replay and see if it's the same guy."

Jazz squeezed my hand. I faked a smile even though frustration colored my mood a darker shade of depressed.

"Hmmm. You've got a bit of reflection on this picture," Frankie murmured.

"You can take away the glare?" I hoped.

"I might be able to do something with it." He worked over a tablet, darkening some of the brighter areas until the man's picture sharpened and came into focus. "Is that a mask?" Frankie said. "A man in a mask. So Scooby-Doo."

"That's him," I said.

"What about this video? Tell me how you took this. What kind of system?"

"Ah…I don't know what kind of system we have."

"The quality of this video screams high end," he said.

"It probably is." Blood warmed my cheeks. The night rushed back into my memories, cresting on a tide of fresh, sharp fear.

"Except the guy took off in a car. It might be too far away to get much."

"Puh-lease." Frankie rolled his eyes at his friend. "Ye of so freaking little faith."

Jazz offered up his hands in surrender. "Sorry, man. What was I thinking?"

On the screen, small sections of the video appeared, snipped out of the larger file, while Frankie typed with one hand and manipulated a tablet with the other. I watched the prowler in profile, and the terror of those minutes contracted my muscles until I couldn't move. Another shot of him materialized; this section of video showed his body angled away from the camera. Then the next one as he ran from the siren I triggered. Finally, a shot of the person getting into a car.

"A sedan—smaller car. European maybe." Frankie squinted at the screen as the picture zoomed in on a set of illuminated taillights. "Yep. Foreign. BMW. 3-series."

My eyebrows shot up. "You're sure?"

Frankie glowered as if I insulted him. "Those are 3-series BMW taillights. Have you seen what I drive? I know my European cars. And I've got two numbers of the license plate."

"What does Patrick drive?" Jazz asked.

"A silver Lexus," I said.

"Damn. Not the same car."

"Nah. I don't think this is your man." Frankie pointed to the screen. "In fact, it doesn't look like a man at all. See?" He brought up a close shot of the person in profile. "Your prowler has boobs."

This was the mic drop. Since the intrusion, I expected a clean shot of Patrick making his escape, except it hadn't been the lawyer unless he'd worn a disguise. But that didn't make any sense either. "A woman? Could Patrick have someone he's working with?"

"Yeah." Jazz laced his hands behind his head and stared up at the ceiling. "Maybe your mom would have an idea of someone he's close to."

"Someone who drives a 3-series Beemer with IC as the first two letters of the plate," Frankie reminded us.

I didn't trust Liz after their kiss, but I'd never seen her drive a BMW, only the Jaguar. "You don't have a way to find out who owns the car?" I asked.

Frankie shook his head. "Not me. I might have a friend who could help us out. I try to stay off government radar—if you know what I mean. But she's expensive."

"Okay. We might need her to check on this for us." If Detective Stephens weren't such an ass, I could ask him. But that wasn't happening.

"What about this other issue? The drone footage of some real estate?"

Apparently, Jazz had taken the liberty of filling in the blanks for our friend.

I nodded. "From what I understand, Patrick has done a lot of these land deals over the years. My mother said he uses an aerial survey company. Drones. They fly over and map the property. If something interesting pops up, he goes in on the ground."

"And you've got something interesting?"

"Yes." I removed the photographs from the file and laid out the pictures on a portable plastic table. He studied the shots for several minutes.

"Yeah, this is definitely drone. There's a couple of companies in this area that do work like this. Pantac Aerial. Friedman Surveys." He tapped on the first picture. "See this? The FSCO in the date stamp? Friedman Survey Corp."

"Do you know anyone over there?" Jazz asked.

He bobbed his head from side to side. "Maybe. A bunch of them went to drone school with me at Carson Drobot. But people like this move around from place to place, following the money."

"You can fly a drone?" I'd judged the epic gamer on his sick video game screens and the way he lived behind the store front. I'd sure shortchanged his abilities. The thought slammed into my brain like an arrow aimed at my stupidity. Hadn't I worried people would do the same when they found out about Jazz? Shame burned up my neck. I was no better than what I believed of others.

If our hacker noticed my discomfort, he made no mention. "Yeah. Who do you think takes those cool beach shots for Fort Myers's website?" He got up and slid a panel back on the wall. Painted the same dark gray as everything else in the room, I'd never seen the hidden door.

I gasped. Behind the panel hung not one but four huge drones, three with four props and one with six.

"Pretty cool, huh?" Frankie lifted one of the four propeller models from the wall. "This is Felix. He's my favorite. I modified him myself. He's got a 20-megapixel camera, and I amped up his batteries. I get over an hour of flying time out of him now. Plus, 8K video."

Jazz whistled in appreciation as he leaned over the drone. "What would someone surveying a property like this use?"

"This is way more machine than you need. A basic camera drone would work. Five hundred bucks, tops. A modified one like this is a couple of grand. But those pictures you have, I'd say the operator didn't care about bells and whistles. They just took the pics. Nothing fancy." Frankie patted Felix like a puppy in need of attention before setting the drone back on its shelf.

"We need to find out who at Friedman took the pictures," I said. "If we know the drone operator, maybe he or she could shed some light on the plane wing in the pictures."

He settled the drone back in the niche and closed the sliding door. "A plane?"

"Yeah. See this? Doesn't this light area look like a plane wing to you?"

"You've got something to clean up this image, right?" Jazz asked.

"I bet I could do something with this." Frankie said. "It would help to have the original picture."

"The only way we're going to get the original is to steal Patrick's laptop and phone." What would the detective say to that plan? How much more danger would I bring into my life if I tried to locate it on my own?

"Unless we can track down the drone pilot, like you said," Jazz added. "We get the pilot, we might be able to get the picture."

"Hang on. Let me see what magic I can cast." Frankie laid the photo on a scanner and then pressed the button. "This baby was designed to scan in artwork. It's got amazing detail."

As I held my breath, the photo appeared on the screen in sixty-five-inch, high definition. The trees leapt off the screen with crystal-clear depth and detail—leaves, branches. But there—the metallic outline of the silver wing. For the first time, the details sharpened into focus including a series of letters which hadn't been visible in the smaller picture. "What's this shading? Some kind of logo?"

The wing of the plane zoomed into view. "I think it's a bunch of letters. E-s-t."

Jazz was already typing in his phone. "Air cargo companies with the letters e-s-t."

"It's a pretty big plane. Search for a company shipping to the Caribbean or Mexico," I told him.

"How would you know that?" Frankie asked.

Self-conscious, I shrugged. "My dad was a pilot. He had a plane at Fort Myers Airport."

"I think I've got something," Jazz said. "Quest Cargo and Transport reported a stolen plane a couple of years ago. The plane and the pilot were never located."

Frankie scanned the article over Jazz's shoulder. "They searched the Gulf. No wreckage. Gave up after a week."

"What do you want to bet that's it?" I jabbed a finger at the screen. "The question is, was the plane stolen, or did it crash and they just reported the plane stolen?"

"We need to know what's on the plane." He tapped the image with his index finger. "See here? There are boating channels running through the woods."

Excitement brewed in my veins. "Are you thinking what I think you're thinking?"

He smiled. "Of course I am. I know a guy with a boat." He fired off a text. "He owes me one for helping him set up a system."

"The more people who know what you're out there doing, the more attention you're gonna have on you. Don't forget…two people are dead because of this, including your father." Frankie's warning settled over the icy room like a dark cloud.

My back stiffened. "Every time I remember, I take a breath and it hurts like somebody's digging a knife in my ribs. Patrick did this. He's not going to get away with murder." The fury and sorrow I suffered when I knelt beside my father surged through my body on a wave of determination.

"Just want to make sure you know what you're doing," he said.

"I have no idea," I confessed. "I'm making this up as I go."

"Well, if we're gonna do this, we better get moving." Frankie got up, slid open the secret door, then took Felix from the space.

"You're going with us?" Hope bled through my anger. With Frankie and Felix in our corner, the chances of finding the plane jumped.

"You think I'm going to miss a chance to fly my bird?"

Jazz showed us the text on his phone. "We're on for the boat. We need to pick it up."

"What did you tell him?" Frankie asked.

"I wanted to go drinking and watch the sunset." Jazz smiled at me, and I briefly forgot the chill of the room around me.

"That works for me," Frankie said. "I'm going to pack up Felix and the rest of my gear." He disappeared into a back room.

Jazz closed the distance between us. I wrapped my arms around his waist.

"It's gonna be okay," he assured me. "No one knows we found out about the plane. Patrick isn't going to expect us to go searching for it."

I swallowed, calming my rushing nerves. "I guess we better pick up some industrial-strength bug spray."

He smiled and leaned in for a kiss as Frankie returned carrying two bottles of water. He'd ditched the turtleneck for a tank and a pair of rugged cargo shorts. Hiking shoes had replaced the Pumas.

"You two aren't kidding anyone. We know you're getting some," he quipped as he removed two machetes from a wooden trunk. "These might come in handy."

Jazz winked as heat rushed into my face, then released me and took one of the blades. He tested the heft of the tool in his hand. "I guess this could do some damage."

"No kidding. Why do you think I packed them? There are snakes out there. Big ones." Frankie shivered for emphasis as he boxed up the drone in a soft-sided nylon case.

"I've got to let Belle know what's going on. She'll never forgive me if we go in without her." I sent a text to my sister. I glanced down at my flip flops and orange toenails. This wouldn't be pretty. "I better get her to bring me different shoes."

Frankie snorted at my dilemma. "That's a great color on you," he said. "Good thing one of us is prepared." He dug in a closet and hefted a pair of rubber boots with tiny yellow duckies from the clutter. "My sister left these the last time she was in. They might fit you."

"I don't care if I have to cut off my toes. Thanks!" I took the boots and wiggled my feet into them. My sweaty toes stuck to the rubber.

Belle texted back that she would ditch our mother and meet us at the property entrance. "Okay. She'll meet us there."

We waited while Frankie loaded a backpack with a laptop and extra batteries. A solar charger went in as well. "Let's go get the boat."

"You mean before you pack one of us in here?" Jazz lifted a bag. "Jeez. We're going for a couple of hours, not a month."

"I'm prepared," he said with a mock-salute.

Jazz threw up his hands, and I stifled my nervous laugh.

Frankie whooped and led the way.

"Who's your friend?" I asked Jazz, amazed at the brand new, crew cab pickup standing four feet off the ground. As if boarding a rocket ship, I climbed up into the cab.

"Rand Cummings," Jazz answered. "He sets up gaming systems for most of the local streamers—plus a ton of business work. I helped him out one time when he was short-handed, thus the favor returned."

"He did mine," Frankie said. "Guy's got skills. He can increase upload speeds like nobody's business."

Jazz glanced at me. "You have the GPS up?" We pulled away from the beach house with a fifteen-foot, flat-bottomed Jon boat in tow behind the massive Ford F-250 pickup.

I skimmed over the map on my phone. "Yeah. We stay on this road for about twenty-five miles."

"Great. Python country," Frankie moaned.

"Good thing you brought your machetes," I said.

"Time to channel your inner Indiana Jones." Jazz laughed.

"Really? Not a good character reference. He hates snakes too!"

We shared a laugh at his expense.

"Belle's bringing a cooler and water," I told them, reading her latest text.

"We'll fuel up the boat at the next gas station." Jazz donned a pair of aviator sunglasses.

I couldn't suppress the laugh.

"What?"

"I guess your aviators are fitting. Since we're looking for a plane." Excitement rippled through my stomach. I felt like a treasure hunter.

We figured out the location of the X, but not what we'd find when we dug. My musings shifted to my Dad, as they inevitably did when I stopped to think beyond our next step. I guessed what he'd say about me chasing this plane lead down. Dad would freak. He'd be super pissed. He'd never let me put myself at risk this way.

But I already was at risk. The prowler and our stalker at the beach proved my precarious situation. I remembered one of his favorite lines; one he used when dealing with a sticky case. "The only way out of a mess is through," he used to say.

Just following your advice, Dad.

"You okay?" Jazz nudged my arm.

I nodded and smiled. "Yeah. I'm good."

"What's the deal with the court case? How does that tie in?" Frankie asked from the back seat.

I glanced over the seat. The drone-flying, video-game-hacking phenom appeared a bit out of place sitting in the back seat of a monster truck. "We're not entirely sure yet. My mother and sister spent a bunch of time going through the files today. Maybe she has something."

We rode in silence for a while, my mind drifting as the dense foliage slipped by on both sides of the highway. I remembered road trips with my parents, when I'd seen the jungles of South Florida and wondered about the people who explored this beautiful and violent land of alligators, hurricanes, jungles, and mosquito-infested swamps. In many ways, I now understood what those explorers experienced and the emotions that might have driven them forward regardless of the cost.

My sister waited for us at the entrance to the access road we'd seen on the drone pictures. Her eyes widened when we parked the truck and boat. "Where'd you get the boat?"

"Jazz has a friend," I said, kissing him on the cheek. I owed him a lot for the past week. Not only had he been there for me, but he'd also jumped into our investigation with both feet. Without him, I wouldn't have Frankie, Felix, or the awesome boat.

And let's not forget the machetes.

"Follow us in for about a mile. We'll leave your car there. No one will see it." Jazz climbed into the driver's seat, and then I scampered up beside him. He eased the truck down the weathered and rutted track with my sister close behind.

"Talk about being in the middle of nowhere," Frankie muttered. "No coffee bar, not even a farmer's roadside stand."

"That was my first impression too." I glanced over the seat. "You're right. Seems like this land can't be worth much on its own."

Gesturing out the window, he said, "There's pythons, cottonmouths, rattlers, and God knows what else out there. What was he gonna do with this? Open Reptile World? There's no development around here. No people. What could you build besides some tourist trap?"

"I doubt he wanted it for the view," Jazz replied. "Once Patrick did the survey for the case and found the plane? Nothing else mattered."

"I bet he did research about the plane and knew it was valuable," I said. "Otherwise, he should have called the cops or the Feds—whoever handles plane crashes, right? I can't wait to see what's in it." A small clearing appeared off the side of the dirt track. "This might be a safe place to leave the car."

The truck bounced and bucked over the rough terrain as we slowed and parked. I hopped to the ground and helped Belle shift the cooler from her trunk to the truck bed. The suffocating air, thick as damp velvet, pressed against my skin, and the pungent aroma of stagnant water tickled the back of my throat.

My sister dragged herself into the backseat. After introductions, we set off.

Frankie tapped on his phone screen. "From what I see on the satellite map, the track ends about a mile farther up."

Sure enough, the road came to an abrupt halt against a copse of trees. To our left, a path had been cleared through the woods to the waterway.

Jazz slowed the truck. "See the dirt path to the canal? Might be a spot to launch the boat that way." He swung the truck around and backed the boat toward the water. "This is as far as I can go without getting stuck. It's marshy in here."

We slid out of the truck into the palpable Florida heat and picked our way back to the boat. It took the four of us, sweating and cursing, to slide the craft off the trailer and to the shore. The guys loaded Felix, while Belle and I grabbed the cooler and loaded-down backpacks.

Sweat dribbled down my neck.

"These bugs suck," she said as she set the bags on board and fended off a dense swarm of gnats with both hands.

"One more thing." Jazz collected the machetes and tossed them into the boat. "I think we're ready." Sweat dripped from his hairline, and he wiped it away with the hem of his T-shirt.

The woods pressed against both sides of the channel, an impenetrable wall of living green. "By the time we get back, we're all going to smell like damp dogs." Frankie wrinkled his nose.

"That's why God invented the shower." Jazz smacked his friend on the shoulder.

Belle eyed the weapons with suspicion. "What are the machetes for?"

"Protection from pythons or other creepy crawlies. And to cut our way through this mess if we have to." Jazz eased the boat from the beach and jumped aboard.

We paddled a short distance from shore. The canal was no more than twenty feet across and of questionable, muddy depth. Vines hung low with leafy tendrils snaking from the dense canopy, and Spanish moss curtained the branches to hang reaching fingers over the water.

"Gotta be careful going through here." He lowered the electric motor into the murk. "At least it's built for mud. I don't want to mess up Rand's baby."

The motor fired to life, and we sat back to ride. The heavy air grew more humid between the trees. A cloying smell of decaying leaves and stagnant water rose from the boat's wake.

"Head southwest." Frankie squinted at his portable GPS. "The pictures of the plane were of the far-left corner of this property."

"This canal leads in that direction," Jazz shouted over the hum of the motor.

We puttered along until we came to a left snaking branch, and the boat slowed. Frankie tied a bright pink strip to one of the trees. "So, we can find our way back," he said.

Getting lost in the canal system was not my idea of a good time, and I silently thanked tech-support for his foresight.

"Did you find anything in the case file?" Jazz asked.

"Yes. There was an issue with some endangered wildlife. A couple of birds and alligators. They like to lay their eggs in here." My sister picked at her cuticles, a definite tell she was nervous about our little adventure.

My eyes widened. An alligator breeding ground. But what part of South Florida wasn't one? "Fantastic," I said.

Our not-so-adventurous friend sucked in a breath. I guessed he didn't like alligators either.

"It is. That's what got them in trouble," Belle said. "I read the owner of the property applied for a variance. Something to let him bring in fill and dry part of the acreage out in order to build. But when the Florida DEP figured out what he wanted to do, they slapped him with a cease-and-desist order. It's been tied up in court ever since."

"How long has this been going on?" Jazz asked.

"Four and a half years."

"How does Patrick fit into this picture?" I asked.

She smiled as if she had saved the best for last. "Patrick came into the case as a special consultant because of his environmental experience. His consult had to be how he learned about the plane. Right after his consult, the shell companies started forming. Patrick set himself up to purchase the land without repercussions. He was very patient— very careful—to set this up without anyone finding out about his unethical finagling."

"Did he make the guy an offer using one of the company fronts?" Frankie typed something into the GPS and nodded.

"We don't know," Belle admitted.

I ducked beneath a low-hanging vine. "Whatever is out here has to be worth the trouble." But was it worth my father's life? Or the fisherman's?

"It's gotta be a plane full of drugs," Frankie said above the drone of the motor.

A cloud of mosquitos closed in, so I doused myself in bug spray.

"We're not going to get close enough by boat to see what's inside the plane. We're going to have to go in on foot," Jazz said.

Using a machete, my sister cleared draping vines. Her shirt hiked up, and her gun peeked from the waistband in the back of her shorts. Either she expected trouble, or she saw an opportunity to practice for the FBI.

I edged to the back of the boat where Jazz kept his hand on the rudder. "How far back do you think this goes?"

He shrugged. "The property is what? Around four hundred acres? But it's long, so a mile or more? Hey, Frankie," he called. "How are we doing?"

His friend squinted at the tablet's screen, shielding the display from the sun. "According to the GPS, we're about halfway there. I think this canal will get us within a quarter mile of the plane."

"A quarter mile?" Belle grumbled, her gaze on the overgrowth. At least she'd worn sneakers and cropped jeans. I hadn't expected to go on a jungle cruise and Everglades expedition when I left the house this morning. Thank goodness, I had Frankie's ducky boots.

"We'll jog," Jazz said with a laugh.

"Great." She swore under her breath.

After about fifteen minutes of sluggish progress, Frankie waved a hand. "This is it. The plane is to our right, in there." He peered into the heavy, dense foliage. "Thanks, but I'll stay with the boat."

"I don't think we should split up," Belle said.

"Who's going to fly Felix?" Frankie asked.

Her eyebrows shot toward her hairline. "Felix?"

"The drone we brought to guide us in," I explained.

"Well that's wicked cool." Scoping out the water behind us, she seemed to consider our options. "Okay. You two take the machetes in with you. I'll stay here with Frankie and the boat in case anyone decides to come snooping up this way."

Nodding, Frankie said, "Yeah. She's got the gun."

Belle whipped around. "How do you know I have a gun?"

With a smirk, he said, "You look the type."

She narrowed her eyes.

"And your shirt rides up."

I stifled a giggle as my sister scowled.

Frankie unpacked the drone and set Felix on a seat. With a press of a button, the props began to whirl.

"Get in, take the pictures, and get the hell out of there." My sister clutched my wrist and squeezed. "I mean it. In and out."

When she released me, I said, "You think I want to spend more than thirty seconds in there? You're nuts." I picked up the machete and an extra backpack Frankie produced from his endless supply of necessities.

"There's a good digital camera in there, too."

Jazz gripped the machete in his right hand. "You think of everything."

Frankie pressed buttons on Felix's controller. The drone set off with a faint whir.

My sister's worried face was the last thing I saw before following Jazz into the jungle. The plants and trees disoriented me as I glanced up at the heavy canopy of foliage. Noises I hadn't noticed before filled the green world in a mass of sounds woven together with the sharp rustle of palm fronds in the breeze and a near-deafening cacophony of insects.

Ahead of me, Jazz traversed over a fallen palm. He reached back to help me climb over. "Thanks," I said as I wiped rivers of sweat from my face. I switched on the walkie talkie and keyed the mic. "Can you hear me?"

A static burst preceded Frankie's enthusiastic, "You bet!"

Jazz chuckled. "This is a big adventure for him."

We picked our way through the dead leaves, and I kept my gaze fixed on the ground watching for snakes. "Don't you have a stream this afternoon?" The last thing I wanted was Jazz jeopardizing his sponsor contracts for my wild goose chase.

"We'll be home by dinner," he said with the grin I loved most, lopsided and wry. "We're going to have to get the band together too. We're due to audition on Tuesday."

I'd forgotten about Sun Runner's and how much the opportunity had meant to me—and the band. I couldn't let them down. "Tomorrow," I said. "Let's rehearse tomorrow."

"Remind me to check schedules when we get out of here," Jazz said.

"Keep going straight," Frankie squawked from the radio. "About a quarter mile."

"I thought he said a quarter of a mile from the boat," I grumbled, pushing aside vines and branches.

Jazz reached back for my hand to pull me through. "Hey, we're alone in the jungle. Enjoy it."

I sucked in my breath, and my pulse kicked into high gear. His body blocked the path. I forgot my fear of pythons and kissed him, leaning against his sweat-dampened shirt. "I like the jungle," I said as we parted.

"To be continued," he said. "Like before."

We trudged through the gloom beneath the trees. Every so often, a patch of sun slipped through the treetops illuminating the ground below. I removed a water bottle from the side pocket of my backpack. The liquid slid down my throat, the only cool thing in or on my body.

"Man, it's close under here," Jazz complained, wiping his face on the end of his tank top and affording me a glance at his stomach muscles. He dropped his shirt and wiggled his eyebrows. "Liking the view?"

"Maybe," I said with a smirk of my own.

Frankie barked from the radio. "Hey! You're almost there. Take a slight right."

"Got it," I replied then stopped short from running into Jazz. "What? Why did you stop?"

He touched a finger to his lips, took the radio from my hands then turned down the volume. He pointed in the direction of our travel. A football field-length away, the silver fuselage of a cargo plane tilted nose up into the trees, balancing on one wheel and the torn remnants of its right wing. Behind it, the shattered spikes of trees belied the plane's last path to its resting place.

ATVs sat beside tents that had been pitched below the craft. New rope looped around the plane's body and nearby trees, holding the craft aloft in place of the missing left wheel.

Deep boot tracks led in multiple directions. Men, not just one, but many had been here. My heart pounded. This was much worse than we had imagined.

"What do we do?" I whispered, taking out my phone. If nothing else, we'd have dozens of pictures to prove the plane existed. But we needed to know the contents inside the plane if we had a chance of figuring out Patrick's motive.

Jazz gestured to our left. "Let's circle around. See that?"

I squinted in the direction he indicated. "There's some kind of chute on the side of the plane. Next to the ramp."

"I bet they're unloading right here. Taking the cargo out on those ATVs."

"Maybe Patrick didn't want to wait for the case to settle." Sweat dripped from my bangs, burning my eyes. Whatever bug spray I wore had washed away. A horde of the flying menaces descended on us. "If he lost the case, he'd lose access to the property."

"Exactly. It looks deserted. Maybe they left for the day?" Jazz's tone told me he wasn't as sure as he sounded.

I spit out a bug and glanced back the way we'd come, our path invisible in the dense bush except for a few bent branches. "We should tell them back at the boat. Warn them to be careful."

He nodded. "Do it. Quiet."

"There's a bunch of people here, working in the plane," I radioed to Belle.

"Get the hell out of there," she snapped.

I ignored her complaints and switched off the radio. "Okay, I told her. Let's do this fast."

We crept around the plane, giving the encampment a wide berth. A campfire smoldered between the mosquito-netting draped tents. "We just missed them," I murmured. My heart pounded as we crossed in front of the plane's battered nose. No time to try Frankie's fancy camera with bad guys lurking in the woods. Instead, I snapped pictures of the call numbers, the ropes, the tents, everything with my cellphone. Our favorite detective might not want to know what we'd been doing, but he'd sure be interested in a four-year-old unsolved crime.

Bugs dogged us, drawing blood. We stopped and hid behind a clump of low palms, near the ramp into the plane. "There's no one inside," he murmured, his hand on my arm. "Stay here. I'll run up there and see what they're hiding."

"I'm not sitting here by myself," I hissed through my teeth as I swatted a mosquito the size of a parasail.

"Yes you are. I need a look-out." He spun around, grabbed me then kissed me. "I haven't had this much fun in a long time." While I regained my senses, he bounded away.

"That wasn't fair," I grumbled as he disappeared inside. "I wasn't prepared." My legs cramped from my crouch.

Minutes ticked by. Where was he? What was he doing? The rumble of a distant ATV engine spiked my pulse. *Oh no!* They were returning to camp.

"Jazz!"

His dirt-streaked face appeared in the doorway.

"They're coming!"

He tossed his backpack over his shoulder, ran halfway down the ramp then leapt the rest of the way to the ground. He slid around the back of the palmetto fronds just as the ATV towing a trailer drove into the clearing on the other side of the downed plane. We flattened to the ground and peeked through the bushes. Two men crawled off the vehicle and trudged up the ramp. Voices echoed inside the craft, but I couldn't make out the words.

Relief hammered in my heart. They didn't know we were here.

"You okay?" I asked. I tried not to think about the critters crawling over my skin.

Wiping the sweat dripping down his temples, he panted for breath. "We were right. It's loaded with pallets of stuff wrapped in plastic."

I gasped. "Is it pot?"

He pursed his lips before saying, "It's worse than pot. A couple of them were broken open. They have powder in them, like cocaine. Or maybe heroin."

"Oh my god."

"We need to get out of here. Now. Keep a watch on the door."

We faded backwards like shadows into the brush but froze as the men appeared in the doorway carrying plastic wrapped bundles. Jazz signaled toward the plane with a jerk of his chin, and we crawled beneath wide palm fronds at the edge of the clearing. He parted the leaves with a hand.

The men stacked their burdens in the trailer before climbing back inside for more. I took more pictures of their labor with shaking hands.

As soon as they entered the fuselage for another load, Jazz whispered, "Now. Go." We took off, skirting the clearing to the place where we'd exited the jungle.

"Stop," I hissed. "They're back."

When the workers descended the ramp, we waited for them to disappear back inside. Three loads later we reached the area where we entered the clearing. I took one last backward glance at the plane and snapped a picture of the loaded wagon before plunging into the dense undergrowth behind Jazz.

Chapter Eighteen

At least on the way out of the woods, I didn't have time to worry about the critters and bugs lurking in the jungle. Once out of sight and hearing of the plane, we ran full speed, jumping over tree limbs and hacking through heavy vines with a machete until we tumbled onto the canal shore.

"There!" We raced down the thin strip of beach. I pretended I didn't see the alligators drifting in the water or sunning themselves on the opposite bank.

We threw ourselves into the boat and lay panting, dripping sweat.

"What happened?" My sister tossed me a bottle of water.

"Did you find it?" Frankie wanted to know. Too concerned with flying Felix, he didn't glance our way. We watched the screen on the tablet as the drone hovered over the plane.

"We saw you on the video feed." She dropped onto one of the seats. "Who are those people?"

"No idea," I said. Sweaty strands of hair clung to my neck. I brushed them aside. "They're unloading the plane. They have tents and supplies. It appears as if they've been here for a while. A base camp." I guzzled water.

A gun shot echoed in the forest, followed by revving engines. Felix dove away from the rifles aimed in its direction.

"We've got to go." Jazz scrambled toward the back of the boat. "Get the drone down, now!" He lunged for the motor and rudder.

My sister drew her weapon.

"You think that's a good idea?" I growled through clenched teeth.

Real fear sparked in her eyes. "You want to get shot?" If Belle was afraid, maybe the rest of us should be.

Jazz spun the boat back the way we'd come. "Someone better

fire up the GPS and tell me where the hell I'm going."

I switched on the unit. "Go straight. A slight left up ahead."

We chugged up the channel as fast as we dared. I kept my gaze fixed on the area we escaped, praying the men wouldn't reach the shore before we made the bend in the river.

"Come on, Felix!" Frankie shouted at the clouds. The drone appeared above the channel and shot toward the boat. Belle and Frankie snagged it out of the sky. "We've got him. Go!"

The roar of ATV motors carried down the narrow channel. "Jazz, go faster!"

He gunned the throttle. Something hard scraped underneath the boat. Alligators slithered into the water, startled by our intrusion. We burst free from the channel into open waters.

"Made it." Triumphant, he throttled back on the motor, and we cruised toward the truck.

I sank back against the hull for a moment before hauling myself to a seat.

"I hope the jungle expedition was worth it." A cloud of gnats tormented my sister. She swatted like mad. "Did you get pictures? Did you see inside the plane?"

Jazz smirked, and my heart did a backflip. "We did better than pictures." His gaze shifted to me. "Check out what's in the backpack."

I tugged on the zipper. "Holy shit. Jazz!"

"The plane's loaded with those."

My sister peered into the bag, her mouth a perfect O. "We're in big trouble. We need to take this to the cops the second we get out of these woods."

"We can't do that," I said. "The second the cops start jumping around out here, Patrick takes off. We still can't prove he wanted this land because of the plane."

"She's right," Frankie agreed. "You need proof the lawyer knew the drugs were in the plane and that he intended to buy the land because of it."

"I know about intent," my sister snapped. "I'm a law student."

Was a law student…

Frankie's expression saddened. "I am truly sorry for you."

Her lips drew back in a garish smile.

Brash sunlight burned my arms. I squinted as the breeze blew over my damp skin. "We still need Patrick's computer or his phone."

"Does he have access to your parents' law office servers?" Frankie asked.

"Yes." Hope surged into my chest. Maybe we could find what

we needed without stealing his laptop.

"Then his tech is how we get in. You get me into the law office, and I can get into his files."

My eyes widened. "You sure you want to get any deeper into this mess than you already are?"

"Are you kidding?" Our talented friend smiled, his eyes sparkling with mischief. "This is a hell of a lot of fun. Way more interesting than screwing around with the ten streams running on my screens. Besides, they won't miss me."

Jazz guided the boat to shore. After checking for marauding alligators, we jumped onto the muddy bank and dragged the boat toward the trailer while Frankie and Belle threw the gear into the truck bed.

"Grab the tie down," Jazz called and tossed me a line.

I hooked it through the loop on the trailer, but I couldn't shake my distraction from his earlier comment.

"You have something on your mind, counselor?" Jazz asked with a tone straight out of *Law and Order* reruns. Mud smeared his tank top and the side of his neck. Both of us needed a thirty-minute power shower.

"Nothing."

"You're full of it."

Struggling for words, I chickened out and said, "Thank you. You didn't have to do any of this. We could've gotten shot. Or captured."

"By who? Them? They're a couple of goons. I'm way too smart to get caught by those guys." He came around the boat and stood in front of me. "But I don't think my safety is what's on your mind."

I glanced back toward my sister and Frankie. They chatted by the side of her car. "I'm trying to figure out what this is," I said, gesturing between us. "What are we trying to do here?"

His mouth twitched up at the corner, and a breeze lifted the sweaty points of his hair. "I'm trying to figure out how to get you to admit you like me."

My mouth popped open.

"See? You didn't deny it." He kissed the side of my face before he walked away toward the front of the truck, leaving me and my heart unsure of what to do next.

~ * ~

We drove home listening to Frankie chatter about how clear the footage of the plane was and how well Felix had done under the circumstances. I kept quiet, trying to process my life today compared to a week ago. How much had my father known about Patrick? He'd suspected his partner. The woman who triggered our house alarm fit somewhere in the puzzle. She could be working for Patrick. Her appearance in our backyard had to be more than an inconvenient coincidence.

Jazz took my hand, drawing my attention back to him. "We gonna sit down with your mom and hash this out?"

"I think we should. She's the one with the information on the case and the real estate sale." Mom would have a fit when she found out we'd been traipsing through the Everglades after a downed drug plane. Add in the sample cargo we brought back, and I couldn't think of any way she'd be happy about what we'd done.

"You might have to turn in the drugs and let the cops handle it," Frankie interjected from the back seat. "I know you guys want to get the guy for murder but proving he's a slime ball might be tougher than you think. Taking away his prize might be all you can do."

"Except he's already unloading the plane. They've got to be taking the drugs somewhere else," I said. That gave me another idea. "Where could you store a plane load of drugs?"

"You'd need a warehouse—just like the shell companies. Someplace people wouldn't notice a lot of traffic going in and out," Jazz said.

"Somewhere isolated," Frankie agreed.

I shifted around in my seat to see him. "You know what we didn't see? A truck. Some way to get the loads out of there. Where were they taking the drugs in those little trailers?"

"There's gotta be another road," Jazz said.

"Or water access. What if these channels meet up somewhere? Out to the Gulf?"

"How they're getting out of here should be easy enough to figure out," Frankie said. "I sent Felix beyond the borders of the property, south of where we were. I'll go through the camera footage and see what I can find."

"We're gonna get him, Lily. Don't worry about it. He's going down." Jazz squeezed my hand then released me as we merged onto the highway.

While we bumbled around playing detective, Patrick sat in my father's firm, and my family mourned what had been ripped away from us. Vengeance burned in my throat. There was no way I'd allow him to be free for much longer.

We left the truck off at Rand's house, promising to come back later to scrub the Everglades mud from it and the boat. Belle left for home, and we dropped Frankie at his vape store.

"I'll go through Felix's footage and give you a shout when I find something worth shouting about," Frankie promised. "After I drink a gallon of water."

"I'll be right back." Jazz left to help carry the drone and gear inside.

The trek through the woods and finding the treasure trove in the airplane had been exhausting. My muscles ached, and the bug bites I hadn't seen in the jungle peppered my skin with itching red blotches. What a nightmare. I should've been sitting in my final week of AP Calculus class, prepping for finals. *Or maybe I should count and celebrate the blessings I can.* The headmaster had exempted me from my finals based on my father's death and my stellar GPA.

I longed for the simplicity of school, the normalcy of monotonous routines. I'd moved so far past high school in these last ten days as if my time there happened to someone I observed from afar.

Jazz returned from Frankie's, and we sat for a moment in his Jeep, tired, dirty, and back at square one. I had to get out of his car and home to confront my mother and the guillotine of uncertainty hanging over our heads.

"You want me to follow you home?"

"I'm good. Thanks for the chivalry."

"You want to talk about it?"

I studied him—his tousled hair, his mud and sweat-streaked face—and knew I was finished. I more than liked Jason "Jazz" Sumner.

"I do." I took a deep breath, prepared for his answer. "Is there anyone else?"

"No," he said with a decisive shake of his head. "There hasn't been anyone since, you know."

I gaped, my heart grinding to a standstill. "Really?"

He laughed.

"What's so funny?" I asked.

"Nothing. Really. I, ah…I couldn't be with anyone else. You're not only a hot sax player, but you're my best friend, and I fell for you. I was so sorry about that night. We got drunk. I didn't want to kiss you that way and—"

"It was perfect," I told him.

He held my gaze for a long moment before leaning across the car and digging his fingers into my hair. We kissed until I couldn't breathe and didn't care. We drew apart, foreheads touching.

"You're the one I want, Lil. There's not going to be anyone else."

I smiled, tears filling my eyes. "Good. I don't plan on sharing." I kissed him once, a light brush of my lips on his. "I'll text you later.

What time is your stream?"

"Seven-thirty." He played with a loose strand of my hair. "I forgot to tell you. Kellison is back on the table. They'll have a decision for me by the end of the month."

I threw my arms around his neck. "That's awesome! I'm happy for you. I'll be there, I promise."

"Text me, so I know you made it home."

He waved as I slipped out of the car and into mine. When I drove off, he eased into traffic behind me, shadowing me until I merged onto the highway.

Chapter Nineteen

Mom and my sister were waiting for me when I hauled my butt through the back door. I ditched my filthy loaner boots in the garage, but my clothes were a mess. Dried mud smears and scabbed over bug bites covered my arms and legs in a nasty patchwork of ick. I reeked of swamp and sweat. At least Belle had gotten home before me. Maybe Typhoon Mom had subsided.

"Lily?" Mom called from the patio.

Or not.

They sat outside, drinking iced tea. Filthy from head to toe, I removed the cushions from a patio chair and sank onto the metal frame. "Hi," I said. My sister's bemused expression set my teeth on edge.

"Are you both crazy?" Mom didn't waste a second, laying into me. "Do you know what would happen if you got caught in there? To you? Annabelle? Your friends?"

"It's fine, Mom." Exhaustion pressed my back into the chair frame. Even though I expected this lecture, I didn't want to experience the upset we'd caused her.

A furious pallor drained her color. "Your sister said the plane was full of drugs."

I nodded. Uh-oh. Mom wasn't using names. Trouble followed whenever she played the "your" insert-family-connection-here card.

"We're taking this to the police. You're done with your escapades." Mom got up as if to end the conversation.

I threw up my hands. "What are you taking to the police? A package of cocaine? Some pictures of a lost airplane? Telling the cops is gonna make sure Patrick cleans out the plane that much faster."

"She's right," Belle said, her allegiances unreadable. *Way to play both sides, sis.*

"Did I solicit your opinion?" Mom asked her. My sister shrugged as if she didn't care. I was pretty sure she didn't.

"Mom, listen—"

"No, you listen." My mother leveled a finger at my face. "Whatever is going on here cost me my husband. It's not taking my daughters too. End of story."

"I need you to listen to me!" I leapt to my feet, eyes filling with tears, chest heaving. "Tell me again. Who filed the lawsuit about the land?"

"No."

"It's important!"

Her eyes flashed in anger. "An environmental group. A bunch of save the planet types."

"Why, Lily?" My sister edged forward in her seat. "What did you find out after I left?"

Mom's lips compressed into an annoyed line. I'd seen this unconscious reaction in court when I shadowed her for career days. "The property is a nesting ground for alligators and a bird called the piping plover. Both are on the endangered list. They filed an injunction to stop the sale and development of the land. Once the case went to court, the original buyers backed out. That's when Patrick's group made a move."

All of this over a tiny bird and some leftover man-eating dinosaurs. "So Dorminy Holdings tried to buy the land?"

"I don't have anything but a handwritten note in the file. Your father's handwriting. Dorminy offered double the asking price in cash." Mom sank into her chair. "The seller agreed to sell the property behind the group's back, in spite of the injunction."

Raking her fingers through her hair, my sister said, "Because there's a plane worth fifty million dollars sitting in the middle of it. I bet the seller doesn't even know it's there."

"The land is not worth that much. It's nothing but swamp," Mom said.

"Oh, really? We looked it up online. That package Jazz took out of the plane is probably worth close to thirty thousand dollars. Maybe more depending on what's in it."

"You took drugs from the plane?" Mom's face went ashen.

I nodded, confirming my sister's claim. "Plus, we have pictures, video, and drone footage of the area. I have pictures of the plane's call numbers. There was an old news article we read. It's been missing for years after being stolen."

My sister picked at her nails, her face thoughtful. "The problem is, we can't tie Patrick to the plane with honest evidence. It's all circumstantial."

"We need proof he knows about the plane," I told my mother. I scratched a painful bite on my knee and drew blood. "We need to get access to his computer and his phone."

Her eyes widened. "How are we supposed to access his phone?"

"Patrick was a consultant on this case for Dad, right?" Belle asked. "He'll think it weird if you cut him off now. Ask him to meet with you at the office. I might have an idea about how to get him to part with his phone and laptop long enough for us to find what we need."

"How do you plan to do that?" Mom gasped. "You do know all of this is illegal?"

My sister smiled, a chilling, cunning smile. "Leave the details to me."

"Maybe you better switch to CIA instead of the FBI," I told her. "You're scary." I rubbed away a mud drop on my arm. "I'm going to shower."

Scrubbing the swamp off my skin and out of my hair, I smiled at the bites, badges of our adventure in the jungle. After I toweled dry and treated my bites with anti-itch cream, I followed the scent of lemons and garlic toward the grill. Mom had chicken and shrimp grilling in her special marinade. She'd been destroyed after being released from jail—drained, exhausted, and grief-stricken—not like this tanned woman in cutoff jean shorts and a ponytail.

If nothing else, our family investigation provided all of us with something to take our minds off the overwhelming sadness weighing down on the house.

I took down plates from the cabinet, startled when I grabbed four instead of three. With trembling fingers, I set Dad's plate back on the shelf, my throat thick with tears. How long would it take to come to terms with his absence? The rest of my life, I supposed.

I hadn't had time to grieve properly. Not the way regular people did. Family members died of cancer. Heart attacks. A million other ways to die that gave closure and an assurance maybe a loved one was at peace.

Where was our peace? Grief nailed me in the chest with a mighty fist. I blew out a breath as I gathered napkins and silverware. Mom didn't need me falling apart over a dish. Not when she was just getting herself together.

While we filled our plates with grilled vegetables, salad, and shrimp, my mother informed us she had scheduled a meeting with Patrick for tomorrow at eight.

"In the conference room, before the new secretary arrives. I hired a temp to fill Monica's position." She poured a glass of iced tea with a shaking hand. I understood how she felt. We had to find out what Patrick knew, but were afraid to at the same time. "I don't like this idea.

There's a lot that can go wrong." Mom directed her comment at my sister, not me.

"Like what? He gets pissed and quits? To me? Probably the best thing." Belle skewered another shrimp.

Mom's phone vibrated, and she scanned the screen. "It's Liz. I have to take this." She got up and retreated to the other side of the pool. Her eyes focused on the water while she listened.

"What do you think the call's about?" I whispered.

Behind dark sunglasses, Belle studied our mother. "I don't know. She doesn't seem happy—it's a pretty serious conversation. You'd think she'd talk to her lawyer here, in front of us. It's not like we don't know what's going on."

"Maybe it's firm business," I offered, even though I didn't believe it.

The way my mother stood, resolutely beside the pool, told me this call was not casual or business-related. This had something to do with my father, the murder, or my mother's incarceration. Maybe all three.

"Hmmm. Don't think so." Belle's observations mirrored my thoughts. "There's more to it."

"I wonder how much she's told Liz."

"About our suspicions? Not much I'd guess, or Liz would have been back over here to rip into us for taking matters into our own hands. And with all the suspicion in the office? Just enough to make sure her name is cleared."

Mom ended the call and stared at the face of her phone.

"What do you think?" I whispered.

"Got me," Belle said.

Several minutes passed before our mother shifted back in our direction.

"Everything okay?" I asked.

She made a rude sound. "No."

My sister removed her sunglasses and set them on the table. "What's wrong?"

"An investigation into the Harmony Firm. Something to do with misappropriating trust funds. I don't understand it." Mom's face had drained of color. "We've always been careful. We never take chances with client money."

"What trust funds?" I tried to imagine another massive stress thrown on top of what she had already suffered. We couldn't catch a break.

She laid her phone on the table. "We have several trusts we

manage. Some small, some very large like the one in question. It had over a hundred million dollars in it."

My eyes went wide. "Had?"

"Yes. Twenty-five million is missing."

I gasped—my brain unable to comprehend that kind of cash.

"Who had access to it?" Belle asked.

"I can see the investigator's wheels spinning in your brain," I said.

"Who Mom?"

Mom paused before answering. "Your father."

We sat in stunned silence for a full minute. My body was paralyzed, my thoughts in chaos. "Dad didn't take the money."

She waved a hand in the air. "I know. I'm not suggesting—" her voice caught, and she struggled to compose herself. "What I mean is your dad had the account numbers and the access codes. Those were in his office, on his laptop. Someone would have to get to the computer to get those codes."

"We have the laptop here," I reminded her.

But we hadn't taken the computer until the day after Dad died. Who had been in his office? The cops and the forensics people. Whoever took those codes did it when he wasn't there.

"Mom, do you know when the transfer took place?" Belle asked.

"Three days before," Mom trailed off, her voice thick with unshed tears.

I figured out what she meant. By the scowl on my sister's face, so did she. Someone had been in there before he died. Maybe Dad had known about the theft. Could the information be another slice of motive stacked on top of the drug plane sitting in the jungle?

"Son of bitch. We wondered where Patrick got the money to make the offer." My sister jumped up. "All he'd have to do is transfer it out of the trust to one of his shell companies." She paced toward the pool, her gaze fixed on the sparkling water. "Follow the money. Isn't that what they always say? We need to know where the money went."

"Liz said it's untraceable. The money left the account and disappeared." Mom wiped her eyes on a tissue she removed from her pocket. "If we don't discover what happened to the trust, the firm will be liable for the missing funds. A financial loss like this will ruin us. Our insurance won't cover a theft this big, even if we add in Dad's life insurance. We'll have to liquidate." Her gaze drifted over the house, the pool.

Anger flooded my veins. The layers of deception, the misleading and twisted plots peeled apart like an onion. "The theft makes total sense.

Don't you see? If they shut down the firm, everybody stops trying to find the murderer. The news would report how Dad stole the money. No one will care about anything else."

Everything had been carefully orchestrated. The theft, the companies, the land, Dad. No loose ends. If one tragedy didn't cripple the firm's ability to pursue the real estate case, another would.

"We're running out of time." My sister tapped her finger on the table. "If we don't get enough on Patrick soon, we're going to be finished."

"Then we have to make sure we get what we need tomorrow." Mom used her hands to push up from the table, exhaustion bruising the skin beneath her eyes. "Can you girls handle the dishes? I've got one hell of a migraine." She ripped the elastic out of her hair and massaged her temple. The carefree look was gone, the haunted look etched on her face as if someone had drawn a dark curtain over her brief peace.

"Belle and I will clean up," I promised as she went into the house. My heart hurt for her. How much should one person have to bear? Patrick would get his if it was the last thing I did.

"We need to find out how to bypass his laptop security. Can your friend with the drone help us?" She stacked the used plates as I switched off the gas to the grill. "We're going to get one chance to do this."

The "how" had been on my mind ever since Mom mentioned the trust theft. If Frankie didn't know how to break into Patrick's laptop, my guess was he would know someone who did. "I'm going to watch the end of Jazz's stream. After he's finished, I'll ask him what he thinks. There's got to be a way."

"If not, we're going to let everything Dad and Mom worked for get taken away. She might end up losing her law license on top of getting sued." The implications of what might happen hung in the air like a murky, twisted peril waiting for one of us to drop our guard.

"Belle, why would someone do this to us? To Mom and Dad? What did they ever do to deserve this?" The picture of Mom and Patrick floated up to the surface of my mind.

If Dad hadn't been killed, seeing the horrible kissing photograph would have devastated him. Even though they fought, I knew my parents were in love—they had been since high school. I trembled at the thought of what the kiss would have done to him. But I wasn't sure destroying their marriage had been the objective.

Belle must have seen the shock on my face. "What? What are you thinking?"

"I don't know, it's crazy. But think about this for a minute. What if the law firm was always the target? After everything we've learned?

The pictures were from months ago. Dad's murder seems almost random unless you look deeper. Now the missing money and this messed up case. What if taking apart Harmony and Harmony piece by piece was always the goal, to stop the real estate case? If the environmental group lost their lawyer in a huge money scandal, wouldn't that have made it easier to sell the land while they regrouped? It's all about the land, Belle. Destroying Harmony and Harmony might have been the goal all along."

She drew back her shoulders. "We need to get that bastard's laptop tomorrow."

"Let me talk to Jazz. I'll meet you outside after. Like ten o'clock."

"Okay."

I hurried back to my room in time to catch the last half hour of Jazz's stream. Every view and subscriber counted now, the closer he got to signing with Kellison. The corner of his mouth edged up when I appeared in his feed. I settled back against the pillows, letting my mind drift and sift through the information we had and the questions we needed answered.

When he signed off, my phone vibrated. "Hey," I said, delighted to hear him. "You had a nice run going there."

"Thanks." He sounded tired. "I had to battle back from an early upset. What's going on with you? Anything new?"

I hesitated, trying to decide the best way to tell him about the missing trust money. When I finished my story, he let out a low whistle. "Holy shit. The hits just keep coming. What's next? An earthquake?"

"I'm standing on quicksand," I told him, longing for his arms and his closeness. "We need to hack into Patrick's computer tomorrow. You have any ideas about how to bypass a password?"

"I might have a few tricks up my sleeve. But I'll also consult with a professional."

"Frankie?" I asked with a smile.

"My sources are nameless," he said with a chuckle. "What time does the fun start?"

"Eight tomorrow. At the law firm."

"Great. Sounds like a good time. You buying the coffee?"

"Don't I always?"

He laughed, stifling a yawn. "Yes, you do. Man, the fresh air today tired me out. I'm gonna crash. Talk to you in the morning?"

"Yep. Oh, park on the roof of the garage. We don't want Patrick to see strange cars. He might suspect something's up."

"Okay. See you then."

I smiled into the phone before ending the call. If nothing else,

I'd get to spend another day with Jazz, and time with him was worth all the iced mochas in the world. I got up to tell Belle the news.

Chapter Twenty

At seven-thirty the next morning, we took up residence in Monica's office pretending to file. I feigned competence better than my sister since I had so much practice over the last six weeks of Saturdays. I picked up a letter opener and sliced through envelopes. Belle sorted documents by case file and searched the filing system for anything suspect. Every few minutes one of us would either glance at the time or the door, waiting for our prey to arrive.

We'd gone over our plan a dozen times in the car on the way over, making sure Mom stayed in the dark on the details. Her surprise was necessary to prove her innocence. Every moment in this charade, we needed to remember we were dealing with lawyers—masters at reading people and their motivations. What we planned required flawless execution and complete shock on our mother's part.

"He's here," Belle whispered out of the side of her mouth without glancing up from the file drawers. I handed her a stack of correspondence and slashed an envelope with excessive force, my senses on high alert.

When he paused in the office doorway, my fingers clenched around the letter opener.

"Lily! I'm glad you're here. And Annabelle too."

"Hey," she growled. I shot her a look that said *cool it*.

"Hi, Mr. Malvern," I said with my brightest smile.

He hefted his laptop bag over his shoulder, and my heart pounded a ragged rhythm. I needed what was in his bag. Three minutes search-time had been Frankie's promise when we told him about our plan.

Patrick wore a dark suit with a pale blue tie and white shirt, accompanied with his customary scowl fixed in place. I tried to guess his age and settled on late forties. He never appeared rumpled, not even in the south Florida heat.

He waved a hand at our piles of briefs and correspondence. "You seem to know what you're doing. Maybe you could help me out? My…ah…secretary has taken another position. We're in dire straits here for office help." When neither of us said anything, he added, "I'll gladly pay you."

Maybe our shock and awe plan wouldn't be necessary after all. Not if he gave me carte blanche access to his office. I swallowed, controlling the nervous flutter in my throat. "Sure. I'm here for a couple of hours. What can I do for you?" I flinched as my sister slammed a file drawer.

"I have a pile of filing and lots of documents to be printed from email and sorted out. And a couple of briefs," he said ticking the items off his fingers. His gaze drifted to a seething Belle. "I could use your help too. Especially with your law background. Do you have time?"

She grimaced as if she might swallow her tongue and replied, "Sure. We're here all day. Whatever we can do to help."

"Great." He glanced at his smart watch. "I'm going to be late for the meeting with your mother. Can one of you tell her I'm here? I have messages to deal with." He flapped a hand dismissing me.

"Sure," I said.

He left without waiting for my reply. As soon as he disappeared, my sister let out a brilliant string of obscenities.

"I'm surprised you held that in," I said, smirking.

"My tongue is bleeding from biting holes in it. Go tell Mom. Change of plans. She just has to keep him busy." She shook her head. "Is he really so fricking stupid?"

"Apparently." My phone buzzed as I hurried back toward my mother's office. Jazz telling me he had arrived. Our plan included him checking out the roof to search for signs someone had used the top floor to access the balcony. Dropping over the side of the roof was the only way we could surmise the murderer had gotten in and out undetected.

I texted him the change in our plan and stepped into my mother's office. She stood at the windows, staring out at the ocean a block away. I recognized her stance. With her chin up, and her shoulders set, she prepped for her performance with Patrick—while knowing someone had seen them kissing in Washington—and knowing he most likely had my father killed over the case he planned to consult on. But when the time came, Mom's lawyer façade would slam down over her emotions making her impervious to the tempest of suspicions swirling in the office.

"Mom, he's here. He said to let you know he's checking his emails." In contrast to Patrick's subdued gray and powder blue ensemble, my mother had worn a red jacket over black linen pants. She'd always told me dressing was about power, and her choice was as intentional as her mask.

"Good. Let's get this over with." She picked up a stack of files. "Tell him to meet me in the conference room when he's through."

"Okay but wait—there's more. He asked me to work for him today. In his office."

She froze, eyes wide. "Doing what?"

"Filing. Printing out emails. Scanning things." My steady tone concealed the excitement building in my chest. If this was going to work without Patrick becoming suspicious, schooling my emotions as my mother had was essential.

She lowered her body into her chair. "Well. This is an unexpected opportunity."

"Yes. I'm meeting him now to see what he wants me to do."

Her eyes met mine, and the mask trembled for a split second. "Be careful. Keep Belle close."

"I will."

My sister waited for me. She drew me deeper into the office. "We need to get his work done so he doesn't suspect. If he takes his laptop to the meeting we're screwed."

"We make sure that doesn't happen." Frankie provided information about bypassing security, and I felt confident I could hack into the secretary's old password. What if I used it in reverse and locked his desk computer sign on screen? Would he leave me his laptop? I'd have precious time to make our ruse work. "I'll need you to distract him when we get in there. Ask him as many law questions as you can. Ask his advice, ask him out, I don't care what you do."

Her brows drew down. "I'm pretty sure I can handle a simple distraction."

"Good. Let's go."

I knocked on his door. Patrick sat at his desk in front of his laptop. Sweat drenched my palms. "Mom's ready when you are. She's in the conference room."

He nodded. "Okay, thanks. Um...if you girls are ready, I can show you what I'm talking about."

From his desk, he handed us at least a dozen files, a stack of unopened mail including overnight packages, and directed us to the overflowing fax machine. "I'm drowning here. I have these cases to deal with, and there's got to be two hundred emails with attachments to download, print, and store in the electronic files."

The piles of filing were worse than what Monica had left behind before her maternity leave. In truth, losing his secretary didn't appear to be much of a loss. Old files had been stacked on most flat surfaces and more mail filled a wicker basket on the corner of his desk. "Okay. Should I use the computer over there?"

"Yeah," he said. "Fire it up, and I'll show you where to find the emails."

I hurried over to the machine and gave Belle time to chat him up about one of the case files. To her credit, she hid her burning hatred of the lawyer well.

Booting up the computer, I waited for the sign on screen to appear then followed Jazz's directions to lock the screen through the guest account. Easy.

Today was not going to be Patrick's day. "Uh, Mr. Malvern? It says this computer is locked. By someone named Carol?" Blaming the absent secretary might be the easiest plan.

"Son of a..." He ran a hand over his hair.

"Is Carol your assistant?"

"Was." His nostrils flared in a huff, and his face flushed scarlet. "How the hell are we going to fix it?"

"Why don't we call the guy who does the IT work at the house?" Belle offered. She fought to control her smile.

Patrick made his decision. "Okay. I'll leave my laptop here." He signed in and accessed his law firm email account. "This is what I need you to do. All of these with attachments, here. Download, print, and then send each one to the correct digital file. Can you do this?" His gaze hopefully searched mine.

"Sure, no sweat. Do you have a list of file numbers?" My father and mother kept lists of their electronic case numbers to make jobs such as this one easier.

He unlocked his desk, an unexpected bonus. "Yes." He withdrew a file and laid it on the desk blotter. "You should find everything in here. If not, just keep a list, and we'll figure it out after I meet with your mom." Patrick glanced at his watch. "I better get in there before she comes looking for me." He went to a filing cabinet and removed a thick file. I made a mental note of the drawer and section where he'd taken it from.

"We've got this," my sister assured him.

"Thanks. I appreciate the help." He dashed out the door and down the hall.

She fist-pumped the air. "And so do we. Where's the case file list?"

My belief in his guilt swayed a fraction. "Don't you think it's odd for a guilty man to grant us full access?"

"No one ever said he was smart," Belle said.

I opened the file with greedy fingers. "It's alphabetical, at least." I ran my finger down the first page of a ten-page list. Nothing. Flipping the page, I gestured toward the laptop with my chin. "See what you can find while I go through the lists."

She dove into the computer files. "Here. This is the case number. 2020-4-75136." She wrote it down on a sticky note.

I leapt up and grabbed the faxes, sorting them alphabetically by client.

"What are you doing?" she asked, confused.

"We've gotta make this look good right?" I took the basket of faxes to his conference table and made neat piles. There were dozens of briefs and continuances, some going back well over a month. Patrick was in trouble. His secretary hadn't done anything in weeks, so a question loomed. If not doing his secretarial work, what had she been doing at the firm?

A pang of unease raised the hair on the back of my neck. We knew nothing about this Carol. Or Monica besides what she revealed working in the office. Both had unlimited access to the firm's clients, cases, and systems. And the person taking pictures of our house had been female. "What do you think about Carol? She left one hell of a mess."

"I would have fired her." Belle stopped me with news of her own. "Here. This is the file from the drone company including the drone pictures we've seen, but not the one with the plane visible."

"I wonder why the picture with the wing isn't here. If you ask me, Carol's departure is convenient and seems to coincide with the investigation into the trust theft. Let's get a copy of this file and the pics to Frankie. Maybe it's been altered." I glanced over her shoulder. "Anything else? Any evidence he's been at the crash site?"

"I don't see anything. There are no extra pictures on the hard drive or in his cloud storage," she said. "It doesn't appear he has anything he shouldn't have."

"So how did he find out about the plane?"

"What plane?" Patrick asked from the doorway.

She didn't miss a beat as she closed the window, leaving the email scans up behind it. "My Dad's plane. There might be someone interested in buying it."

I sucked in a shaky breath, stunned by her swift cover and more than awestruck.

"She's a beauty." Patrick agreed with our make-believe conversation. "I wish I'd learned how to fly. I'd take it off your hands in a flash. Your dad took me up once, did you know?" His jaw set when he mentioned my father. My hackles rose on a gust of suspicion. "How are you making out?"

Suppressing my dislike for him, I motioned to the sorted faxes on the conference table. "Those are sorted by case number. I have to scan them in, then file them."

"I'm downloading the email attachments. I'm about half done." She typed and clicked like mad. "We called our tech guy. He can't be here until later this afternoon."

Patrick observed my work on the table and actually cracked a smile. "Wow! Looks great. Tech support will work for me—make sure he leaves a bill. I've got a hearing this afternoon. I appreciate you girls handling this disaster." He removed his wallet from his inside jacket pocket and peeled off three hundred-dollar bills. "Consider this a down payment. If you can come back this week and get your tech guy to unlock this computer, I'll give you each another three hundred on Friday."

"Thanks," I said, astounded at the kind of money he'd pay for filing and sorting.

"You girls are lifesavers. I'm heading over to the courthouse. I'll be back in an hour or so." He left with a wave.

We stared at each other. "What the hell just happened?" she murmured.

"This doesn't make any sense. He's not worried about us in here with his computer or his files. He's left us to do what we want. He's sure not acting guilty." My thoughts and emotions churned like the angry Gulf under a tropical storm—frothy and without direction.

"What about the picture with Mom? He's guilty," she snapped.

"I agree. But what about the plane? If he were hiding something, why would he pay us to be in here with full access?"

She said nothing as she faced the laptop and returned to the hidden tab. "Because he had nothing to do with it," she said, her tone glum. "Look at this."

I hurried around the side of the desk. "He sent Mom and Dad an email? Telling them he believed the drone company was withholding information?"

"Apparently."

"Or is the email to cover his butt?"

She slouched in her chair. "Doesn't matter. We're not any closer to figuring this out or what he was doing kissing Mom." She glanced up at me. "Have you heard from Jazz?"

I'd forgotten about the second part of our investigation, the one occurring upstairs. "Let's go for a walk." We found him on the roof, peering over the side of the building. My father's balcony sat directly below.

"Hey," he said when he saw us. "How are you two making out?'

"Better and worse than we expected," she told him.

At his confused reaction, I explained, "Patrick asked us to work for him. His secretary quit."

"Well that's handy."

I chuckled. Jazz's sarcasm was my normal in a life full of crazy. "And so far, it looks like he might not be our guy."

"Why? What happened?"

"There's nothing here," Belle grumbled. "Not one shred of incriminating evidence."

"Did you find anything?" I asked.

His smile widened. "Yeah. Check this out." He waved us over to the edge of the roof. "You see this black mark here? Something was set here, maybe to protect a rope from this sharp edge."

"Could be a rubber scuff. Like from a tire." Belle studied the black marks.

"Right. And over here," he said as he led us to the flagpole. "They tied it off here." Jazz dug a hand into his pocket. "It's a carbineer clip."

"Like from a climber?" I asked.

"I think so. Had to be someone with experience going over the edge of the roof. I found this at the top of the fire escape. Someone must have dropped it as they left." He handed the clip to me. I took a shallow breath. The person who killed my father had dropped this—I was sure of it.

"Is there anyone who works here who climbs? Belongs to a gym, maybe?"

I gave the clip back and wiped my hand on my shorts. "Mom never mentioned it. Liz is a runner—she's always doing half marathons. I don't know what Patrick does."

"He has a used golf ball sitting on his desk," Belle noted.

Her perceptive skills stunned me again. "How did you notice that?"

"It's what I do," she said.

"Doesn't sound like he's climbing anything but the hills at the golf course," Jazz said.

I threw up my hands. "What is with the freaking dead ends? Why can't we find a piece that fits?"

"We're closer than we were before," my sister said without enthusiasm. "And the cops are working this angle too. See?" Bright blue marks were painted near the scuff. "The cops did this. They know what's going on. They're just not telling us." Her expression was laced with the same frustration burning in my chest. Our prime suspect was shaky.

Belle left to bring our mother up to speed, while Jazz and I went back to Patrick's office. I took a stack of faxes to the filing cabinet and rapidly filed what I could. One thing I picked up about him—he was organized when he had good help. No wonder he freaked out about the condition of his office. The man was all about one-inch margins and dotting his I's.

Maybe we *were* hunting in the wrong place.

When my sister came back, I asked, "Do you remember when those drone pictures were taken?"

She pulled up the information on the computer. "March 19th. Why?"

"When did Patrick hire Carol? His secretary?"

"February 2nd," she said, straightening. "No kidding."

My emotions flipped like I crested the big hill on Space Mountain. "Maybe we should check into the mysterious, vanishing secretary."

"The timeline fits," Jazz said. "Write down what you have on her. I'll go over to Frankie's and see what we can run down."

"Thank you," I told him.

Jazz crossed the room and drew me into his arms. "Don't give up, okay? We still have some angles to play here."

"Okay. Text me if you find something."

"What will you be doing?"

I waved my hand over the piles of paperwork. "Working for a living."

He kissed me before leaving.

"I don't like this," Belle grumbled. "We were so sure he was dirty."

"It doesn't mean anything," I pointed out. "We're digging. And now, we have access to his files."

"What's wrong?" she asked, her eyes on mine.

I couldn't hide the distress I felt—not from my sister. "Access doesn't mean anything if Patrick isn't the killer."

"This secretary worries me. I admit, her departure was oddly timed." She pursed her lips, studying the abandoned desk in the corner. "I wonder if she left anything behind."

"Did you finish those downloads?"

"Of course not. I don't want his money."

Regardless of his involvement in my father's death, he'd drugged Mom, kissed her, exposed her to blackmail. "It doesn't matter if you want his cash or not. We need to make this look good."

"Fine." She ripped a file off the desk and slammed it into the cabinet drawer.

"It helps if you put it in the right place," I told her between my clenched teeth.

With a sigh, my sister relented.

An hour later, we'd finished most of the filing. My phone vibrated in my pocket. I swiped a finger over the screen to see a text from Jazz. "They've got something."

Chapter Twenty-One

We left my mother on a multi-hour conference call, promising to catch her up after dinner. I drove toward the beach and the vape shop. My sister stared out the window, quiet on the drive—so not Belle. Finally, when even retro Imagine Dragons couldn't bridge the gap between us, I asked her what was bothering her.

"It's just this whole thing." She lowered the volume on the radio. "After seeing the picture of Patrick with Mom, I wanted him to be the one." Her breath exhaled on a hiss. "I wanted him to suffer. Now that doesn't look like it's going to happen."

I took a left onto Estero Drive and drove past The Whale. A bustling, late afternoon crowd gathered on the upper deck, and music filtered through the car windows. So innocent. We'd been innocent the night we waited for the fisherman.

"We didn't have all the information. Only part of it," I reminded her.

"Yeah. The part that made him look damn guilty." She smacked her fist against the dashboard. "Now what do we have?"

"We'll find out soon enough." I parked the car in the lot then after we got out, I led her around to the back entrance.

"This is an interesting place. Who'd think a hacker would hang here?"

"Are you kidding?" I gestured to the faded beach balls hanging in the windows. "How cliché can you get?"

"I guess you've got a point." We laughed as we entered the dim shop. She shadowed me through the now familiar maze to Frankie's lair.

When he saw us, Jazz approached and took my hand, dragging me over to a central screen. "You need to check this out."

"What's this?" Belle studied the website on the screen. "Isn't this the drone company?"

Frankie nodded from his chair. Today he wore a neon orange

shirt and khaki shorts like he should be holding a stop sign on a road work crew. "You bet it is. And guess what Patrick's secretary's maiden name was?"

I stared at them, waiting for the punch line. "I don't know…"

"Friedman!" the boys shouted in unison.

"You're sure?" my sister asked.

"Positive," Frankie said. "Check this out. Her picture's even on the website."

We stared at Carol Friedman Orson's picture, listed as co-owner of the company with her brothers Alan and Connor Friedman. My heart stopped. "His face is familiar," I said. "This Alan Friedman guy."

"Who?" Belle squinted at the screen.

"You think so?" Jazz asked.

I took out my phone and showed her the fuzzy picture of the man. "It might be him. The guy who tailed us in Fort Myers. On the beach."

Alan Friedman's smiling face filled the screen. "This is nuts," Jazz murmured. "So, what is she doing working in a law office as a secretary if she owns this big drone survey company? The website says they work with FEMA after hurricanes to survey the damage. Drone surveying is a big deal." He paged through the company information on one of the smaller screens.

"And what's he doing stalking us?"

Belle folded her arms across her chest. "She wasn't there for the paycheck. She must have seen the drone footage. Maybe she wanted to know what Patrick and the firm knew about what was on the property?"

"It doesn't add up. There has to be another reason for taking the job."

"We need to talk to Mom. Maybe she can come up with a viable theory. Something we haven't considered." She paused, thoughtful. "I wonder what Patrick had to say in their meeting this morning."

I removed my phone from my pocket to text my mother. She answered quickly. "Uh, well. Asking her is gonna wait. Liz is picking her up and they're going to dinner. She said they have things to discuss."

"That can't be good." Belle groaned. "I feel so bad for her."

"Why? What's wrong?" Frankie asked.

"The firm has some other issues. There's a bunch of trust fund money missing. We thought we would find something on Patrick's computer, but there wasn't anything incriminating," she said.

"We're missing something." Frustration made my chest tight. "I just wish I knew what."

Jazz tugged me toward him, his hands on my shoulders. "We'll figure this out. Maybe not today, but we will."

I smiled into his face, wishing I could catch some of his enthusiasm. "You're right," I lied, not believing the words. "But we're out of time."

"Hey, wait a minute." Frankie dropped a new page onto the middle screen. "Friedman got sued last year. Big time. Check out this news article."

My sister moved in closer to the screen. "They were working on new technology, and someone said they violated a patent. This is big time trouble. They could be on the hook for millions. According to this, they were going to lose."

"Drones are big business and innovation is guarded technology. Like state secrets," Frankie told us. "There's a ton of companies out there trying to be the next big thing."

Jazz nodded. "And Friedman wanted to be the next thing by stealing someone else's tech."

"Here's another article, a couple of months later. Friedman filed for bankruptcy. This company is in big trouble." She gestured to the screen.

"When was the article written?" I asked as the gears in our investigation turned in sync.

She smiled, triumphant. "December of last year. Right before Patrick ordered the drone survey. Carol applied for the job at the end of January and started in February. By then, Friedman would have known about the plane and edited out the pictures that showed the wing sticking out of the jungle."

"Dad became suspicious and hired the fisherman," I said, thinking the timeline through out loud.

"And the fisherman saw the real drone picture, somehow," she finished with a triumphant *whoop whoop*.

Exuberant, Jazz high-fived me. "Looks like we have the connection."

"Now we need to get the police to believe your story," Frankie said.

"A Herculean task, for sure." Connecting the dots made me feel better than I had in days, but a worry tickled the back of my mind. A missing link still eluded us. What was it?

"What? Is there a problem with the logic?" A disheartened frown tugged at my sister's mouth.

"No," I said. "But Patrick had something to do with this and the picture." I struggled to make sense of the pile of damning evidence we'd collected. "Think about it, Belle. How did the picture of Mom happen? I mean, the setup."

"Patrick drugged her," she snapped. Rage flashed in her eyes—a banked inferno ready to erupt.

"But why?" I asked. "It's not like he was taking a selfie when he kissed her. And he doesn't seem to have any interest in her now."

She took a step closer to me. "Are you defending him? After what's been done?"

"Take it easy," Frankie said, calling time out with his hands. "She's processing. Let's see where this goes."

"Think," I said as my idea coalesced into a theory. "Why would he do it? Would sleeping with Mom be worth losing his place in the firm? Not if he knew about the plane."

My sister stared at me as if working out the problems in her own mind. The grimace on her face told me she didn't like not hating Patrick. But something about the entire situation screamed *set up.*

"Who took the picture?" I asked.

The room got very quiet.

"Dad didn't hire the fisherman until April. The conference was before then. All along, we assumed he took the picture. But he couldn't have. He found it somewhere else and planned to pass it to Dad."

She swore, and I echoed her with one of my own.

"We're hunting for someone else." Frankie groaned. "When will it end?"

"I bet Carol Friedman could fill in the blanks. We need to talk to Mom," I said. "This can't wait." I picked up my phone and texted my mother and waited. Five minutes gone. Ten dragged into twenty.

A tremor of unease filtered into my composure as the time expired on our family five-minute text rule. Five-minute reply to texts. No questions asked. At least we'd always know a follow-up would come. But my phone remained silent.

"I don't like this," I said, dread filling my gut.

"Where were they going to dinner?" Jazz asked.

"She didn't say."

"I'm sure she's okay," he said. "Liz isn't going to let anything happen to her."

Belle grabbed the car keys from my hand. "Let's go home. Maybe she forgot her phone when she left to meet Liz?"

I nodded, humoring her. But deep down, I didn't believe Mom forgot her phone. She'd never be so careless at a time like this. And with the way things had been going in this family? I followed my sister out with Jazz on my heels.

He squeezed my hand. "I promised to help Frankie with a server install. Call me when you find her. We'll figure out the next step with her. It's gonna be okay."

"I know," I said with a half-hearted smile. Mom's text silence was deafening.

Worse than the lack of reply, her car sat in the driveway when we arrived home. Belle leapt out as soon as I put the car in park and rushed over to the car. She tried the handle with the edge of her tank top covering her fingers.

"What are you doing," I asked.

"Preserving prints—haven't we learned our lesson? It's locked. Her purse is on the seat."

"Mom always keeps her phone in the cradle," I said, fear swirling in my brain.

"It's not there," she said.

"If she has it, she would have texted me back."

"Pull up the app for the security cameras."

I glanced at the camera mounted on the front of the garage. Wherever Mom had gone, she'd been caught on video. My fingers flew over my phone screen.

"Come on. Do you have it?" She paced from the car back to me.

"Almost. Hang on a sec." The video popped up. "Here. We need to go backward. How long?" I checked the time on my mother's text about going to dinner.

"I don't know. A couple of hours, maybe. Can we watch it as it rewinds? We can see when she got home."

"Okay," I said.

"Can you please hold it steady?"

"I can't help it. My hand is shaking." The frames whipped by until my mother's car appeared on screen.

"Stop. Okay. Play it from there." Belle studied the screen. "See? Right there."

Mom parked her car and removed her phone from the cradle as if she were searching for something on the screen or reading a text.

"That had to be when she texted us about going to dinner," I said. On the video, a second car drove in behind her. Mom glanced in her rear-view mirror and got out of the car. She waved at the driver. "Belle, do you see that?" The driver leaned out of the car and waved back.

"It's Liz," she whispered. "They were going to dinner."

Mom walked toward the SUV and the driver's window. She didn't seem worried or upset as she dropped her phone into her suit jacket pocket. They spoke for less than ten seconds before the back door of the SUV flew open. A man leapt out, grabbed Mom, then threw her into the back. Liz had the car in reverse before the man had a chance to shut his door.

"Mom," I whispered. "Belle... Call the police! We have to get her back!"

She took out her phone to make the call but froze as she stared at the screen. "Lily, look." My sister showed me the text message.

A picture of our mother, bound and gagged, sitting on the floor of a boat. A second text chimed into her inbox. "No cops," she read.

"What are we going to do?"

"Whatever it takes to get her back," she said, typing a reply. "What do they want?"

We waited, huddled together over the phone.

Bring the package and all evidence
Port Sanibel Marina sunset

"What do we do?" I asked her the same question but now with more dire circumstances.

She stared into the distance like she always did when the wheels of her mind worked overtime. "Call Jazz. Tell him we need the package we took from the plane. We'll pick it up on the way."

"We don't have a lot of time," I said, my gaze lifted to the sky. The sunbeams grew longer as the sun drifted toward the horizon.

"Come on." She rushed into the house.

I followed, my heart thudding in my throat.

"Go change. T-shirts, jeans, sneakers. We need to be ready for anything."

"Okay," I said with more conviction than I felt. "What if we call Stephens? Don't you think someone should be there? Backing us up?"

She gripped my arm, her face intense and steady. "They'll kill her, Lil. You know they will. We don't have any choice." Her words cracked on the last syllable. "I'm not ready to be an orphan."

"Me neither."

"Call Jazz. Hurry!"

I dashed into my room my vision blurred by tears. How had this happened? How had our lives been so upended? I was at the center of a maelstrom, clinging to the edge of my childhood by my fingertips. My family didn't deserve this, not for money, not for a load of lost drugs. Knowing where the plane had crashed made us liabilities, just like our mother. And what about Jazz? And Frankie? Did our investigation put targets on their backs too?

According to the time on my phone, Jazz was in the middle of a stream, but it couldn't be helped. I texted him with shaking fingers. *9-1-1 at Frankie's. Bring the backpack.*

His response was immediate. *I'LL BE THERE.*

God, I didn't want to involve him anymore. What if my friends got hurt because of my messed-up family business? I couldn't bear losing anyone else.

I yanked on jeans and a black T-shirt then slipped my feet into a pair of Adidas. Belle would make a great FBI agent if we survived the night. She had great instincts and a practical sense of what needed to be done. I had methodical logic on my side and not enough bravery.

But our combined talents would have to do.

She stood in the dining room, a backpack over her shoulder and the envelope of photos in her hand. "These are meaningless. They don't know about the drive, and that gives us leverage. Frankie has it. We have scans of all of this. They're getting pieces of paper."

"You think that's enough?" I asked, unsure. "Do we give away the fact other people know about this?"

Her gaze hardened. "They'd be stupid to not believe we didn't involve others since they know we've been to the plane."

"Hopefully their fear is enough to keep us alive." I didn't say what was on my mind—the one way they would know we've been to the plane was if Mom told them. What had they done to her to get that information if she did?

"You have that cop's cellphone number?"

Our gazes met. "Yeah. You want me to call him?"

"Not yet. When we park at the marina. We send him the video of the kidnapping and the texts. Have him bring in the cavalry behind us."

"I'd feel better knowing they were coming," I admitted.

We locked the doors before setting the alarm system on the way out. "You get in touch with Jazz?" she asked.

"Yeah. He's meeting us at the vape shop with the package from the plane."

She yanked me into a fierce hug next to the car. We clung together for several seconds. "I'm sorry, Lily. I should never have blamed you for Mom and Dad's problems. None of it was your fault."

I stepped back, amazed by her sudden affection. When this was over, maybe we would be friends. I'd like that. "Thanks," I said.

My sister smiled and touched my cheek. "We need to get in and out. Take the package and leave. You can't tell Jazz what's happening. You hear me? We don't need anyone else involved."

The truth sat on the tip of my tongue to tell her they were already involved, but I relented...for now.

Chapter Twenty-Two

We made it to Frankie's in record time. Jazz waited for Belle and me in the parking lot next to his Jeep. As soon as I got out of the car, I hurled myself into his arms and locked my teeth together to keep the ugly truth from spilling out into the light.

"What the hell is going on?" He drew back and studied my face.

I'd stopped crying a couple of blocks from the house, but now the treacherous emotions screaming for release opened the dam of terror.

"What's wrong?"

"We need what you took from the plane," Belle told him, her tone brooking no argument. "We need it now."

"What's happened?"

"Jazz," I said, laying a hand on his chest. His heart beat against my palm, a steady rhythm of comfort, a port in the storm. "Please. We need it."

He jammed his hands in his pockets. "Not until you tell me what's happened."

Belle pulled her gun from under her shirt and leveled it at him.

To his credit, he stood his ground as I gasped, "What are you doing? You said we should keep this quiet."

"I changed my mind." She gestured with her chin toward the door, her gaze cool, calculating. "Let's go inside. We don't have time to screw around."

I stepped between them. "Put it away, Belle."

"Move," she commanded, her hand steady.

This was the future Agent Harmony in action. I'd never been so terrified of my sister.

"Come on." He gripped my hand and led me toward the store.

Inside, we made our way through the office and into Franke's domain. The odor of pot tickled my nose.

"Frank?" Jazz called.

"'Sup," came the reply. The pot-glazed hacker waltzed into the room and stopped in his tracks. "What the hell is this about?"

"Something happened. They need the package." Jazz edged away from Belle. I followed him.

"Where is it?" she demanded.

Unfazed, Frankie didn't move an inch. "In my freezer."

"In your freezer?" I whispered. Odd place to store a package of stolen drugs, but also the last place I would have thought to search.

"Let's go get it," she told them. When Jazz and I didn't move, she motioned with the gun for us to walk. "All of us."

We trailed him into a tiny kitchen behind the main gaming room. He opened the freezer door on an apartment-sized refrigerator and set aside a box of frozen pizza and a couple bags of vegetables. Reaching inside, he removed the kilo of drugs.

"I don't know what you think you're gonna get for this," he said, gaze fixed on her and the gun. "But whatever you're trying to accomplish, handing this over is not the right call."

"They took my mother!" I blurted out. If my sister could wave a gun around, then I could tell the truth.

Belle's face blanched. "Lily!"

"It's true. They kidnapped her from our driveway." I burst into tears, the stress and fear overwhelming my control. "If we don't give them the drugs and the drone pictures…"

"Who?" Jazz demanded.

"Liz and some guy," I choked out.

"What are they going to do?" Frankie asked, his eyes on the gun.

"They didn't say."

Belle scoffed. "Does it matter? We know what they're capable of. My dad? The fisherman? What's one more dead Harmony?"

"You can't just walk in there and hand them everything they want." Jazz advanced, no longer deterred by the gun in her hand as if the truth presented a greater threat than a bullet. "Lily…you can't."

"We have no choice," I said, my words as bleak as our prospects.

"Give me the package," my sister demanded. She slipped the backpack off her shoulder and handed it to Frankie. "Dump the drugs in there. We can't be late."

"Who said you both have to go?" Jazz asked.

"You mean, just send Belle?" I'd never let that happen. She looked like she wanted to smack me for suggesting it.

"Right. She goes in, we follow. You'll have more leverage. If they know the whole thing is being videotaped, for instance, that might keep them honest," Frankie said.

"Don't go, Lil." Jazz's fingers drifted over my arm.

A strange calm settled over my thoughts as what we had to do next became clear. "I have to." Friendly Liz Monroe, turned cold-blooded killer, had my mother. We had what we needed to buy her back. "We'll be fine," I told him.

Did I believe that? I searched under the layers of my emotions for hope, but instead brushed the edges of my fear for her, for us.

The false courage I promoted didn't affect Frankie. "Or you're really going to piss them off, and they send out a death squad to hunt us down."

Jazz smirked, but the gesture didn't reach his eyes. "You're such an optimist."

"Belle—it's a way to make this work without involving the cops. Let them help."

"I don't like it." Her gaze traveled from Frankie, to me, to my boyfriend, and back to me.

Squaring my shoulders, I waited for her decision.

"Please, Belle. It's a better plan. We just want Mom. They can have their drugs and pictures. We need this to go away."

She lowered the gun and tucked it back into her waistband. "What if they kill her? Can you live with her blood on your hands? Or mine?"

"It's not going to happen," I said with determination I didn't know I possessed. "I'm going with you. We have to go. If we're going to do this, we have to go now."

"Are you all good?" Frankie asked.

"Yeah," she said.

"Okay. I've got some camera equipment I've been wanting to try out. A big zoom lens that should do the job." He hurried away as hope bloomed like first morning sunshine in my heart.

Belle's shoulders slumped, defeated. I left Jazz's side and draped an arm around my sister's shoulders. "You won't be alone."

"Why did they text *me*?" she asked. I didn't have an answer. It's true, they could've just as easily texted me. Instead, they'd chosen Belle.

"How did they get your number?"

"Mom had to give it to them. Or they got it from her phone."

Instead of offering an opinion, I told her, "It doesn't matter. You're not going alone. We're going together. Jazz and Frankie can handle the documentation." Fear shone in her face, all traces of her FBI agent-in-training bravado vanishing. I squeezed her shoulders. "We're going to be okay."

Frankie hurried back in with a monstrous black nylon bag in tow.

"Okay. Let's roll."

"Where are we going?" Jazz asked.

He'd been wonderful through the chaos. I didn't want him within ten miles of our plan, but there was no way I would be able to get him to stay away. "Port Sanibel Marina."

"All the sunset cruises leave from there. That's a good thing. Lots of witnesses. It'll be easier for us to blend into the background."

"We ready?" My sister tapped her foot. "The clock is ticking."

Jazz hugged me. "Be careful. We have your back. Text me the detective's phone number. I'll keep him on speed dial."

"You'd be better off calling 9-1-1," I told him as we walked out of the store into the late afternoon sunset. "After he hears this, the detective wouldn't put me out if I was on fire."

At my car, Jazz kissed me, his arms tight and protective around me. I never wanted to leave this moment. "Stay safe, okay?"

"You too," I told him, my resolve melting. He jogged toward Frankie's white Range Rover.

I slid behind the wheel as my sister clipped her seat belt. Everything I'd eaten over the last week crowded into the back of my throat.

"Any new texts from the kidnappers?"

"No." She shook her head. "I just checked."

Merging into the traffic, I cruised north toward Summerhill Road. "How did Liz get in the middle of this? Why didn't we see it?"

She sighed as if a thousand pounds squeezed the air out of her lungs. "Because we fixated on Malvern. And she was so helpful when Mom got arrested. I mean, she's the one who got her out of jail."

Except I'd been awoken by the dark shape outside my window—the one we later determined had been female. "The stalker had to be her; the night the alarms went off. What did she think would happen if she broke into the house?"

"Who knows? She might have been armed that night. We won't know what she was digging for until we see her. If she was involved in the murder, anything is possible."

"What about the climbing gear? Who did it belong to?" I asked as I picked up Summerhill Road. To my left, the sun dipped closer to the Gulf of Mexico, showering the sky in shades of gold and pink. Within the hour, the sun would set. We'd have our mother back. I couldn't let any other outcome color my perceptions. "Somehow she got tied up with this drone company. That's the one mystery we still have to solve."

"When we find Liz, let's ask her."

I parked the car in the marina parking lot. As we'd suspected, tourists and rental cars jammed the place. Two tour boats boarded passengers. A third waited just offshore to dock. In the distance, lightning zipped across the horizon, rending the sunset with electric arcs.

"Storm's coming," I said without fear. The impending storm didn't matter. Nothing mattered but finding our mother.

"Here goes nothing." She took out her phone and texted the kidnappers. In less than a minute, her phone buzzed back. "They want us to go toward the gift shop and bathrooms." She squinted out the window. "Over there, away from the people." The gift shop windows were dark. No help there.

I took a deep breath and got out of the car. Behind us, the Range Rover slipped into the lot like a pale ghost. I caught Jazz's eye and nodded once. They parked as we strolled toward the bathrooms.

"What are we supposed to do when we get there?" I asked.

"They didn't say. Wait for more instructions?"

I didn't like it. Down at this end of the marina, away from the Outfitter's shop, there was less traffic. A couple of sunset tour stragglers waiting for the final boat milled around. I glanced over my shoulder. The guys had taken up position halfway between the loading area and the bathrooms. They pointed to the sky and set up a tripod as if they were preparing for a photo shoot. As we drew closer to the souvenir shop, they picked up the equipment and repositioned their shot.

"We're too isolated here," she grumbled, as a distant lightning bolt mingled with the purple hues of sunset, turning the clouds molten. "We're away from all the tourists. With the storm coming, everyone else has gone home."

"They don't want any witnesses." I grasped her hand like my six-year-old self when she didn't want me to hang with her. This time, she didn't screech and pull away. We held hands until we reached the shop and sank onto the bench outside. We sat, tied together by blood, fear, and hope. "Did you ever ask Mom why Aunt Claire is angry at her?"

"She said something about Dad wanting to move north when Grandma fell sick. Mom wouldn't go. Aunt Claire dealt with most of it. I guess she blames Mom." She typed out a text. "Here goes," she whispered.

Less than a minute later, her phone buzzed.

"We're to go to the end of the dock. Last slip on the right."

I stood on boneless legs and took the backpack from her. "You need your hands free in case."

She squished her eyes shut before she opened them and met mine. "Let's end this."

I didn't dare glance back at my friends now, assuming the

kidnappers monitored our every move. I walked a few paces in front of my sister, past the shuttered gift shop and onto the marina dock. Fiddler crabs scurried out of our path, darting underneath the boards. Others clung to the pilons, ready to scuttle if we got too close. The last tour boat chugged by, sailing into the harbor beneath a darkening sky, past the mansions clustered on Connie Mack Island.

At the end of the deserted dock, far from the tourist loading platforms, a small fishing boat sat in dock with its canopy up. I recognized it from the pictures on Liz's wall. A single figure stood on the deck.

"Mom!" I yelled.

She was gagged, her hands bound and lashed to one of the canopy braces unable to move or warn us. A purple bruise colored her left cheek beneath her eye.

I sprinted up the gangplank, reaching my mother first. She fervently shook her head as I slipped the gag from between her teeth. "Lily, run!" she gasped.

But her warning came too late. I hadn't seen the person seated at the front of the boat until she rose from her seat. Liz smiled as if greeting an old friend stopping by for an evening on the water. Except friends didn't greet friends with a gun in her hand.

"Lily. You didn't have to come too. I expected Annabelle alone." Her gaze swept toward my sister.

"Let them go," Mom insisted.

Liz smirked. She had no intentions of letting any of us off the deck. "Do you have what I need?" Her stare drilled into me.

"Yes, it's all here." I slipped the straps off of my shoulder and dangled the backpack in front of me like a shield. Not that it would offer much protection from a firearm.

She glanced from the bag to us. Maybe with three of us, we'd thrown her plan off track.

"Put it over there." She directed me toward the front of the boat. When I set the bag on the deck and returned to my sister's side, Liz smiled. "Give me your cellphones."

"Why? We gave you what you need." My sister sneered.

She cocked the gun and leveled it at our mother. "I'm not going to ask again."

We handed over our phones. Without hesitating, Liz chucked both phones into the water.

"Great. Now we can get underway. Toss off those lines," she commanded. Neither of us moved.

"You got what you wanted. We're not going anywhere with

you." My sister set her jaw, her expression unyielding. I prayed she wouldn't do anything stupid.

The chilling smile widened. "Really? You're wrong." Behind us on the pier, fast moving footsteps announced a new arrival. I jerked around to see a man jump into the boat and toss off the lines. "You ready?"

His voice! From The Whale. As we'd suspected, the fake fisherman was the owner of the drone company and the man who tailed us at the beach. Alan Friedman.

"Friedman?" My sister gaped.

"I have to thank you for your help covering my tracks," he said to me with a smile. The boat moved beneath us, chugging out into the channel and away from our friends.

My gaze strayed to his left hand. No tattoo—but tats could be faked. "You pretended to be the fisherman the night at The Whale. And you followed me in town." I wanted to wipe the self-satisfied smirk off his face with a softball bat. "You're not the man who gave me the pictures."

"He's the dead guy from the dock." Belle said, aghast. "They killed the real fisherman, dumped his body, and this guy pretended to be him at the restaurant."

Nodding, I confirmed her ideas. "All to get away with killing Dad."

The man chuckled. "So you do know who I am. Alan Friedman, of Friedman Surveys. And you know my wife." He gestured to Liz who stood at the helm.

"You're his wife?" The implications spun my brain like a ship tossed in a maelstrom.

Liz was married to the man whose company discovered the plane. Her sister-in-law, Carol, had been Patrick's secretary. I stared out across the boat, trying to comprehend where this new information fit into the ten-thousand-piece jigsaw puzzle. The thick mangroves had gone dark on the shore. Few lights shone on the water, and the sky menaced with leaden clouds burning in sunset.

"What the hell?" Belle murmured.

Liz wiggled her ringless hand. "I don't wear my rings to work. I'd rather not have it known I'm married. Professionally, I use my maiden name." She smiled at her husband. "On the other hand, when William was trying to find a reputable drone surveyor, I knew a great company. Who knew what we'd find out there in the middle of the jungle? Lost after so many years?"

At the helm, she guided the boat between the navigation lights.

When I was little, my father kept his boat at this marina. The narrow channel's depth went down ten feet and could be treacherous if the skipper didn't know what they were doing. As a sailor, she seemed to know this. Liz had many talents we'd overlooked.

Alan watched us closely. "Sorry about the fisherman. I had to prevent him from telling you the truth. He caused enough trouble, don't you think?"

"How about untying my mother," my sister snapped.

"How about shutting your mouth?"

My fingers dug into my sister's arm when she swayed toward him. "Belle, don't."

He jerked his head in my direction. "Listen to your sister."

I breathed a sigh of relief when she relented, choosing to glare instead of attack. Had Jazz seen us taken and called the police? I prayed Stephens was on his way with the cavalry.

"What are you going to do?" I asked as we slipped past dark mansions adorned with heavy hurricane shutters as if their eyes had been permanently closed. Other houses were full of light but without visible people.

"Poor Patrick," Alan crooned ignoring my question. "After this is over, he'll be locked up for a good, long time. Thanks to the two of you for leading the way to him. I have to say, you followed the trail we left to that loser like a couple of bloodhounds. There's no doubt the police will suspect he planned this—the murder, the theft from the trust—from the pictures of him with you." He pointed to my mother. "By the way, Patrick never touched you. Not with the dose we slipped the two of you at the conference. He has no idea what you suspect him of."

I gripped the back of Belle's shirt. Mom's face quivered. How dare he torture her this way. Belle's gun was inches from my hand. He had to pay for what he'd done.

"Let's not forget the fake shell companies we created in his name. He'd already had a few sketchy plans in place to shelter some of his shakier personal investments. Not too difficult to tie them to the new ones we created once Carol took the job. We needed him to trust her and be too busy to read what he signed. He signed all of the paperwork, and we filed it, with some help from Monica." He smiled a ghastly slash filled with artificially white teeth—a Friedman family trait. "New babies are expensive, fragile things."

My brain spun. They threatened Monica's babies. No wonder she refused to call my mother back.

Mom shifted toward her former partner, her face streaked with tears and sweat. "How could you do this? How could you have William killed?"

Liz sighed, a trace of reluctance in her eyes. "I truly respected him. William wasn't supposed to know what was happening. When Connor and Alan found the plane, we intended to buy the land quickly, quietly. How could I know William would agree to work the case? He should've helped the environmental wackos file their paperwork—that's it. Instead, he made it a personal campaign to save the birds." She rolled her eyes.

"You knew what was in the plane. Was it worth killing my father for?"

"Not at first—not until William decided to take the case pro bono. He called it a worthy cause. Then he filed for the full environmental impact assessment. We had to act before the authorities caught on to us."

Pride warmed me. My father had been a good man. A smart, shrewd attorney who called BS when he saw it.

"But William guessed you were up to something. He hired an investigator. You knew he'd figure it out." Mom wrapped her hands around the braces as the boat hit swells.

I willed her to stay strong. *Don't give up, Mom. Jazz is coming.*

"William was the smartest lawyer I knew. Past tense of course." Liz's lips crested in a sickening sneer. "No doubt where these two got it. Once we'd taken care of the investigator, Alan impersonated him at The Whale. He led you out to the pier, so you'd think he'd been killed while I dumped the body into the water. Another death should have been enough to scare you off the trail."

"We don't scare easily," I snapped.

Alan laughed.

"But you?" Liz swung the gun back toward my mother. "You were too easy. Don't you remember? I was out of town the weekend you and Patrick went to D.C. I stopped by your table when you'd gone to the ladies' room. Slipped a little something special in your drinks. Patrick never noticed. The rest was a matter of time."

Mom turned her face away in shame.

Relief swept through my blood. She never cheated on Dad. "You bitch," I snarled. "You killed my father!"

"Now, we're going to finish off the rest of the family. What a tragedy. The entire Harmony family killed within a week of each other." She made a tsk-tsk sound in her throat. "Guess I'll inherit the firm. First thing I'm going to do as the new owner? Fire Patrick and change the name."

My sister edged toward Liz, but Alan stopped her with a leveled gun. "Uh-uh. Stay put."

The boat cleared the mangrove-lined channels and set out toward open water. "Fortunately for us, we don't have to go too far. The wildlife in this area will take care of the evidence. Cayo Costa isn't the only uninhabited island out here. By the time they find the three of you, there won't be much left to identify."

For a moment, giddy relief rushed up my throat. They weren't planning on shooting us and dumping us overboard. But leaving us on an island off the coast? With no water or shelter? She was right. We wouldn't last long. Except she didn't know our friends knew where we were.

Please find me, Jazz.

"How did you do it?" I asked Alan. "How did you make me believe you were dead?"

His mouth twitched. "Easy enough to dress the investigator in a duplicate of my shirt. Take away his ID so the police would have a tough time figuring out who he was—place an anonymous call to make them think he was a vagrant. You saw what I wanted you to see."

"Who did you kill? What was his name?" Their claims made a lot of sense. I'd been looking for the fisherman's obituary. I'd been searching for the wrong person.

"He was nobody. A hired hack your father picked up on the internet. He didn't matter."

His cold, callousness staggered me. He was devoid of conscience.

The boat cruised across choppy swells birthed by the storm drifting inland from the Gulf. Clouds in ominous shades of orange and gold roiled above dolphins dancing on the surface. For a moment, I feared the impending storm more than Alan's gun. How far would they take us before forcing us from the boat? Miles? Numerous islands dotted the coastal waters, some named, some too small to matter. Those dense mangrove patches loomed indistinct in the deepening gloom. A perfect place to leave us for dead.

Another boat skirted the horizon, sending up a blast from its horn. One of the last tours, beating a retreat back to land before the wind and rain. The radio snapped to life. "Severe thunderstorm warning for the southeast coast including Sanibel, Captiva, and Fort Myers. Return to port. Seek safe harbor."

"Check the radar," Liz ordered Alan. He moved around us until he stopped beside her. They stared at his phone. "We need to get this done and get back."

"We have ten minutes. Maybe less before it's on us," he told her.

The skies heaved a massive bolt of lightning off the starboard side. Curtains of rain hid the clouds like gray sheets enveloping the coast.

"Then this will have to do." A dark island of mangroves sprouted out from sandbars on the port side. Low tide. Otherwise those tiny patches would have been below the water. "Untie her. You two. Over to the side, now."

Alan advanced on us. I tugged Belle to the side. We needed Mom free before anything else happened. My sister set her face, determined. The thought of her wielding the gun terrified me, but we were running out of options. A death sentence awaited us if we got off the boat. No one would ever find us.

Had Jazz called the police? Maybe the Coast Guard was searching for us. We needed time before they sent us into the water. But the encroaching storm wasn't waiting for the police to arrive.

Alan cut through Mom's restraints with one slash of his knife. She peeled the gag from her throat and threw it at him. "You don't believe we're the only ones who know about the plane, do you Liz? Of course others are involved."

"It doesn't matter. By the time they find your bodies, the plane will be empty, and we'll be gone."

"Move," he commanded.

With careful steps, Mom crossed the boat to stand in front of us, blocking their view and the line of fire. She didn't know about the gun Belle carried, but she was the tiger shark. We were her pups.

Belle's hand ducked around behind her waist, and she removed the gun from the back of her shorts. As she held the weapon close to her side, her body shielded the gun from view.

My heart hammered concussively. Thunder rattled the sky and fat drops of rain hit with impressive force.

"We're out of time. Do it!" Liz yelled over the storm's tirade. The boat coasted to a forward stop but bobbed on the swells like a child's lost top.

"Over." Alan waved his gun at Mom and gripped the rail to stay on his feet.

"No." She took a step toward him on the bucking deck.

"You can go over, or I can put some holes in your kids. Your choice." He leveled the gun at me.

Mom held up her hands and backed toward the rail.

"Mom, no!" I lunged forward.

Behind the curtains of rain, a boat's engine revved on the starboard side, and a blast of light illuminated the deck. Alan whipped around as Belle lifted her hand and fired.

The bullet caught him in his right shoulder, and the gun tumbled from his hand. I dove to the floor of the boat as the weapon skittered away, at the edge of my reach.

The boat leaned hard to port into a sandbar, and the deck tipped as the storm barreled down on us, crashing swells against the already unstable craft. My fingers closed on the gun as the boat struggled to right itself.

Lightning poured from the sky in a fiery screen.

"It's going over!" he yelled.

I held onto a deck box as the boat pitched and tilted. The roar of another engine filled me with unprecedented hope. Whether the Coast Guard had arrived or a ship full of Boy Scouts didn't matter. Someone knew we were here.

Liz abandoned the helm and lunged for my mother. They fought to regain their footing on the slippery deck. Alan yanked himself up and slid to the rail, his shirt a crimson stain against the storm. His gaze fixed on my sister and the gun she held.

A swell crashed into the starboard side, driving us into the sandbars. I flew backwards as the boat ground to a stop.

"Lily!" my mother screamed.

One minute, my body was weightless, careening through the storm. In the next, I was over the rail, one with the rainfall and the sea. Deep water closed over my head, blocking out the storm, the blood, the rain.

A lightning flash told me which way was up. I kicked for the surface with everything I had.

My name rang out as I broke free of the swells. Water rushed up my nose, down my throat. Taking my air.

"Lily!"

"Jazz!" I choked back.

A low-slung motorboat dove through the swells, slicing a path toward me. A furious wave swamped me, driving me down. I struggled back to the surface, gasping and retching saltwater and mud. He waved an orange life jacket. I kicked toward the boat as he threw it into the storm.

Inches from my fingers lay safety. A line back to solid ground. I barely hooked a finger on the vest as another bolt rent the sky. Somehow, I looped my wrist through the straps. Jazz hauled on the line, dragging me through the water. I'd swallowed a gallon by the time his hands reached down, hauling me into the boat. I laid on the deck, unable to move until the water I choked down found its way back up my burning throat.

"Can you breathe?" His face hung against the black churning clouds, inches from mine.

I'd wretched up what felt like gallons of water, and lights danced in front of my vision. Lightning? Spots? I couldn't be sure.

A scream pierced the storm. Mom or Belle?

"They're going over!" Frankie yelled from the front of the boat. A man I didn't recognize stood beside him at the helm.

Jazz helped me to my feet as the other boat capsized against the sandbar.

"Mom!" Stinging rain lashed my face.

She leapt free from the side of the craft.

"Rand! Over there! Toward the island." I followed Jazz's gesture to starboard.

My mother had made it to one of the sandbars, but swells threatened to wash her away. I scoured the leaden water for a sign of my sister. White caps drew my gaze only to disappoint when the foam dissolved. "Where's Annabelle?"

Jazz readied the life jacket and line. "I don't see her. Maybe she's on the other side of the boat."

Rand maneuvered the boat as close to the sandbar as he dared. "Can't get any closer than this, before we get stuck too."

With a mighty heave, Jazz launched the jacket toward the sandbar. My mother's gaze followed the arc, and she lunged toward the jacket, taking the orange vest and the line back into the water. I held my breath until her face broke the surface. She had one arm through the vest, enough to keep her afloat.

"You got her. Pull!" Rand yelled.

We lugged the line toward the boat until Mom came close enough to grab our outstretched hands. Blood trickled from the side of her face. I clung to her as she climbed into Rand's bucking boat.

"You're bleeding," I said.

She touched her face and stared at the blood. "It's nothing. We need to find Annabelle."

We scanned the dark, restless water for signs of my sister. *Come on Belle.* Not her too. I couldn't survive losing her.

"There she is!" Frankie yelled.

Belle had managed to drag herself up onto the side of the sinking vessel. She clung to the deck of the pitching boat, just as Liz surfaced. Her fingertips gripped a railing, holding on for all she was worth as her gaze found my sister.

Rand pushed the throttle forward, and the boat closed on her position.

"Belle!" Mom waved both of her arms. "Behind you!"

Liz clambered onto the side of the boat. Her furious stare fixed on my sister.

Belle's head came up. She dragged herself to her knees, waiting for her adversary to approach.

"Rand! We have to get closer!" I rushed to the rail. If he could get alongside the sinking vessel, she might be able to jump aboard.

"I'll try." He edged the boat forward, trying to avoid both the sinking boat and the sandbars lurking just beneath the waves.

We closed the distance to twenty feet. "That's as close as we're gonna get. It's too risky."

The radio crackled with static. "This is Coast Guard Motor Unit 426, search and rescue. What is your position?"

The guys let out a shout. Rand yanked the microphone to his mouth. "Mayday! Mayday! Coast Guard. We are two miles north of Port Sanibel Marina. Near an unknown barrier island. One craft sinking. People in the water. Need immediate assist!"

"En route. Five minutes from your position."

Five minutes. Somehow this would be over before they arrived.

I searched the water for signs of a Coast Guard cutter before tearing my gaze back to the sinking fishing boat. Liz had made progress, reaching the hull. She shuffled forward in a crouch, a wicked, curved blade in her hand. My sister watched her, face intent, as if she wanted the lawyer to come after her. My heart thundered.

"Oh my God," Mom whispered.

With a final effort, the mad woman lunged. My mother gasped as the blade dove toward my sister's chest.

Belle blocked the blow with her left arm like she'd done the action a hundred times before, landing a sharp cut to the lawyer's face with a right fist. Her opponent stumbled backward, her footing unsure on the bucking hull. My sister attacked with an elbow to the nose. The blade left Liz's hand and succumbed to the waves. Off-balance, she grappled for footing to fend off the assault. Belle landed hit after hit as waves crashed over the sinking hull until the boat disappeared beneath them with a groan.

A blast from an air horn sounded behind us. Rand let out a jubilant shout. I spun as a Coast Guard motor lifeboat rushed toward us. Flood lights momentarily blinded me before I searched out my sister in the melee.

"Belle!" I screamed into the darkness. Frankie swept the beam of his flashlight over the water. There was no sign of my sister.

"Help!" Mom waved to the Coast Guard boat. "We need help!"

Lights swept over us. Rand eased our boat out of the way to make room for the Coast Guard vessel. Beneath the waves, the stricken boat hung up on the sandbar. The lights flickered from its watery grave, but there was no sign of my sister.

Tears streamed down my face, blending with rain. Brave, fierce Annabelle was gone.

Divers hit the water, swimming with rapid strokes toward us. They dipped below the surface, their progress toward the sinking boat.

How long had it been since I'd last seen her auburn hair bobbing on the surface? Minutes? Seconds? Lights reflected off swells, and a shout rang out above the crash of the storm.

A head bobbed in the fray. The Coast Guard boat swung around.

"Who is it?" I called out. No one answered.

Please. Please. Please.

Another diver leapt into the water. Moments later, he guided a struggling form toward the Coast Guard craft. We waited, tense, soaked to the bone, rain and spray streaming from our hair. A woman's face broke the surface. *Belle.*

Cheers and hugs erupted. Rand's fist shot into the air. Jazz clung to me and my mother as we sobbed in relief.

With help, Belle climbed into the Coast Guard vessel, and a crew member wrapped her in a blanket.

"Where are the other two?" Rand wondered.

"In hell," Jazz said. "You okay?"

I leaned into his embrace. "Yes. Now I am."

The radio crackled to life. We watched the divers search around the sinking boat while Rand confirmed two more people were missing.

Mom sat by herself, staring into the water.

A half hour later, the storm blew out to sea, and the first rescue diver clambered aboard the cutter.

"Looks like they're abandoning the search," Frankie said.

The other divers surfaced, swam to their vessel, and had a discussion with the Coast Guard skipper. We couldn't hear any of it, but their lack of haste spoke volumes. Alan Friedman and his wife were gone, lost beneath the channel.

Mom approached and laid her arm over my shoulder. I hugged her back with an arm around her waist as the Coast Guard vessel moved toward us. Rand steadied his boat, and the larger craft inched closer. When a few feet separated us, I sank to the deck bench. With the ordeal over, the truth would be told, and this time, the authorities would listen.

Rand picked up the microphone and acknowledged the order to follow the Coast Guard back to port. By the time we arrived at the narrow straights to Port Sanibel Marina, the storm had shifted well to our west, lighting up the sky with golden flame. My damp clothes clung to me, and I shivered despite the muggy night air.

The conversation on the radio had been stark in its frankness. The talk was of recovery not rescue. From the sound of it, another vessel en route to the crash site would continue the search.

Stephens was going to lose it. How would our detective friend take our investigation and involvement? The deceit, the dead-undead fisherman. The conspiracy to hide their tracks and frame Patrick for all of it. The decision to murder my father in cold blood.

He'd have to believe me now or arrest me for meddling in police business. I didn't care either way.

Jazz came up behind me as Rand guided the boat toward the dock. "How are you doing?" He brushed wet hair from my face.

I settled back against the rail. "Better than I was on the way out. Thanks for coming to our rescue."

"When I guessed they were going to leave with you, I called Rand. His boat was docked just up the coast. He picked us up, and we floored it to you. Broke most of the "no wake" rules."

I narrowed my eyes. "You better not have hit a manatee. I like manatees."

"I assure you. No manatees were harmed in your rescue."

Rand docked. Jazz leapt ashore and tied the boat to the pier. The Coast Guard followed suit, tying up on the other side of the dock. On shaking legs, I climbed out of the boat. It would be years before I had the desire to ride in a boat again.

Our group huddled together on the dock, waiting for two members of the rescue team to disembark.

"Mrs. Harmony? I'm Captain Cleary. Are any of you injured?" A stern woman, who I assumed to be the boat's skipper, scanned over us.

"Cuts and scrapes," Mom told her. "We'll be all right. Where's my daughter?"

"We're treating her for a gash on her forearm. She said your kidnapper cut her in a struggle." She took stock of our injuries. "You're both bleeding. I'm going to insist you take a ride to the emergency room."

On cue, an ambulance and patrol car roared into the parking lot, lights flashing.

"Thank you." My mother offered her hand.

"Glad we were able to assist."

"Captain?" I stopped her. "What about Liz Monroe? And Alan Friedman?"

The captain's expression softened a fraction. "We have a crew out now, trying to recover their bodies."

The horror of the last hour hit me broadside. The persons responsible for my father's murder were dead, lost in the storm-furious waters of Peace River or swept out into the Gulf.

Belle reappeared at the side of the Coast Guard vessel and stepped wearily onto the dock. Mom and I rushed her, collapsing into a group hug. A bandage covered her left arm from wrist to elbow, and a scarlet stain bled through.

"She cut you?" I asked.

"Yeah. I might need some stitches." Belle choked back a relieved sob. "I'm sorry Mom."

"For what? You, Lily, and your friends are the reason we're standing here instead of floating out there." She glanced around, her face streaked with happy tears. "Where is the young man who came after us? Jason's friend?"

We spotted the guys hanging out in the back of Rand's boat. Although soaked and bedraggled, their smiles were wide.

Heavy footfalls on the dock announced Stephens's appearance. Better late than never, I supposed.

"Mrs. Harmony. I heard you and the girls were abducted." His contrite tone irritated me. I held in my growl.

Mom nodded and tucked her blanket closer. "We were. Those young men came to our aid."

The guys waved from the boat.

"Would someone like to explain what happened?" He glanced from my mother to Belle's bloody arm, until his wry gaze landed on me, like he thought I had been the instigator.

"I tried to tell you." I clenched my fists at my sides. "You didn't want to hear what I had to say on the pier. If you want to hear now, we're on our way to the hospital. My sister needs stitches." I marched past him without another word and headed for my car.

Chapter Twenty-Three

I dangled my pink polished toes in the silky water. Sunlight glittered off the surface of the swimming pool making me drowsy. Water tinkled over the rock wall, dropping sparkling beads that glimmered and spun. How beautiful water could be. How serene when the waves weren't storm tossed.

The search crew discovered Liz's body about a half mile from the boat wreck, drawn out toward the Gulf by the tide. Her wrecked boat would be removed later, after a team of marine biologists determined the environmental impact on the surrounding, fragile mangroves.

Alan Friedman and his brother Connor were nowhere to be found.

Had Alan been washed away in the storm, drowned in the channels, or swept out to the Gulf? If so, they might never locate his remains. A nagging dread followed me the day after the kidnapping. What if he made it to one of the mangrove islands? There was always a chance he'd been saved by some unsuspecting boater. But he'd been shot. The blood would draw predators. If he had survived, time and exposure would likely finish him off.

The Friedman offices had been raided, and Carol arrested on her way to the airport. I forced myself to watch the coverage on the news. Investigators carried boxes and computers from the drone company. Mom heard the cops were hunting for the drugs removed from the plane, but there was more trouble for the surviving Friedman. According to the detective, the smugglers who lost the plane were also after the cargo.

After her arrest, Carol implicated Alan in the murder of both the investigator and my father, claiming the entire plot had been his doing. We learned he was an avid climber, having traveled around the world on expensive climbing trips before his company ran out of money. Stephens suspected the financial trouble was why Alan Friedman took a chance on getting control of the plane. Bankrupt and under heavy pressure from their competition, the Friedman family seized the opportunity to buy the property and the millions of dollars in drugs hidden there.

In the end, the fisherman hadn't given my father the drone picture. Friedman Survey had sent the unredacted footage to Patrick by mistake, and he passed it on to my father as part of discovery in the case. Unfortunately, Patrick hadn't known what he was looking at. Dad, a seasoned pilot, had picked the wing out of the shot and known the moment he saw the shape hanging in the mangroves.

Had he researched planes lost in the area? Seen the articles about the smuggler's plane? Did he call Friedman to let them know?

Some questions may never have answers. Sometime between the drone survey and my father's death, the plot had been hatched to implicate Patrick as the bad guy. Putting Carol on the inside of the firm had been a brilliant move. She planted the evidence; she'd known about the trip to Washington. I'd wondered about who had taken the picture of my mother and Patrick. Thanks to Liz's admission on the boat, we were sure of her guilt.

"Hey. What are you thinking about?" Belle dropped to the side of the pool and plopped her feet into the water.

"Lots of stuff. How they put this whole thing together. They were so careful. So evil." A shudder ran through my body. I lifted my face toward the searing summer sun to banish the thoughts.

She removed her sunglasses and swept them through her hair to sit on top of her head. "I bet they freaked out when Dad saw the picture. The one thing that could have messed up their whole plan."

"That and the lawsuit," I reminded her. "Dad had filed to block the sale. I wonder if he knew about the plane then, or later? No way to know when he saw those pictures."

"They must have been frantic." Her voice took on an edge in renewed anger. "They ended up sneaking in there and taking the cargo. Why didn't they just do that in the first place before Dad knew about the drone pictures? No one would have known they stole it. No one would have died."

With Liz gone, answers to some of our questions remained elusive. "Maybe they were afraid someone would catch on," I said. "But the longer the case dragged on, the more likely those environmental people would be out there hoping for a reason to prevent them from buying. Someone would have stumbled upon the plane sooner rather than later."

"Then Dad's investigator started digging. Somehow, he came across the staged picture of Patrick and Mom. Finding the photo was a big problem which might have made him hold off giving Dad the file."

I had a theory about the picture. Dad had hired the deceased fisherman—we now knew his name was Daniel Armstrong, Private Detective and ex-Marine—to keep an eye on his partners. Armstrong had worked in security for several firms over the years. I suspected he'd found the picture the same way he'd gotten the drone footage. By accessing Patrick's personal computer. By then, Carol Friedman had planted the incriminating picture in Patrick's files.

As Alan said, Armstrong had seen what the Friedman siblings had wanted him to see.

I splashed my feet in the pool. "But now we know making Patrick appear guilty was a distraction. Liz knew we were upset about Mom being accused of Dad's murder. They just added to the mess to keep everyone off their tracks."

"Thinking we'd lose it over the picture was a mistake. The photo and the implication made us more determined to figure out what the hell was going on." She glowered at the water.

I smiled at my sister. We'd come far from the day I made the call to tell her about Dad. We'd become sisters. Friends. I dreaded the day she'd leave for Georgia.

"Mom's planning a hell of a party tonight. Never thought I'd see her hanging out with a bunch of video gamers." She laughed, an honest-to-goodness happy laugh. "She's got about twenty pounds of chicken in marinade. I don't know who she thinks is going to eat all this food."

Mom had her way of healing. Cooking. Entertaining. Bringing life back into the too quiet house. I'd taken to painting lightning arcing over the Gulf and playing my saxophone next to the pool. On canvas and in song, the ordeal we'd been through terrified me less.

"You should go back to school." My sister had worked her butt off so long. She'd sacrificed so much to excel.

"I know. It's been on my mind these last few days. I only have a couple of months left. Maybe they'll take me back." Her fingers skimmed the surface of the water. "But I still don't want to be a lawyer in a practice. I asked for an extension on my application for the FBI until I finish school. I hope they agree. Besides, Mom's going to need some help until they find that trust fund money Carol took."

"That's awesome," I told her. "I'm happy you're going to go through with school." Later, she'd make a fabulous agent. Pre-law in Boston was off the table for me—I planned to switch to a Florida school. Maybe I'd study music. Or I could go "undeclared" and find my own path like Belle had.

But I'd wait to tell my mother about my decision. At least for a couple of days.

Today, Jazz was coming over, and I'd show him my paintings. Tonight, we'd run our last practice before our audition at Sun Runner's.

Belle climbed from the side of the pool and kicked water from her feet before donning her flip flops. "I have to run to the store for Mom. Want to tag along?"

All the times I'd wanted to be part of my big sister's life—to have an invitation to tag along. My heart filled with love and loss, but mostly love.

"Sure."

~ * ~

Patrons filled every seat at Sun Runner's as we took the stage for our audition. My stomach launched into Simone Biles-worthy backflips, and my sax slid in my sweaty palms.

"We've got this." Jazz leaned toward me and bumped knuckles before waving to the crowd.

No pressure. Sun Runner's was only the biggest venue in Fort Myers Beach. Plus, out there in the blinding lights sat everyone we knew.

I wet my reed and nodded to our drummer. He counted us off, and we dove into the first measure of *Brown Eyed Girl*.

I leaned into every note while Paul kept the beat and belted out the vocals to our version of Van Morrison. Across the stage, Jazz caught my eye and wiggled his eyebrows. Our set flew by in a blur, and before I knew what happened, we were accepting a standing ovation. Out in the crowd, I saw my mother and sister seated with...Detective Stephens? What the heck was that about?

Half an hour later, we celebrated, cheered, and cried backstage. Several members stood off to the side reliving the set while our guitar player, Taylor, and bass player, Kayla, kissed passionately. I wiggled the neck off my sax and leaned against the wall, enjoying the feel of air flowing up my nose without having to force it through my horn.

My sister appeared backstage a few minutes later. She pulled me into an embrace.

"I'm all sweaty," I warned.

She hugged anyway. "I don't care. That was freaking amazing. You guys rock. If this place is smart, you'll play every Saturday night from now on. Did you hear that crowd?" Her eyes sparkled.

"What did Mom think?"

"Are you kidding? She's out there telling everyone she gave birth to you."

I rolled my eyes. Kayla threw me a clean towel, and I wiped the sweat off my face.

"Did I see you sitting with Mr. I'm-smarter-than-all-of-you-except-I'm-not?"

She lifted a shoulder like it was no big deal that the cop who brushed us off for weeks had come to see our band. "He's okay."

"Really? Are you running a fever?" She laughed, and I relished this new easiness between us. No longer just my formidable sister, but a friend. A supporter.

"Are you ready to get out of here?" Jazz appeared from the hall behind the stage and grabbed me around the waist, spinning me. His skin glistened with sweat. "You need me to teach you how to take your horn apart or what?"

I elbowed him in the ribs. "Nope. But we have to find Rich and see what they thought." The entertainment director and the owner had been in the crowd tonight. I was thankful the detective had shown up. He'd taken my mind off our true audience.

As if on cue, Rich stepped backstage dressed in khakis and a black Sun Runner's polo shirt. He wore his hair slicked with gel and spiky on top—every bit the business owner. I wondered if I should have my mother present for the meeting.

We stood waiting for him to say something. This was it. The moment that decided our future. Would we have a job here? Or would Brass Tactics have to go back to the graduation party circuit?

Finally, his face broke into a smile. "You guys booked next weekend?"

Acknowledgements

Years ago, sitting beside my grandfather and reading his poetry, I decided to become a writer. It's been a long and winding road to get from then to now, and there have been so many people who have walked this journey with me. I need to thank you all.

To Cassie Knight and the entire Champagne Book Group staff: Thank you for believing in me and my work.

Cindy Dorminy: Thank you for talking me off the writing ledge more times than I can count, for reading on a moment's notice, and for being there.

Kate Foster: We've been through a lot together. Thank you for always being the voice of reason in the writing chaos.

To the entire Pitch Wars team and mentor support staff: Thank you for letting me be part of an amazing group of writers.

To the March 39, Hymn Day ladies (Fiona, Kim, Lynnette, and Monica): You rock and you are my rock. Hugs.

Thank you to Dawn Husted for your sharp editorial eye.

Thank you to Erin Gunti and Cass Scotka for starting as my mentees and becoming my dear friends.

To my Creative Writing kiddos and especially Brooke, Dani, Liam, and Lilly for being great writers and better humans. You make me so proud.

And to my family, Dave, David, and Kelsey. All of this is possible because you believed in me. Much love.

About the Author

Kelly Ann Hopkins fell in love with mysteries as a teen and still can't resist a good "whodunnit". She spends her days as a high school librarian and creative writing teacher where she challenges her students to read with abandon. When Kelly isn't creating perilous adventures for her characters, she is dreaming of her next trip to the Florida Gulf Coast.

Kelly lives in Pennsylvania with her husband, two children, Auggie the dog, and too many books.

Kelly's loves to connect with her readers. Find her at:

Website/Blog: https://khopkinswriter.wordpress.com/
Facebook: https://www.facebook.com/khopkinswrites/
Instagram: https://www.instagram.com/khopkinswrites/?hl=en
Twitter: https://twitter.com/khopkinswrites

~ * ~

We hope you enjoyed *Gulf of Deception* as much as we did. If you did, please write a review, tell your friends, or go give one of the other terrific offerings at Champagne Book Group a try.

Now, turn the page for a peek inside Kelly's newest book, *High Vices*, where the daughter of one of the most feared cartel kingpins is recruited to take her father down.

High Vices
By Kelly Hopkins

Hiding in witness protection is getting old. The only way out for Antoinette? Take down the mob boss who got her there—her father.

Antoinette Lombardi is not your average daddy's girl.

She didn't ask to be the daughter of one of the most feared cartel kingpins in the world, and she sure didn't ask to be recruited to take her father down. But when the cartel finds Antoinette and her mother hiding in witness protection, her mother agrees to become the government's bait to protect her daughter, leaving Antoinette in the care of agents who despise her family line.

Given a new identity at a super-secret boarding school, Antoinette is introduced to the other teens in a diverse posse, all of whom have lost parts of their lives to the murderous cartel. Together, this cast of criminal teens will infiltrate the cartel's ranks at its most vulnerable levels and secure the revenge they seek—if they don't kill each other first.

Excerpt

Outside the mansion, purple-velvet shadows deepen beneath a thick stand of pines lining the flagstone path. Fresh cut grass fragrances the air. Against the foundation, dormant mulched gardens await summer plants. Everything is neat, clean, and green. Not a dead leaf in sight. We make our way through the lush backyard, away from the house toward the serenity of the woods.

At home, we never had much property for gardening. Once, when we didn't live in an apartment, we planted a bunch of zinnias and marigolds from seeds behind our tiny bungalow, right before we relocated away from the best summer of my growing up. I kept one of the marigolds in a pot on my bedroom windowsill at our latest home. Maybe our landlord will take care of it.

"Flynn owns all this?" I inquire.

Many of the outbuildings dotting the property weren't visible behind the house. Now, with an unobstructed view, the expanse of the facility Flynn and her agents control hits me hard. It's not just a house. It's a freaking compound. Where does the money come from to support an operation like this? The marshals? WITSEC? DEA? Who else has enough cash to keep this school running?

"Yeah. It's an old boarding school that sat abandoned for years," Phil says, pausing at the edge of the lawn. "I've checked into the records. They got a good deal on it. Fixed it up."

The offer of information raises my eyebrows. "Who are *they*?"

"Well, it's a company name. Vice Industries. Not like she'd put her name on this place."

"And you know this how?"

He tugs on the hem of his shirt. "Oh, sorry, you don't know. You want something or someone found, I'm your guy."

I store the detail without comment. My interest shifts to Jackson. "What's your specialty?"

He smirks and rubs his palm over his cheek. "All things automobile."

"Like…" I prompt him.

"Like *Grand Theft Auto* without the cool soundtrack and X button," he says with a grin.

A car thief and a tech nerd. Important, necessary details, but the information could be part of a cover story, just like my meth dealing. "Really? So how long have you guys been here?"

"Three weeks." Jackson scuffs the toe of his Converse in the dirt.

"A bit longer. Two months," Phil adds. "Karma and Corrine got here right after I did."

"What about you?" I throw the hook at Boots.

"Two years," he says with a non-comital shrug. The house looms behind him, as dark and haunted as his gaze.

"Two years?" I struggle to disguise my shock. What's he been doing? More importantly, what did he do to earn a two-year sentence here? I open my mouth to ask how he ended up sitting in my math class, but I'm interrupted.

"So, what did you do?" Phil asks me, his eyes bright with interest.

The boys fall silent, waiting for my answer. I wonder if they're aware of the Lombardi glue tying us together. I'm guessing that's a no. Time to heave out my new identity and try it on for size. The stories they've shared sound plausible, but if their stories are full of lies like mine, I have to wonder why they are hiding here in the mansion.

In reality my bet is we're all liars. I can't trust any of them. But none of them act as wary about these introductions as I feel. Too much is at stake. My life—my mother's. This is not a conversation I wanted to have so soon. I try to sound convincing. "I was selling meth at school. I got caught."

Jackson lets out a low whistle. "Cranking it up, baby. How the hell did you get mixed up in that nasty business."

"It wasn't my business," I say, irritation sharpening my tone. At least the next part of my cover is sort of true, but Boots must know it's a lie, unless Flynn kept him in the dark about my true identity. "My mother's sick. I was paying for her medicines."

"Oh, wow. Sorry about that. What's wrong with her?"

"Drop it," Boots snaps. He seems capable of speaking only if he's barking out commands through his clenched teeth.

As he moves to leave, Jackson steps in front of him, blocking his path. They stop and stand face to face. Although Boots has a few inches on the other boy, the car thief isn't backing down. "What the hell's your problem, man? We asked her a question. She's got a voice. She doesn't have to answer if she doesn't want to."

"It's okay." In an effort to calm the guys down, I recite the details from my file. "My mother had cancer. It sucked." I tug on Jackson's sleeve. "It's over, okay?"

He hurls one more loathsome look at Boots before letting me lead him forward. The others follow. I have no idea where I'm going, but the worn path through the woods might be promising. The air thickens behind me with unspoken words. I can't figure out why Boots wouldn't want to hear the answers to my questions—unless he already knows the truth. A thread of terror tugs at my mind. I need to know more about this group. Knowledge is power—the best way to protect myself.

"What about you guys?" We exit the woods at an enormous brick garage with four white roll-up doors. One of the doors stands open. I peer into the dim interior. The car parked inside is fast, red, and expensive.

Jackson stares into the open bay with a wolfish longing. "Like I said—I stole a couple of cars."

"A couple? Sheeee-it. What do you call a lot?" Phil asks. His curly hair puffs out from his head in the breeze. He has deep blue eyes the color of a late summer sky and an easy way of talking.

"Okay. Eighteen."

"Eighteen?" I gasp.

He blasts me with a proud smile. "Give or take."

"And one very sick speed boat," Phil adds.

"What did you do with so many cars?" I gain a new respect for the lanky kid who looks like he'd be vying for an athletic scholarship if he wasn't a felon. He's one slick dude to pull off that many jobs before getting caught.

His hand slips down my arm. His fingers brush mine, sending tingles over my skin. The touch was no accident. I fold my arms across my chest in a message of *keep your hands to yourself.*

"I delivered them to a garage. They gave me a couple hundred per car. I needed the money too."

Phil exudes nervous energy like a Labrador on a fresh bag of Beggin' Strips. "Chop shop. They stripped the cars for parts." His gaze shifts to our housemate. "You never told me what you were going to do with the boat, though."

Of course, I must ask, "How'd you get caught?"

Wrinkling his nose, Jackson admits, "Boat ran out of gas."

"Maybe you should've stuck to cars." I hide a laugh behind my palm.

He rubs the side of his neck. "Yeah…well…"

"In the middle of a monster lake." Phil laughs. "Jackson says he can't swim."

"Shit happens," he agrees with a shrug as we laugh together.

Still, suspicion of my housemates nags me. How much of his story is reality? Is this a cover? I suspect there's some fact to his story, as there's a fiber of truth in mine. The gleam in his eye when he stared into the garage wasn't contrived. Why would a kid who got nabbed for swiping cars be here, hidden away from the Lombardis? Maybe the chop shop was another of my family's side-businesses.

The back of the school towers over the yard as we walk on. Boots trails behind, pretending to ignore us. Every so often I catch his scrutiny as he keeps to himself. Frowning, I file the suspicions away for later.

"What about the girls? And what's Boots's deal?" I say, lowering my voice. "He acts like a real sweetheart."

"Karma's ex-gang, in case you didn't figure it out. Maybe still gang. They picked her up off some corner," Phil says.

"What's with the baby bump?" I ask.

Jackson grimaces. "It's a fake. She's practicing in case she has to go undercover. My guess? Flynn's never going to let her loose on the world. No freaking way. She's messed the hell up." He taps the side of his head.

My eyebrows lift. "You think? The blonde girl seems twitchy too."

"And she's hyped up," he says, his words clipped. "She's from some prep school near Philly. Lots of money. Lots of toys. She got messed up—almost died. Her parents checked her into some rehab and walked away."

"They left her?"

"Yeah. That's what she said. They paid the bill and disowned her." Jackson winces and rubs a hand over his hair.

Wow. Abandoned. So much for being a rich poser, but is it true? Again, I consider why the girls would be hiding here—why Flynn would choose them to join this school. I have no doubt Corrine is on something. The part about her parents leaving her rings of falsehood. As far as Karma goes, well, maybe she was in a gang with the vicious attitude, tats, and piercings.

A steep hill leads toward what must be the stable. I can smell the horses before I see them grazing in the fields. It's not a bad smell, not even a zooey smell. Kind of like fresh cut grass mixed with old leather. Golden split rail fencing extends in every direction right up to the tree line where horses stand drowsing in the late day sunshine. Dark pines shield the woods from view. I wonder how far back Flynn's slice of heaven goes.

At the fence, I lean against a post. The horses eat and swat flies with their tails. Phil jumps up on the fence to sit on the top rail. Jackson is quicker. He hops to the top rail, scoots across, then over and down the other side.

"Parkour too?" I ask him. I can't find adequate vocabulary to express how cool his lithe and graceful movements are.

He walks up a bench and tilts it like a teeter-totter, first up one side before following the other end to the ground. "Yeah. I've got some skills." His feet float over a stump and back up onto the fence rail.

"That's nothing. I'm into identity theft. I got one guy for fifteen grand before he knew what hit him," Phil says, puffing out his chest as Jackson hops to the ground. "I can find anyone too. Nobody hides from me."

"Wow," I say, feigning interest but worried because he's mentioned his tech skills before. What if he dug into my story? Would he find my real identity or my mother's location? These two make my trumped-up, intent to distribute charge look like jaywalking. Maybe I should be afraid of these kids.

My former classmate has been quiet through our exchange of offenses, but his jaw tightens as the techie expounds on his hacker creds. Phil's gaze finds mine. A *don't ask, don't tell* warning flashes in his eyes. I can't stop the words already spilling from my mouth. "What about you? What did you do?"

He picks up a stick and snaps bits from it as we near the barn. For a moment, I suspect he's not going to answer, then he says, "I was born."

Stunned, I stare at his retreating form. "What the heck do you mean? Born?"

"Forget it," he snaps.

I open my mouth to say something but catch Phil's slight shake of head just in time. There's more to this story. A lot more. How will I determine if the tale is truth or some fabricated reality? Boots regards me from the barn door. He growls low in his throat before he stalks into the building.

The boys glance at each other, but I don't care what's the big secret I'm not supposed to know. My teeth clash together. Fine. I'll figure it out later.

"You okay with this?" Jackson asks, his tone brimming with sudden irritation. I can't tell if he's mad at me for preventing the fight or at Boots for picking one.

I nod even though my insides do somersaults. "I'm fine." Defiantly, I march into the barn with the boys in tow.

Outside one of the stalls, Boots strokes the neck of a huge, brown horse with a white dot dead-center of his forehead. The horse yanks his head back as we approach, retreating to the inside of his stall with a wild call somewhere between a whistle and a squeal. When I think about sitting on one of these monsters, my heart lodges in my throat. No freaking way.

Pretending our conversation never occurred, Boots says, "We have seven horses here. That means seven stalls to muck every afternoon. We take turns. Now there are more of us, we'll get two weeks off in between our shifts." He watches the horse paw at his hay. A massive turd pile sits in the back corner, like someone piled miniature brown cannonballs in a mound on the straw. A small cloud of flies alights on the manure.

Fantastic. Yuck. Rhymes with muck and... Okay, maybe I could pick up poop. I might not like it, but I could do it. Wearing gloves, super-thick boots, and a hazmat suit.

"You can help me. This is my week," Boots says, his gaze on me.

He's challenging me. Daring me to wimp out. I'd love to. But— *no way.* Flynn's warning sounds in my ears. I can't show weakness, I can't show fear. "Whatever," I say instead. It's my defense. My brick wall of *I don't care anymore.* Even if I do, I'm not telling him.

"We better get to it before it gets dark. You two got trash. Tell the other girls they're on laundry."

"Right," Phil agrees, shaking his head and acting like the world isn't about to blow up around us. "I'm not telling those two nasties anything. Let Flynn or McCord land on them for not carrying their weight."

"Yeah, I'll stick with the trash." Jackson wrinkles his nose, but his furious glare drifts toward Boots.

Goosebumps rush over my skin. Why is he defending me?

Phil clamps a hand on Jackson's shoulder. "Better than dealing in this crap." He cracks up at his own joke as they leave.

Then I'm alone with Boots. Painfully alone. He's brooding, angry, dangerous—especially with a pitchfork in hand. Who's he annoyed at? Me? At something the other guys said? I'm about to explode with wanting to ask him when he says, "There are muck boots in the closet over there. Rakes in the empty stall. I'll go get the wheelbarrow." He stalks around the corner.

I let out a frustrated sigh when he's out of range. He doesn't want me to ask about his issues. Why? What's his deal?

A honey-colored horse with a white mane pops a head over the stall door as I rummage in the closet for muck boots near the correct size. "Hey there," I say. The horse snorts and withdraws. Great. Another critic. I slip out of my shearling heavens and gingerly slide my foot into a pair of black rubber jobs that have seen more than one stall cleaning.

Classy.

"Those look great with leggings," he says behind me.

I glower at him over my shoulder. He manhandles a monster wheelbarrow loaded with three bales of hay. The bales tumble as he dumps the wheelbarrow over. I snag a couple of sketchy rakes and follow him to the end of barn. It bothers me we're going to throw poop in the wheelbarrow that doubles as a food truck. I sure wouldn't want to eat the hay.

"So, what do we do? Take the horses out of their rooms?" A big, black brute of an animal occupies the room we stop in front of. The horse tosses his head, flinging his mane into the air. The wild whites of his eyeballs terrify me.

"Rooms? They're called stalls. And no," he says. "It's not best practice, but you *can* clean around them."

Wide-eyed, I point to the horse. "You think I'm going in there? With him? You're freaking nuts." The horse snorts and stamps his massive, hard hoof in agreement.

Boots shakes his head as he opens the door. The horse backs away, head down. "He's not going to hurt you." He pats the horse on the shoulder, calming the animal.

I guess it's a shoulder. Horses have shoulders, right?

"I'll hang in here with you. Take the rake and pick up the big stuff. Manure goes in the wheelbarrow. This old straw too. Dig into this area to get the wet stuff. There's a rubber mat underneath the bedding. When you can find the mat, you'll know you've taken enough old bedding out." He gestures to some matted, wet straw of questionable scent. I poke at it with the rake, then dig in. I guess I can do this. It's like cleaning a cat litter box. Only elephant-sized.

He watches me work, pointing out places I missed until he's satisfied with the job I've done. My muscles warm from the physical activity, and my mind has grown surprisingly calm and clear. Boots dumps a white powder on the wet spots.

"What's the powder?" I ask.

"A little barn lime. It helps with the urine smell."

"What's this flaky stuff?" I ask, toeing my borrowed boot into the bedding.

"Wood shavings. We'll need more of them in here. I'll show you where they are."

I follow him through the barn with a wheelbarrow of fragrant horse manure. He dumps the contents in a wagon-like device hooked to a big, red tractor. The wagon has what appears to be metal teeth crusted with old manure and hay like someone forgot to brush.

"What does that do?"

With a wicked smile he says, "Manure spreader. Wait ''til it's full. Then the fun really starts."

"Thanks. I'll pass on the demo."

He loads two bales of plastic-wrapped shavings into the empty wheelbarrow. We head back to the cleaned stall. After he slices through the plastic with a knife, I help him spread the aromatic bedding around the stall until it covers the limed areas. The horse sniffs and snorts. As soon as we latch the gate, the horse lowers his big body to the ground and thrashes in the wood shavings. His shiny hooves flail in the air.

"He always rolls. This guy loves a clean bed."

I warily watch the legs thrash as the horse snorts in delight. "Did you always like horses?"

"Yeah," he says. "They're great listeners."

"You talk to them?" I smirk.

He laughs once in his throat. "Don't worry. You will, too."

I can't think of an answer. Instead, I ask, "Okay. Are we done with this one?"

"As soon as we water. Then we have to feed fresh hay and

grain." He deposits the empty bucket from the stall on the floor then grabs slices of hay out of the bales. I pick up two buckets to fill them from a hose. A door next to the sink stands ajar. Dim light shines from inside. My hand is resting on the knob when Boots comes up behind me carrying buckets of grain. "You ready with the water?"

Uh-oh. I've been caught spying. His curved left eyebrow has me wondering if he's waiting for me to say something. "Yeah. Ready to go." I kick the door shut. If he doesn't want me in there, that's his business. Doesn't mean I won't check it out later when he's not around.

An hour later, seven stalls are cleaned, bedded, watered, grained, and hayed. I'm itchy from the shavings that have crawled down my shirt into my bra. Boots picks hay out of my hair with careful fingers.

"Thanks," I tell him, and it isn't just for plucking the hay out of my hair. He's been so patient. Kind. Conflicted. There are a thousand questions I want to ask him—most of them about why he ended up in my math class, but I suspect this is not the time for truth-telling.

Why is he here? What does he have to do with my family? One minute he's ready to kill Corrine and Jackson—the next he's patting a horse. Talk about a short fuse.

His chin tightens. I suspect he guessed what I'm thinking. His blue eyes go stormy. "Yeah, well you get to fight with the wheelbarrow tomorrow."

"Fantastic." I smile. His expression softens by degrees.

Tomorrow will be another chance to figure out what makes this bizarre school's senior resident tick. Even with the hay itch and manure, I'm looking forward to working in the barn with him again. I'm betting he has the answers I need. I'll get them even if I have to push the poop.

What's next on your reading list?

Champagne Book Group promises to bring to readers fiction at its finest.

Discover your next
fine read!
http://www.champagnebooks.com/

We are delighted to invite you to receive exclusive rewards. Join our Facebook group for VIP savings, bonus content, early access to new ideas we've cooked up, learn about special events for our readers, and sneak peeks at our fabulous titles.

Join now.
https://www.facebook.com/groups/ChampagneBookClub/

Made in the USA
Middletown, DE
18 April 2022

64180034R00126